HER EYES

Matthew was fast asleep in his desk chair.

God, but he was beautiful. The computer screen slightly lit up half his chiseled face and shone highlights on his dark, thick hair. His rolled-up shirtsleeves revealed tanned, strong forearms, lightly covered with dark hair.

He was tall and lean and muscular. And he had to be uncomfortable in that position.

Suddenly, he lurched out of the chair and practically flung himself on the bed, his eyes closed.

He was still asleep.

And he was lying down right next to her.

He turned toward her and burrowed his face in the crook of her neck, his warm breath dancing along her collarbone. She could smell his soap, his musky aftershave, the masculinity of him. An arm snaked around her waist, then inched up, dangerously close to her breast.

Mia held her breath.

They were so close they could be making love.

What do I do? What do I do? What do I do?

His eyes opened.

And then opened wide.

He bolted up, and so did she.

"How—" he began, two spots of color forming on his hard cheeks.

"I don't know," she said, her face flaming. "I guess we both fell asleep. I'll just call a cab."

"Stay," Matthew said. "I mean, you can have the bed, and I'll take the couch."

"I—"

"It's"—he glanced at his watch—"three in the morning."

So I guess I'm staying, Mia thought.

DON'T GO HOME

Janelle Taylor

ZEBRA BOOKS
KENSINGTON PUBLISHING CORP.
http://www.kensingtonbooks.com

Dedicated to my nieces Diane, Robyn, Lisa, Julie, and Lynn.

ZEBRA BOOKS are published by

Kensington Publishing Corp.
850 Third Avenue
New York, NY 10022

First Printing: December 2003
10 9 8 7 6 5 4 3 2 1

Printed in the United States of America

Prologue

Robert Gray slipped his wedding ring into his pocket, sucked in his gut, and checked out the women sitting at the bar and the small, circular tables dotted around Chumley's, his favorite nightclub. *Not bad,* he thought, eyeing a young, busty redhead in a midriff top and a miniskirt. Perched on a bar stool, the babe leaned over to shout an order to the bartender. Thirty-six C, tiny waist, and hips a guy could hang on to for ten or fifteen minutes. He'd buy her a few cheap drinks, offer to drive her home, "show her the view" at the far end of Lover's Cliff, then screw her senseless, and be back at Chumley's in less than an hour. A quick washup in the men's room, and he'd be ready for babe number two.

Robert liked to have sex with at least two women on his Saturday "Boys' Night Out." The boys had abandoned him a few years ago for serious girlfriends or marriage, but Robert didn't mind driving into Center City to make the nightlife rounds alone. Less competition for the ladies that way. As long as his wife thought he was out with his buddies, watching a game at a sports bar or shooting pool, she didn't give him much grief about going out on Saturday nights. He always showered first thing when he got home, making the excuse that he reeked of other people's smoke. His wife thought that was very sweet, especially because Robbie, their two-year-old son, was asthmatic.

When the redhead's girlfriend headed toward the ladies' room, leaving his dream girl all by her lonesome at the bar, Robert made his move. One classic line later, he had the redhead smiling and leaning closer to him. Two very strong gin and tonics later, he had her crossing and uncrossing her long legs, the sign that he was definitely going to score.

Until her friend got ditched by the guy she'd been flirting with.

Suddenly his redhead was putting on her jacket and getting up. Leaving. He couldn't take his eyes off her chest. Man, what he wanted to do to her.

"Hey, beautiful, why don't you stay?" Robert said in his sexiest and most sincere voice. "It's only nine o'clock. I'll drive you home later."

The redhead giggled and eyed her friend, who looked jealous. "Sorry, but I've got to get going. Thanks for the drinks, though. You're a sweetie."

And then she was gone. With eight bucks of his money in her enticingly flat stomach. *Bitch.*

Robert sat back down at the bar and ordered a scotch. *Forget her, man,* he told himself, running a hand through his thick brown hair. There were plenty of other good-looking young women in

Chumley's tonight, and a few were checking him out. At thirty-eight, Robert was in his prime to attract women in their twenties. He had the looks, money, confidence, and experience to seduce them. Sometimes he'd go for a woman in her thirties—if she was hot enough—but it wasn't much of a challenge. Unmarried women in their thirties were so desperate they'd latch on to any man and give it up too easily.

Scotch in hand, Robert turned and looked around Chumley's.

Whoa.

Whoa.

The best-looking piece of ass Robert had ever seen had just walked through the door.

Twenty-something. Long, silky blond hair. Light brown eyes, like a doe's. Red lipstick. Little black dress—very little. Lots of cleavage.

She sat down alone at a table near the bar. Robert couldn't take his eyes off her. *A babe like that has to be waiting for someone,* he thought, noting she wasn't wearing a wedding ring. But ten minutes later, she was still sitting there by herself, sipping a drink, not paying the least bit of attention to the door. Probably got into a fight with her boyfriend. Probably could use a little male attention. Probably could use a little of the Robmeister's very talented tongue tonight.

Robert downed his scotch, popped a breath mint into his mouth, sucked in the ole gut, and made his way over to Blondie's table. Ten seconds later he was sitting down next to her. A few minutes later, she was sipping the cosmopolitan he'd bought for her.

Her name was Candy. Twenty-five. Administrative assistant. Aries. She told him a bunch of other stuff about herself, but he'd been so busy fantasizing about whether he wanted him or her on top that he missed the rest of what she'd said.

He inched closer, and she murmured that his cologne was very sexy . . . which was his invitation to get even closer, slip an arm around her shoulder. She smiled and took a sip of her cosmo. Giggled. Crossed her legs. Uncrossed them.

"I'd do anything for a kiss," he whispered into her ear.

She smiled shyly, then tilted that beautiful face toward his and closed her eyes. The zipper of his pants strained against his erection. He wanted to rip off her clothes, lay her down on the table right here and now, and wrap those long legs around his waist.

He settled for a soft, slow one on the lips, no tongue to show her he was a gentleman, then blew into her ear and—

Suddenly he was dragged up from his chair by powerful arms. He tried to twist away, but the guy's grip was too strong. "What the—"

"I can't believe you're all over some woman in public. What the hell is wrong with you, Robert?"

At the all-too-familiar voice of his brother, Robert relaxed. "Get the hell off me, Matt," Robert growled, trying unsuccessfully to shake loose. Despite being four years younger than Robert, Matthew Gray was a good three inches taller and all muscle and managed to drag Robert over by the jukebox.

Robert glanced at Candy. The blonde was stirring her drink as though nothing out of the ordinary had just happened. Now there was someone who knew how to mind her own business. Any other woman would be watching them and probably hoping a fight would break out so she could screw the victor.

"What the hell are you doing, Robert?" Matthew hissed over the blare of a rock and roll song. "You've got a wife and baby at home, for God's sake," he added, tightening his grip on Robert's arm. "You're lucky I don't tell Laurie that you cheat on her."

Damn buttinsky. He'd had to put up with Matt's butting in his entire life, and he was sick of it. "You want to break your sister-in-law's heart and watch your little nephew grow up with divorced parents, Matthew? Bug off, little brother. Mind your own damned business."

Matthew stared at Robert, then shook his head and shoved Robert up against the jukebox. "It's your life, man. Go ahead and wreck it. You don't deserve it. You don't deserve your own wife and child." Finally, Matthew stormed out.

Jerk. Robert rolled his eyes, straightened his shirt, and headed back to his table. "Sorry about that little scene, darlin'," he told Candy. "Why don't I buy us a fresh round of drinks, and we'll continue what we were doing before we were so rudely interrupted by my holier-than-thou brother."

Candy glanced at her watch, then slipped on her cardigan sweater. "Um, I'd like to, but . . . I'd better get going," she said, offering him a tight smile.

No way was this piece of feminine perfection going anywhere before he nailed her. She was so hot she was worth two lays in one. "Look, baby, why don't we go somewhere more private for a drink where no jealous relatives can bother us." He smiled and leaned close so he could whisper in her ear. "There's a little motel a few doors down that has a very nice bar and an intimate little dance floor—"

Candy stood and picked up her purse. "I'd really better get on home. I have an early start tomorrow. Thanks for the cosmopolitan, honey."

Damn. Damn. Damn! This should have been an easy score. He stood and forced a smile. "I'm here every Saturday night, Candy. Will I see you here next weekend?"

"Um, I'm not really sure," she said.

"Well, how about your phone number?"

She hesitated for a second, but then smiled and wrote down her name and number on a cocktail napkin before sashaying that heart-shaped butt of hers out the door. He folded the napkin and slipped it into his wallet. At least he could call her one night this week and go over to her house and finish what he'd started tonight.

Robert sat back down at the bar and ordered another scotch. While he drank, he fantasized about what he'd do with Candy when he saw her again. In the middle of a particularly hot visual, he suddenly had the sensation that someone was watching him. *Please be a busty babe,* he prayed heavenward as he glanced over to his right.

But no one seemed to be paying him the least bit of attention, not even the average-looking trio of women a few seats down the bar. Considering the three of them could hardly fit their ample asses on the bar stools, they should be all over him.

He angrily gulped the rest of his scotch. What a waste of a Saturday night. Between his two lost scores and his jerk of a brother, he wasn't in any mood to try his luck with anyone else, even for a super easy score like one of these bimbos promised to be with a free drink or two in her system.

He slapped a few bills on the bar and stood, wobbling a bit. *Shouldn't have had that last scotch,* he thought as he headed outside, the muggy June air hitting him full in the face. "Heyyyy, pe-peeeople," he called over his shoulder to the door, "bring your drinksies outshide. No von out here at all and all this roooom to d-d . . . dance and fu—" He tripped over his own feet, straightened, then stopped still, looking around at the lot packed full with parked cars. *Which one mine?* he thought, zigzagging a few feet. *Ah, there it is.*

He staggered toward his car, figuring he'd sleep off the worst of his drunk in the air-conditioning before getting on the road. Tomorrow was his son's second birthday, and he didn't need Laurie yelling up a storm about his coming home drunk or with a totaled car.

He felt eyes on him again, that same creepy feeling that someone was watching him. He turned around. No one there. He must be drunker than he thought.

Footstcheps, he thought, the word slurring even in his mind. *I definitely hear footstcheps.*

And as he neared his car and fumbled for the keys in his pocket, he felt the plunge of a knife in his back.

Then another. And another.

Robert dropped to his knees and put his hands

out to break his fall, warm, sticky blood spurting out of his mouth and dribbling down his chin onto his fifty-dollar shirt. *Damn, damn, damn*—blood didn't wash out easily. Laurie was going to have a cow over this.

He heard the soft tap of shoes on the pavement and thought of calling for help, but he couldn't find his voice. And anyway, wasn't the sound coming from right behind him?

He strained to listen. Yes, someone was right behind him. Whispering something now. Chanting, almost. He tried, but he couldn't make out the words.

He tried to turn his head to see who it was, but the knife plunged into his back again, low, and then high, and then lower still.

His face hit the hot pavement. And then he felt a hand reach into his pocket, fish around for something. His wallet?

No. His wedding ring.

Damn. Don't take the ring, you asshole, he thought. *Laurie will have a cow when I come home without it. She'll withhold sex for a month over this one.*

Robert closed his eyes. He was suddenly tired. Very tired. He felt the way he did before he was falling asleep, before he was about to slip into a wonderful dream about Pamela Anderson or Nicole Kidman naked.

And then he felt his wedding ring being slipped onto his ring finger. *Good,* he thought. *And thanks, since Laurie always bitches like crazy when I come home with it in my pocket.* His excuse that beer made his fingers swell didn't always appease her.

The warmth was spreading through his entire

body. He felt lighter and lighter. And as another and another plunge of the knife split open his back, he finally could make out what the person behind him was whispering: *"Cheaters never prosper."*

Chapter One

One week later

Please don't ask me out on a date, Mia Anderson prayed as she spied Norman Newman, belly jiggling, plodding toward her classroom with a wilted bouquet of lilacs. *Please, please, please have gotten the hint after all these months!*

Mia ducked back inside the room, staring longingly at the water fountain just across the hall. It was unseasonably hot for late June—eighty-six degrees and equal humidity—and of course, the air conditioner in her classroom had broken that morning. But a cool drink of water meant a hallway of students and faculty saying their goodbyes to each other would witness Norman's final attempt at asking her out.

And what was he doing here, anyway? It was three-fifteen on a Friday, the final day of school, so perhaps he'd come back to say his goodbyes, too. Norman had been given special permission to cram all his unused vacation time into the past two weeks in order to care for his mother, who'd had a terrible stroke and was all alone, save Norman. The staff had banded together and taken care of his finals, grading, and all the administrative duties that had to be performed in the final days of school.

The smell of the fragrant purple flowers was getting closer. Why had she ever told that traitorous bunch of students that lilacs were her favorite flowers! The entire school knew that Mr. Newman—voted Most Absentminded Teacher per the unofficial school poll (quickly confiscated by the vice principal during lunch period)—had a longtime crush on Ms. Anderson, who'd been voted Favorite Teacher and, to Mia's embarrassment, Prettiest.

Prettiest. Mia shook her head. If everyone, including Norman, had seen what Mia had looked like before she began teaching at Baywater five years ago, they would have voted her Most in Need of a Makeover. Most Mousiest Brown Hair. Most Blah Brown Eyes. Most Blah Schoolmarm Clothes. Most *Blah.*

After all, she'd been awarded that title by her own husband before she'd changed to please him. Before she'd turned into someone else. Before she'd become someone who could win "prettiest teacher" four years in a row.

Yes, she thought, catching her reflection in the pane of glass on the classroom door. *The long blond hair. The pale brown doe eyes enhanced by a light dusting of makeup. The fitted dress and stylish sandals. The hoop earrings and large sterling silver ring. It all adds up to* pretty.

A pretty lie.

But tonight, after the makeup came off for good and the Miss Clairol Ash Blonde hair dye was rinsed clean from her hair, Mia would once again be a fresh-scrubbed ponytailed brunette. Add the clothes she preferred—long, comfortable cotton skirts and pretty blouses, the pearls she'd inherited from her mother her only adornment—and she'd once again be the Mia she used to be. The Mia she was before David Anderson had come into her life.

You don't see your sister *wearing pearls, do you, Mia?* her ex-husband had asked every time Mia even *looked* at her pearls. *They're a little matronly, don't you think?*

Five years ago, she hadn't had the self-esteem to tell David that no, she most certainly *didn't* think pearls were matronly, that in fact the pearls were her most precious possession, that they were all she had left of her mother besides wonderful memories. She'd simply stopped wearing them. She also hadn't had the self-esteem to tell David that if he wanted her to dress like her twin sister, Margot, maybe he should have *married* Margot.

Five years ago—heck, *one* year ago—she hadn't had the confidence to tell David Anderson to go to hell. And it had cost her dearly.

"Afternoon, Mia! Hot enough for you out there?"

Norman Newman. He was hovering in the doorway of her classroom, the wilted lilacs in one hand, a sweating can of iced tea in the other.

At least he was a respite from her thoughts. The last thing she wanted on her mind was her ex-husband.

Problem was, Mia didn't want Norman on her mind, either. She wished she could feel more kindly about Norman, but the man *wasn't* a sweet, "absentminded" chemistry and physics teacher.

Mia hated to think it, to say it, but Norman Newman was a real pain in the butt. Six months ago, when word had spread that Mia's divorce was final, Norman had begun asking her out immediately—and upon being turned down had continued to ask her out every Monday morning for the following Saturday night. She'd nicely told him she was flattered, but that it would take her a long while to get over her divorce and that she had no interest in dating, now or in the near future, which was every bit the truth. So Norman had asked about the *distant* future. She'd let him know that, too, was out. And yet every Monday morning, in the faculty dining room, in the office, in the hallway, at the water fountain, in the parking lot, anywhere, Norman Newman would ask her if she would like to have dinner and perhaps see a movie that upcoming Saturday night.

Norman had begun to make her feel the way her ex-husband had. As though her wishes, her thoughts, her *words,* had absolutely no bearing, no impact. And instead of finding his "crush" sweet, she began to find it unbearable. What a relief his absence had been these past two weeks.

Norman smiled, revealing a mouthful of clear braces. "I was hoping to speak with you alone about—"

"Sorry we're late, Ms. Anderson! We had so many kids to say goodbye to."

Relief. The Farley twins, Amy and Anne, came barreling into the classroom behind Norman and rushed for seats in the front row. Only the Farley twins would manage to get detention on the last day of school.

Mia glanced at her watch. "Afternoon, girls—I'll be with you in a moment." She turned her attention back to Norman. "Afternoon, Mr. Newman. Yes, it certainly is warm out there. Well, I'd better get these two students' detention started," she told him. "I don't want to stay later on the last day of school, especially in this heat wave, than I have to." She tidied a stack of very tidy papers on her desk. "How's your mother?" she added out of politeness.

Norman frowned. He glanced uncomfortably at the girls, then slid his beady-eyed gaze back to Mia. "Mother is recuperating slowly but surely, thank you." He cleared his throat and lowered his voice. "I was hoping you might want to go out for a cup of coffee to celebrate the last day. There was something I wanted to ask you."

Mia had no doubt what he wanted to ask her: out for Saturday night!

"Well, thanks, Mr. Newman, but I've got my hands full for the next hour, and then I've got quite a busy few weeks ahead, so . . ."

Norman's face fell. "In that case, I'd better ask part of what I intended now."

Amy Farley was stifling a giggle.

"I was wondering," Norman began, clearing his throat again, "if, uh, you were free this Saturday night, if you'd like to have dinner. There really is something I'd like to discuss with you—*off* school property."

Amy burst out into laughter. Mia gave the girl a sharp glance, then turned to Norman, whose cheeks were tinged with pink.

Mia hated to reject him in front of the girls, but he'd given her no choice. He had put himself in this position. "Mr. Newman, I'm terribly sorry, but

I'm afraid the answer is no. I have a very busy summer ahead of me and doubt I'll have any free time."

He narrowed his eyes at her, his expression darkening for just a moment. "Very well, Ms. Anderson," he said, running a hand through his wiry brown hair. "Perhaps I'll call you over the summer. I'm not coming back to Baywater in the fall. Mother needs me." He awkwardly handed her the lilacs and plodded back out the door with the can of iced tea.

He wasn't coming back in the fall! Mia tried to suppress her joy, given his terrible circumstances, but she couldn't help the *hallelujah!* that echoed through her mind.

Amy opened her mouth to speak, but Mia beat her to it. "Not a word, Miss Farley. Your detention began five minutes ago. Am I making myself clear?"

Amy smiled and made a show of clamping her mouth shut. Anne darted a glance at Mia, then stared back down at her folded hands.

Mia let out a deep breath. "Okay, girls. Your detention assignment is to write a five page essay on the importance of paying attention in class—even on the last day."

Amy groaned; Anne immediately opened her loose-leaf binder and began writing.

"Anne, can I have a sheet of paper?" Amy asked, making a noisy show of getting up from her desk and retrieving a piece of paper from her sister. Upon sitting back down, she began staring out the window at a group of boys playing basketball without their shirts on.

Mia mentally shook her head. An hour with the Farley twins would feel like *two* hours. The twelve-year-olds had been writing notes back and forth in her morning English class during the entire period, had been warned twice, and had still passed folded-up pieces of paper. And then Mia had had the "fortune" of cafeteria duty and had witnessed Amy spoon green Jell-O down the back of her sister's shirt, resulting in a furious-faced Anne uncharacteristically flinging mashed potatoes on Amy's lap, which had started a food fight at their table. And now both the girls *and* Mia had to stay an additional hour. At least Mia wouldn't have to grade the essay. She *would* have to drop off Amy and Anne clear across town because they'd miss the school bus home.

Amy was now trying to get her sister's attention without Mia noticing. An impossible feat, given that both girls sat in the front row, just a few desks over on the left from Mia's desk. Mia bit back a smile as Anne nervously glanced at Mia to determine whether Teacher was aware of her sister's shenanigans.

The angelic-faced, white-blond twins reminded her so much of herself and Margot, her own identical twin. Amy Farley was mischievous, an instigator, and so charming that she often got herself out of trouble. Anne Farley was cautious and unable to tell a lie, which meant she got herself into the trouble Amy started. Mia's heart went out to Anne, who sat straight up in her seat, diligently writing her essay, pink tongue sticking out in concentration. And there was Amy, staring at the basketball players. She was probably writing her essay on the importance of paying attention to which boys were the cutest.

When Mia was twelve, she'd been too shy to

sneak peeks at the boys who did funny things to her stomach. And despite the fact that she and Margot looked exactly alike, well, save for their use of cosmetics, their hairstyles, and clothes, Mia hadn't been a hit with the boys the way Margot had been her entire life.

I just don't get *Mia,* she'd heard girls say all during her school years, while she was behind bathroom stalls or just around the corner from or a table away in the cafeteria. *Why would she choose to look like* that *when she could look like her identical twin? All she has to do is buy the clothes Margot buys and style her hair like Margot's and put on some make-up, and she'd be one of the most popular girls in school. Why would Mia purposely want to look so plain and dowdy?*

Mia's ex-husband had the same question for Mia when he'd met Margot for the first time.

"*Hel-lo,* Miss Anderson. Earth to Miss Anderson."

Mia blinked and suddenly realized that two sets of bright blue eyes were staring at her. "Yes, Amy?"

"How do you spell *gorgeous?*" Amy asked, staring out the window at the boys, a dreamy expression on her face.

Mia sighed. "Amy. Amy, face forward, please." The girl dragged her attention to Mia. "What are students supposed to do when they want to know how to spell a word?"

"Um, look it up?" Amy responded, her gaze once again out the window.

"Exactly. You know where the class dictionary is—if you can stop looking at the boys long enough to actually get up and get it."

Anne suppressed a giggle, and Mia smiled at her. Amy trotted over to the bookcase under the clock, noisily flipped some pages and let out an "oh, it's '*e-o-u-s*.' I forgot the '*e*.' " She slapped shut the heavy dictionary and skipped back to her seat. She took one more look at the boys; then her own tongue darted out in thought as she began writing.

Mia wondered if Amy and Anne would soon start to look different, so different that their classmates would forget they were twins, the way Mia and Margot's classmates had forgotten. If when puberty set in with all its demands, Amy would dress like the teen pop stars on MTV the way Margot had and Anne would hide her personality behind baggy jeans and baggy sweaters and ponytails the way Mia had. If the boys would notice Amy and ignore Anne. If the girls would envy Amy and be disdainful of Anne for giving up what she could so easily have, the very thing they all wanted.

What the *boys* wanted. And continued to want for as long as Mia could remember. She was ignored in junior high and high school, except by one or two Norman-like guys in her extracurricular activities. She'd had a few boyfriends in college, but when she refused to sleep with them, they drifted away. And so five years ago, when Mia had been a twenty-four-year-old virgin who truly wondered if she'd *die* a virgin, she'd been an easy target for a manipulative man. A handsome, charming, intelligent man whose manipulations were at first so subtle, Mia wasn't sure if *she* or *he* had had the critical thought of her.

She'd been easily seduced, easily changed into the flashy, stylish woman he wanted her to be. The woman he wanted her to look like. And so within a few months of his constant criticism, she'd gone from mousy brown to blond, from chin-length to shoulder-length, to a new wardrobe bought in stores she'd never think to enter, to perfecting the make-up application tips she'd learned from the sales-women at the cosmetics counter at the mall.

Sometimes, when Mia looked at her wedding album, she was sure it was *Margot* who stood smiling next to David.

Their marriage had lasted as long as David thought he could also change her personality. Oh, he'd tried, but no matter how he berated her for shyly glancing down every time she was introduced to someone new, a client or friend of his, no matter how he criticized her for how dull her small talk was at parties, she remained the same old Mia. The same old boring Mia.

He'd finally considered her a lost cause, told her she'd never be the woman of his dreams. Margot, essentially. On the surface, anyway. Of course, David had nothing but criticism for her sister, who ran too wild for his taste, intimidated him with her reckless ways. *The two of you combined would make the perfect woman,* David used to say. *But alone, you're both off. She's a reckless whore, and you're a schoolmarm bore.*

David had always added a chuckle with that line, proud of his clever rhyme.

The first time it had come out of his mouth, Mia knew their marriage was over. She might not have had confidence or self-esteem, but she'd been smart enough to know that her husband couldn't possibly even *like* her, let alone love her, if he could even think such a thing, *say* such a thing. It had taken her four years of marriage to figure that out. *Four* years.

She had never been enough for David. But what

hurt, what really hurt, was that she hadn't been enough for *herself.* At twenty-nine, Mia was just starting to believe that she was enough. More than enough. Just the way she was.

She glanced at sweet, quiet Anne Farley, in her baggy jeans and baggy T-shirt, her blond hair in a neat ponytail, and Mia wished on every star in the galaxy that the girl would have more self-esteem than Mia had had. That it wouldn't take Anne into adulthood to realize how very *right* she was *as* she was.

Finally, tonight, Mia would *look* right again, look like Mia Daniels, the person she'd been before she'd married David Anderson—the person she had grown into since him.

She'd been dying to change her appearance for many months, even and perhaps especially before David had moved out last Christmas. But she hadn't wanted to dramatically change her appearance midway through the school year, so she'd kept up with the hair color, the makeup, the clothes.

Her appearance was about to change so dramatically there was a very good chance that even Norman Newman wouldn't recognize her.

Mia smiled.

Fatherless at two years old.

Matthew Gray closed his eyes and held his little nephew, Robbie, tight against his chest, breathing in the smell of baby powder, baby shampoo. Innocence. He pushed through the screen door of his brother's house—his sister-in-law's house now—stepped onto the porch and carefully sat down on the white wooden swing he and his brother had installed a couple of years ago, when Laurie had been pregnant with Robbie.

Robbie wound his chubby arms around Matthew's neck and fell fast asleep, his warm, tiny body rising and falling with each breath on Matthew's chest. Matthew shut his eyes against the unfamiliar sting of tears and rested his chin on the baby's head, on the Yankees baseball cap he'd given Robbie that morning as a belated birthday gift.

This is some party, Matthew thought bitterly as he opened his eyes and looked around the front yard. There were no toddlers running around squealing with delight. No silly clown or talking mule. No nursery songs.

There were only the sounds of grief, of sobbing, of soothing words.

And there was only little Robbie, sweet, innocent Robbie. The only blood relative Matthew had left in the world.

Matthew squeezed his eyes shut again and looked up at the sky. *I'm going to watch over Robbie, you bastard,* he told his brother. *I promise you that. He'll never want for anything.*

You bastard. You damned bastard!

Matthew knew he shouldn't be thinking this way, looking heavenward and using language that wouldn't sit well with The Man Upstairs. But Robert had gotten himself killed, left a grieving wife and a beautiful son who'd never know his father.

Robert might have been a Class A jerk when it came to how he led his life, but at least he acted the good father to Robbie. Robert seemed to truly love the boy, as much as he could love anyone.

And Robbie had adored his father, had laughed and squealed and crawled the distance of the house to find him and throw his arms around him.

Robert had given that up. *Gave* all *this up*, Matthew thought, looking at the white colonial house that Robert had been so proud to be able to buy. Robert had given up a chance at a perfect life, the life Matthew would never be willing to even shoot for.

Because it couldn't exist.

Matthew and Robert's father had proved that.

And now Robert had proved that.

Identifying his only brother, a tag around his big toe, in the county morgue a week ago had proved that.

Last Saturday night, Robert Gray had been found stabbed to death in the parking lot of a small night-club in Center City, right next to his own car.

On the eve of his son's second birthday.

Laurie had gotten the call and had immediately called Matthew, who'd driven the half hour from Center City to Clarkstown so fast he was surprised he wasn't pulled over for speeding. Surprised he'd actually made it there alive.

His brother couldn't possibly be dead; after all, Matthew had just seen him with his own eyes a couple of hours earlier. Had *talked* to him.

Had *fought* with him.

Again, Matthew blinked away the sting of tears. He'd cried only once in his entire life and had vowed long ago that nothing would ever make him lose control of his emotions like that again. Besides, Robert didn't deserve Matthew's tears. Robbie was all that mattered now, and Robbie needed strength, needed his uncle to be there for him now and always.

Robbie needed his family to celebrate his birthday. His second birthday. Matthew had been the one to call the Grays' friends early last Sunday morning to explain that Robbie's birthday party was cancelled—and the reason why. That day and the days that followed, gifts for Robbie, pots and pans of hot and cold food and baked goods, cleaning services, and sympathy callers had flooded in. Laurie had a small family, but they immediately drove and flew in for the funeral. Matthew had been the only member of his family present. His parents were gone, and there were no other Gray relatives. Only Robbie.

Laurie had decided to hold a small birthday party for close friends and family today, Friday, since tomorrow, she and Robbie were going to stay with her parents in Pennsylvania for a couple of weeks.

Matthew gently patted the baby's back, once again breathing deeply of the scent of baby powder. *Thank God you're too young to understand, Robbie, because I don't know how I'd explain it to you. I don't know why your daddy is dead.*

I do know why, Matthew amended. *I saw why. Over and over again.*

"You and Robbie okay out here?"

Matthew turned around and nodded at Laurie, standing behind the screen door. She offered a weak smile and disappeared back inside the house. In her early thirties, pretty and kind to a fault, Laurie Gray had deserved better than a husband who didn't appreciate her. Who'd cheated on her constantly. Who'd made her a widow. Had she known about Robert's philandering? Robert was sure she didn't, but maybe Laurie just kept quiet about it to keep the family together.

Like Robert and Matthew's mother had done—until the secrets and lies had destroyed her, destroyed their family.

You bastard, he bitterly thought again. *You damned bastard. If you weren't dead, Robert, I'd kill you myself for what you've done to your family.*

He let out a deep breath. He knew that the police, in fact, wondered if he *had* killed Robert. The thought made him shudder. But he understood their suspicion. He'd been seen arguing with Robert just a half hour before Robert had been found dead in the parking lot of Chumley's. Questioned for hours about the argument at the Center City Police Precinct, Matthew had finally been allowed to return to Laurie's house. He wasn't a suspect, the officers had said, not yet anyway, but they would appreciate it if he didn't leave town.

Matthew had been shocked more than a few times in his life. But nothing had come close to someone, anyone, thinking for even a moment that he might have killed someone, let alone his own brother.

And when the police were through with the questions for him, he'd had his share for them. The detectives weren't very forthcoming with him, but they had told Laurie that were no clues, no fingerprints. Nothing to go on. No similar homicides. Because Robert's wallet containing over a hundred dollars in cash, car, car keys, expensive watch, and gold wedding ring had not been taken, the police were operating under the assumption that he'd gotten into a drunken brawl in the parking lot and that the perpetrator, freaked by what he'd done, had fled the scene.

But what about the blonde? Matthew had asked

over and over. *She's your link. Either she killed him, or a jealous boyfriend or husband saw her and Robert together and ambushed him in the parking lot. You have to find the blonde,* he'd pleaded.

But they'd been unable to trace her. A cocktail napkin with a telephone number and the name Candy written inside a heart had been found folded in Robert's wallet; but the number belonged to a nearby pizza joint, and no one named Candy or any blondes worked there. A couple of witnesses and the bartender had been sure they'd seen the blonde before, in Chumley's or around Center City; but Center City *was* a city of over a million people, and there were a lot of good-looking plastic blondes out there. The only reason anyone had remembered her from last Saturday night was because of the little scene Matthew had caused.

Are you sure you're *not the blonde's jealous lover?* the police had asked Matthew with narrowed eyes.

Matthew's stomach had turned at the absurdity of it. He'd pleaded with them to keep the information about the blonde a secret from Laurie; there was no need for her to know that her husband had been kissing another woman in a bar a half hour before his death. On the night before their baby's birthday. There was no need, Matthew had pleaded.

The detectives had agreed that there was no need because there was no link between the blonde and Robert's death. According to the bartender, Robert had been talking to a couple of other women that night; the blonde had simply been the last.

Matthew knew in his heart that the woman he'd seen Robert with was involved. He felt it in his bones like he'd felt every other terrible truth in his life. According to the detectives, the blonde had left the bar twenty minutes or so before Robert did. Had she killed Robert? Had a jealous boyfriend of hers? *Had* Robert gotten into a random drunken brawl, a brawl that had gotten terribly out of hand?

They didn't know.

And all Matthew knew was that Candy, if that was her name, had been draped over Robert a half hour before he was murdered. She was the last person to be with him. And she hadn't reacted normally when Matthew had barged in on them and dragged Robert away from her. She'd barely paid them any attention, in fact. She'd simply stirred her fancy drink and glanced around the nightclub as though the men she was with got yanked out of their chairs and dragged across the bar every night.

That was probably the case.

Either she killed his brother, or a jealous husband or boyfriend had seen them together and killed Robert. Matthew knew it.

The police weren't going to do anything. But Matthew was. He'd vowed in the early morning hours of last Sunday to find out what happened to Robert. He was going to do that much for the brother he'd never gotten along with. That much for the brother with whom his last communication had been a terrible, terrible argument.

But Matthew had turned up nothing. It was now Friday, almost a week since Robert had been murdered. His own private investigation had resulted in nothing but what the police had already shared with him. No one at Chumley's knew who the blonde was. No one saw or heard anything in the parking lot.

A week of nothing but wasted time. He'd walked

miles around Center City searching for Candy, looking for her in every store window, every coffee shop, every bar, every restaurant. Nothing. He himself had lived in Center City for the past twelve years, and he knew every nook and cranny. He was positive he'd find her. He'd known from the start that he'd have better luck searching for her once Friday night rolled around and along with it the "Happy Hour" that attracted throngs of men and women to Center City's many bars and nightclubs. If he didn't find her this weekend, he'd just keep searching. Matthew knew a thing or two about being relentless.

As president of his own small, successful marketing company, Matthew had left the daily running of the business to his second in command. There was no way he could concentrate long enough on work to even check in with his executive, let alone spend a single second thinking about campaigns. Over the past eight years, he'd put together an excellent team of people who he trusted, and he was never so grateful for that fact.

Robbie stirred in Matthew's arms, and he took the tiny Yankees cap off the toddler's head and caressed the wispy blond hair. *I'm going to find her, Robbie. I'm going to find out who took your daddy away from you if it's the last thing I do.*

Chapter Two

With a deep yawn, Mia washed and dried her dinner dishes and glanced at the clock on her kitchen wall. Eight-thirty P.M. The last day of the school year should have been a light, stress-free day, but instead, today had felt like one of the longest of her life. There had been the extra hour for detention, that uncomfortable scene with Norman Newman, and then she'd been deluged with comments and questions by Amy Farley as she drove the twins home at four.

I can't believe that Mr. Newman thinks he's your type, Ms. Anderson, the girl had said in one breath. *I mean, come on, he's such a dork, and you're so beautiful and well put together. Who is he kidding! Hel-lo! Haven't you noticed that the biggest losers and geeks have no problem asking out the prettiest and most popular girls? It's like they're too dorky to even know there's a hierarchy. Like . . .*

Mia hadn't had to reprimand Amy for her way of thinking; her twin sister had taken care of that, and the girls got into one of their famous arguments on the subject of looks and popularity and integrity. By the time Mia had dropped off the twins and said her hellos to Mrs. Farley, she'd had an enormous headache. And so she hadn't gone out of her way and driven to the shopping center in Bridgeville, the next town over from Baywater; she'd gone to the strip center smack in the middle of town. And of course, the moment she'd entered the drugstore to pick up a hair-color kit and some toothpaste, she'd been engaged in three conversations by parents of students. In the supermarket, she'd encountered four students, six sets of parents, and her avoid-at-all-costs neighbor, Mrs. Wriggles, who complained for fifteen minutes about how their neighbor's poodle was destroying all the flowers in their gardens and what did Mia propose they should do about it?

By the time Mia got home, put away the groceries, went for her forty-minute power walk, made herself a light dinner of a tuna sandwich, returned a phone call from her elderly aunt, slipped into an old paint-splattered T-shirt and sweatpants, cleaned the kitchen and repotted an outdoor plant that the neighbor's poodle had toppled over, it was eight-thirty.

She picked up the hair-color kit and headed into the bathroom. *In just a half hour, I'll be me again*, she thought, a smile forming on her lips. *I'll be me again and truly free of David, truly free of being someone that I'm not.*

Humming a song that Amy and Anne had blasted on her car radio earlier, Mia unpeeled the plastic gloves from the instructions of Medium Brown #7 hair color.

Twist off cap of color developer. Open bottle of color crème. Puncture cap—

The phone rang.

Let the machine get it, she told herself. *This is your time, Mia.*

But it might be important, she argued with herself. *What if it's Aunt Bessie and she's fallen or is locked out of her house, or what if it's Margot with an emergency?*

Aunt Bessie might have been seventy-two, but she was strong as an ox and had never once lost her car keys, let alone her house keys. And when had Margot *ever* called Mia with an emergency?

Just once, Mia thought, her gaze falling on the photograph of herself, Margot, and their parents that Mia had blown up and framed and hung on the bathroom wall. A strange place for a family photograph, yes, but Mia liked to look at the photo, her favorite, while she was enjoying her nightly ritual, a lavender-scented bubble bath.

"Just once," she repeated aloud in a voice so low she wasn't sure she'd spoken at all.

Eleven years ago. Eighteen-year-old Mia had moments ago arrived at the sleep-away camp where she'd been hired as a counselor when she'd been summoned to the camp office for an emergency telephone call. Her sister had been on the other end of the line. Margot had been crying so hysterically that Mia could barely understand her. But she'd heard the words *Mommy* and *Daddy* and *car accident* and *gone.* And she'd heard Margot cry like she'd never heard Margot cry before.

Tears streamed down Mia's face as the memories flooded her. The hair-color instructions and gloves fell from her hands onto the floor, and she dropped down on the toilet seat lid and covered her face with her hands. *Oh, Mama and Daddy. I miss you so much. So, so much.*

The phone continued to ring, snapping Mia out of her memories. The word *emergency* echoed in her mind, and she raced into the living room and grabbed the cordless.

"Hello?" she practically yelled. "Hello?"

When she heard whose voice it was on the other end, a wave of anger overtook her. If only she'd let the machine handle the call.

Norman Newman.

I don't believe this! Won't he ever learn? she asked herself in exasperation. *Enough is enough!*

"Mia, uh, I really did want to talk to you today, get to the bottom of this little mystery, but with those students in your classroom, I was unable to—"

"Norman, I'm right in the middle of something . . ." The only little mystery they had in common was why he kept pursuing her, despite her repeated *nos.*

"I'd just like to know why you've been lying to me, Mia," Norman said, his voice cold.

"Excuse me?" she asked, surprised by the tone of his voice.

"Why pretend that you aren't interested in dating when *dating* is all you do?" Norman said. "Why couldn't you just say, 'I'm sorry, Norman, but I'm already seeing someone else.' A *few* someone elses, for that matter."

What the heck was he going on about? "Norman, I really don't know what you're talking about. Not that it's any of your business, but I haven't gone on a date since before I was married five years ago." Mia glanced impatiently at her watch. She wanted to do her hair and be in bed by ten o'clock to get an early start on her garden tomorrow morning.

"I saw you out on the town in Center City Tuesday

night and again last night, Mia," Norman all but growled. "You were all over some guy. A *different* guy both nights. I was surprised enough to even see you in a place like Joe's Pub, but there you were. And when I saw you in LuLu's Lounge last night, I figured, yeah, this is more Mia's speed, but I was shocked at your behavior. I wonder what Principal Ashton would have to say if he saw you dressed that way, acting that *way.*"

What the—

And then Mia realized what Norman was talking about.

Margot.

"I tried to get your attention, Mia. Last night, I saw you notice me staring at you in absolute shock. But you acted like I wasn't even there, like you didn't even know me. Nice, Mia. Very nice."

How dare he! He didn't deserve the truth; he deserved the phone slammed down in his ear. But Mia had never hung up on anyone, and she wasn't about to lose her temper because of Norman Newman. "Listen to me, Norman, and listen *clearly.* I happen to have an identical twin sister who lives in Center City. I have no doubt that it was *Margot* you saw last night, and—"

He snorted. "You're really appalling, Mia. A twin sister? *Please.* Middle school is really the place for you if you have to resort to that kind of preteen lie. What kind of fool do you take me for? I happen to have a *master's* degree in *physics.*"

Mia gripped the phone, her anger getting the better of her. "Norman, I am hanging up right—"

"I was hoping we could discuss the matter and move on," Norman interrupted, "but your attitude on the phone right now—You can just forget it.

You can consider my invitation to date me withdrawn, *Ms.* Anderson. I no longer have any interest in someone like you."

Thank God.

The dial tone buzzed in her ear. Mia was so relieved that he'd both lost interest and had hung up that her anger started to ebb.

"You know what, Norman Newman?" Mia said aloud. *"Amy Farley was right about you. You are a total dork!"*

Shaking her head, Mia started back to the bathroom. Speaking her mind, even if no one heard but her, made her feel like the Mia she'd been with her family as a child and teenager. She'd never been afraid to say how she really felt with her parents or her sister.

And in moments, she'd soon *look* like the Mia she used to be when her parents were alive. Before Margot, in her private grief, had shut her out and gone off to live in Center City, doing who knew what, and before Mia had let herself be molded into something she wasn't by someone who didn't even care about her.

The sisters had never quite gotten back to the closeness they'd once shared before the death of their parents. But spending more time with Margot was at the top of her list for what she wanted to do with her summer vacation.

Mia took a deep breath and picked up the hair-color instructions. Yes, this promised to be a very good summer. Especially because it looked as though Norman Newman was finally out of her life!

Matthew drove the half hour home from Laurie's house, the twinkling lights of Center City reminding him suddenly of last Christmas. There had been no such thing as overboard for Robbie Gray's second Christmas. Matthew and Robert had strung thousands of white and colored lights inside and outside the Gray house, had brought home the tallest, most robust evergreen they could fit through the front door, and had bought more toys for Robbie than he could ever hope to play with.

It was the best Christmas Matthew had ever had. The first Christmas that had felt like Christmas. Matthew and Robert's parents had always celebrated the holiday season with a tree, a turkey dinner, a few gifts, and a lot of screaming, tears, and fighting. Matthew had stopped celebrating Christmas the moment he'd left his parents' house at age eighteen and joined the army. There had never been any reason to start celebrating thereafter, until an eight-pound reason came into his life. And so last Christmas, for Robbie, the Grays had given him a holiday befitting a prince.

Last Christmas, Matthew had truly loved his brother. Yeah, he knew he wasn't supposed to pick and choose, wasn't supposed to love his own brother conditionally, but Robert's disregard for people, for his own family, had made it impossible to love him any differently.

That was exactly the way Robert and Matthew had felt about their own father.

But the brothers were supposed to grow up to be different than their dad, *better*. Instead, Robert had become him.

Matthew didn't have any experience at parenthood, nor did he ever want any; but he'd vowed to do what he could to set a good example for Robbie, so that Robbie would grow up with at least one positive male role model in his daily life.

It had been so hard to say goodbye to his nephew an hour ago, so hard to place his warm, sleeping body back in his crib and walk out the door. He wouldn't be able to see Robbie for two weeks. Two weeks. Since Robbie's birth, *two* days hadn't gone by without Matthew visiting his nephew.

Matthew had wanted to stay for a while longer, to at least baby-sit his nephew for a few hours after the party so that Laurie could have private time to grieve, private time to cry. But she had a house full of family and friends and seemed to be holding up remarkably well. And so Matthew had felt all right in leaving.

He'd had strong motivation to leave. He wanted to get on the road, be back in the city by five-thirty at the latest.

Happy Hour.

Prime time for a woman like Candy to be out on the town on a Friday night after work, if she worked at all.

If she was out tonight in Center City, Matthew would find her. He'd recognize her in a heartbeat because he'd never, ever forget that face.

And not because she was unforgettable. Had Matthew been in Chumley's with a couple of buddies last Saturday night, having a beer, playing a round of darts, appreciating pretty women—not that he hung out in nightclubs—he never would have looked twice at Candy. Plastic Barbie types with caked-on makeup and revealing outfits weren't his type. Never had been and never would be.

No, he'd never forget her face because he *had* to

remember it. That face was his link to his brother's murder. To his brother's murderer. That face might even be the *face* of his brother's murderer.

While his brother was dead, while his nephew was denied a father, *she* walked around. She was probably on her way to Happy Hour right now. Matthew had no doubt that he'd find her perched on a bar stool in some skimpy outfit, her tongue down some married man's throat.

The thought of her made him sick.

He turned off the highway, anger burning in his gut. But by the time he drove the half mile to his high-rise apartment building in Center City, pulled into his parking spot, and turned the key in his apartment door, he felt only the weight of sadness.

He stood in front of the wall of windows that looked down twenty-five flights onto the city. *You're out there, Candy, or whatever your name really is. And I'm going to find you.*

Matthew let out a deep breath and turned from the window, his gaze falling on a mantel photo of his brother's family—Robert, Laurie, and little Robbie. Matthew had taken the photo just two months ago at his brother's birthday party at a steak house.

Matthew headed into the bathroom, stripped out of his Robbie-sticky clothes, and stepped under the spray of the shower. He mentally ran down Center City's most popular bars and nightclubs and came up with a list of five to start with. A few he'd been to before, with clients or for a staff member's birthday celebration. But never just to hang out, to pick up women. That had always been Robert's thing, and anything Robert had done, Matthew had always veered to the opposite.

As he shaved, he noticed the dark circles under

his eyes were clearing up a bit. Aware that he'd have the best luck tracking down Candy on the weekend, he'd gotten his first decent night's sleep last night since Robert's death.

He dressed in black pants and a pale blue shirt, ran his hands through his thick chestnut brown hair, and left the apartment.

It was time to find a killer.

Matthew found the streets of Center City crowded as usual for Happy Hour on a Friday night. Men and women, young and not so young, headed up and down the main drag, some dressed to the nines, some casual. Everyone suddenly looked so carefree, headed out for a night of fun. Matthew had never been that carefree. Never.

First stop, Chumley's. Last Sunday, when Matthew had started his search for Candy, he'd started in Chumley's. He'd thought it would be difficult to walk into the bar, the last place he'd seen his brother alive, the place his brother had been killed, the *reason* his brother had been killed. But it hadn't been difficult. Instead, being inside the nightclub filled him with a sense of peace, a sense that Robert's spirit, whether or not Matthew approved of that spirit, had been alive and well there for the last time.

Matthew pulled open the door to Chumley's and was greeted by a welcome blast of air-conditioning. The small nightclub was hopping. Men and women were three deep at the bar, and the small, round tables were nearly all filled. Two of the pool tables were in use, and a bunch of women and a few couples were dancing. Matthew ordered a club soda and looked around, slowly and carefully. His eye stopped at every blonde, but none was Candy. Once, he was sure he'd spotted her on the dance floor, but it wasn't her.

I'm going to find her, Robert. I promise you that. I promise Robbie that. I'll find out who took you from us, Robert. And I'll see justice done.

Matthew headed over by the jukebox and stood in the same spot where he'd stood when he'd argued with Robert. He closed his eyes.

"Like this song, huh?"

Matthew felt a tap on his shoulder and opened his eyes to find an attractive brunette smiling up at him. She was swaying to the music.

"Excuse me?" he asked over the blare of the jukebox.

She giggled and shook her head. "So what's a girl gotta do to get a good-looking guy like you to buy her a drink?"

Matthew noticed the gold wedding ring on her left hand. "Why don't you ask your husband that question?" he all but growled.

She stared at him for a second and let out a giggle, then seemed to catch on that he was serious. "I get enough of a holier-than-thou attitude from my boss at work. I don't need it at Happy Hour, you jerk." And she turned around and stomped off.

He was the jerk? Matthew shook his head and set his club soda atop the jukebox. He took another look around. *Where are you tonight, Candy?*

The door opened, and a group of women came in. Candy wasn't among them. He gave Chumley's another fifteen minutes, then headed outside. *Left or right?* he asked himself. He hated the idea of going left only to think of Candy coming from the right. He went left and headed into LuLu's Lounge, a popular nightspot with the twenty-something crowd. Just the kind of place his brother liked to prowl for young women. Matthew felt the familiar burning in his gut at the thought of Robert, married to a wonderful woman, father to a beautiful, healthy child, taking his good life for granted.

Cheating.

Just like their father.

It never ceased to amaze Matthew that two brothers could be raised in the same house, by the same parents, under the same terrible circumstances, and grow up with such different personalities, different hearts. Matthew had vowed never to marry, and Robert had always been looking for the right woman to make his wife. Matthew had vowed never to cheat on a woman, no matter how casual their relationship—and all of Matthew's relationships with women were casual—and Robert had been cheating on women since his first girlfriend at age thirteen. The Gray brothers were as different as night and day.

Matthew sat down at the bar at LuLu's and ordered a club soda and a plate of buffalo wings.

"I love buffalo wings!" chirped the woman to his right.

"Uh, I'd share, but I'm meeting someone," he told the redhead, who smiled and nodded and turned back to her friends.

Is it this easy to meet people? he wondered. Come to a bar, sit down, and voila, you're in a conversation with a stranger, making a date. Suddenly it all seemed a little creepy. You had no idea who you were talking to. A married man. A married woman. A psychopath. A neurotic rage-a-holic. You thought you were having a pleasant conversation with someone you were attracted to, and two weeks later, you were wishing you'd never laid eyes on the person.

Matthew met most of the women he dated through work. He didn't date at the office, not since his mistake four years ago, but instead liked to take out female clients who he found attractive and who expressed an interest. Clients always kept up enough of a shell to protect the business relationship, and therefore, things never got too personal, never got messy. If a woman asked where the relationship was heading, Matthew would be honest and explain he wasn't looking for a relationship. Usually, the woman would end things, but it wouldn't hurt the business relationship, since he'd been honest from day one.

Once, though, someone had fallen for him hard, and he'd ended up hurting her. Matthew had been through hell and back in his life, and breaking someone's heart had been right up there with the worst of times.

Yet his brother had risked breaking his own wife's heart every day. *How? How did you do that?*

As a plate of wings and blue cheese was served in front of him, Matthew put the past out of his mind and dug in to a hot, tangy piece of chicken. His seat at the side of the bar gave him a good view of the entire bar. No Candy.

And she wasn't at the next five bars he went into, either. By eight-forty-five Matthew had done the circuit twice. It was hardly time to give up; some people had only begun their Friday nights at this hour. But he couldn't stand the thought of another club soda, another smoky bar, another disappointment.

He breathed deeply of the warm, muggy June air and ran a hand through his hair. There were a few hotel bars he wanted to try over on River Boulevard. He slipped his hands into his pockets and headed down the crowded avenue. A long line was snaked out the door of an ice-cream parlor featuring fifty flavors. Fifty flavors. He chuckled. Robbie would eat only vanilla. It was Matthew's favorite flavor, too. Maybe he'd stop back on his way home and pick up a pint and drop it over at Laurie's as a goodbye gift—

Matthew froze. Standing at the counter with a chocolate ice-cream cone in one hand and a five-dollar bill in the other was Candy.

Chapter Three

Matthew rushed inside the ice-cream parlor to a few jeers about his cutting in line.

"Candy, right?" he said to the blonde.

Her eyes widened for just a moment; then she lost all expression. "Excuse me?" she asked, pocketing her change.

"Candy. It's Candy, isn't it? You were having a drink with my brother, Robert, in Chumley's last Saturday night."

No expression. The blonde slowly took a napkin from the dispenser and glanced up at him. "I'm sorry, but you must have me confused with someone else."

Matthew put his hand on her forearm. "I know it's you," he said coldly. "I'd remember you anywhere."

With that long, bleached blond hair, the make-up, and that fake-innocent expression, he had no doubt that the woman standing before him in tight jeans and a cropped tank top with her navel exposed was the same woman he had seen with Robert last Saturday night.

"I'm sorry," she said, "but my name isn't Candy, and I don't know what you're talking about."

And then she darted out the door.

He followed her and caught up with her on the street. She was walking very quickly. Staring straight ahead.

"My brother is dead," he said, enunciating every word. "The man you were with that night is *dead.* You left, and then twenty minutes later, he was found stabbed to death in the parking lot."

She froze for just a second, then resumed her quick pace. She said nothing.

"Lady, my brother is dead. I saw you with him." He grabbed her by the shoulders and stopped her in her tracks. "Did you kill him? Your jealous husband or boyfriend maybe? Or maybe Robert saw you with some guy in the parking lot and he got angry and started a fight, and your boyfriend ended up killing him in self-defense. I just want to know what happened. Tell me what happened, dammit!"

"Get your hands off me," she hissed, darting a sharp glance at him. "I don't know what you're talking about."

But he saw the fear in her eyes. She *did* know what he was talking about. "My only brother, the only relative I had left, is dead. And you were the last person to see him alive. Tell me what happened!"

She kicked him so hard that he saw stars for a second. And in the one moment that his eyes were closed against the pain, she ran.

Frantic, he spun around, trying to spot her. The

streets were so crowded with cars and people that he couldn't see straight down the block in any direction.

He ran to the left and strained to see, then to the right.

And just as the rain started coming down in buckets, he knew he'd lost her.

Twist off cap of color developer. Puncture and pour contents into color cremé—

The phone interrupted Mia again. Furious, she marched into the living room and snatched the cordless.

"Norman, I've just about had it with—"

"Mia, it's me. Margot."

"Margot? Is something wrong? You sound—"

"I didn't do it, Mia. I swear I didn't. I didn't do anything wrong! I just wanted you to know that before—"

Mia's heart was beating a mile a minute. "Margot, slow down! What are you talking—"

"Mia, I've got to go away for a little while. I'll contact you when it's safe. I just don't want you to worry about me. Okay?"

"Margot, I'm coming over right—"

"I love you, Mia. Goodbye."

Click.

Margot had hung up. Paralyzed, Mia listened to the phone buzz in her ear before punching in Margot's number.

"You've reached Margot at 555-3612. I can't come to the phone right now, so please leave a message and I'll return your call as soon as I can. Beep."

"Margot, pick up the phone. Margot! Please!"

Nothing.

"Please pick up, Margot. Please!"

Nothing.

Mia's knees started to wobble, and she dropped down onto the sofa.

I didn't do it. I swear . . . I have to go away for a while . . .

Didn't do what? What didn't she do?

Get up, Mia. Get up and go after her. Maybe she's still in her apartment, packing. If you hurry, maybe you can catch her.

Mia shot up and grabbed her purse.

The rain started coming down heavily just as Mia pulled off the exit for Center City and turned onto Bridge Avenue. She found a spot a few doors down from Margot's apartment building. Slinging her purse over her shoulder, she wrapped her arms around her, dashed into the lobby of the luxury high-rise, and headed for the elevator bank. She jabbed the *up* button five times.

"You'll break it!"

Mia turned around to find an older woman holding a miniature dog.

"Patience!" the woman snapped, scowling.

Mia closed her eyes and prayed for the elevator to hurry up. *Come on, come on!*

Finally, the elevator door opened, and Mia flew in and pressed the button for the seventeenth floor. The older woman pressed twelve. Mia groaned.

When the doors finally slid open on seventeen, Mia ran down the hall to 17K and pounded on Margot's door.

Come on, Margot. Please be there. You've got to be there!

No answer.

Mia knocked even harder, tears welling up in her eyes.

The apartment door to the right of Margot's opened suddenly, and a woman holding a baby stepped out and glared at Mia. "Ah, I'm strangely glad you're back, Margot. You left so fast earlier that I barely got my door unlocked before you were in the elevator, and I need to speak with you." The woman's expression was ice-cold. "I've had it with how loud you play your stereo at night. Twice I've asked you nicely to keep it down, and now I'm going to complain to management."

You left so fast earlier . . . So she was gone. Mia's heart sank.

"Actually, I'm not Margot," Mia told the woman. "I'm her twin sister, Mia—"

The woman rolled her eyes. "Just keep the music down, Margot. Or I'm going to petition to get you out of the building." She stepped back into her apartment and slammed the door.

Maybe she's wrong about Margot leaving, Mia thought, frantically shoving the spare key Margot had reluctantly given her into the lock. *Maybe Margot is still inside. Please still be inside, Margot. Please!*

The huge apartment was silent. Mia ran into the bedroom, into the bathroom, opened every closet. There was no sign of Margot. She searched for a note, for anything, but there was nothing out of the ordinary. Nothing to indicate that Margot was in any kind of trouble or had left in a hurry. But clearly, she had.

Mia checked the answering machine. Two messages. She pressed Play.

One call was from Margot's dry cleaner to let her know her clothes were ready. The other was from Mia.

Shaking, she stood in the center of the apartment. She'd never felt so alone in her life. Never.

She looked out the window. Seventeen stories up, people and cars looked miniscule. *Am I safe in here?* she wondered. *Is someone after Margot? Someone who might have access to her apartment?* Shivering, Mia wrapped her arms around herself. *Is someone staring up at the window right now?*

Trembling, Mia ducked away from the window. There was one of those trendy coffee lounges across the street. Maybe she could go there and sit by the window, watch for Margot. She'd be able to see the door to the apartment building, and she'd be in a public place and safe.

Taking a deep breath, Mia let herself out.

Where the hell was Candy?

Hiding, that was where. She was probably curled up on her sofa at home, laughing at the notion of Matthew wandering around in the rain, searching for a woman he'd never find.

Exhausted and soaked to the bone, he finally stopped walking and ducked under the awning of a closed electronics store. He'd searched everywhere for Candy, looked in every bar, every store, every doorway, every alleyway, but he'd lost her. And now that she knew he was looking for her, she'd be that much harder to find.

Damn. Damn. Damn.

At least the rain was letting up. Maybe he'd better just head home and think strategically about how to find her. He'd built a company from scratch; he could find one bleached blond bimbo.

As he walked toward his car, he noticed a coffee lounge was still open. That was what he needed: a tall cup of strong black coffee. Matthew headed inside and shivered from the blast of air-conditioning.

But it wasn't the cold air that made him freeze. It was the woman sitting at the long granite counter along the window, looking nervous and worried and every bit the lying murderer.

Candy.

Chapter Four

"I want answers. Now."

Mia started. A man was staring at her. No, *glaring* at her.

"Excuse me?" she asked him. Had he even been talking to her?

Mia glanced around her; she was the only person sitting at the long, narrow bar in front of the expansive window. At least six or seven stools sat empty to her left; a wall was to her right. The man was clearly talking to her.

"You kick me again," he said, "and I'll kick you back. Hard. Woman or not. Understood?"

Mia stared at the man. Was he a psychopath? She glanced behind him at the two teenagers behind the counter. Singing along to the loud alternative rock music blaring in the background as they prepared cappuccinos and lattes, the superthin duo hardly looked capable to swat a fly, let alone hurl this six-feet-plus muscular lunatic out the door.

"They're not going to come to your rescue, Candy," the man said, his dark blue eyes intense upon her. "And don't even think about running again. This time, you won't get away."

Mia grabbed her purse with one hand and shot up, but the man clamped a hand down on her forearm.

"Take your hand off me this minute!" Mia shouted, panic setting in. Her heart was racing so fast she couldn't quite catch her breath.

"Hey, no lovers' spats allowed in here," trilled the male teenager from behind the counter. The boy shook his finger at them and grinned. His female coworker giggled; then they both went back to preparing coffee drinks.

Mia was about to scream at them to help her, but the man tightened his grip on her arm and startled her.

"Please," he said, desperation in his voice. "I just want to know what happened last Saturday night. Please."

"I have no idea what—"

Oh God, oh God, oh God. This had to have something to do with Margot.

"Stop it with your lies, Candy," he said. "I want the truth, *now.*"

Candy. That was the second time he'd called her that. Maybe he was just some psycho and this had nothing to do with Margot.

Her heart slowing a bit, Mia took a deep breath and looked the man square in the eye. "Look, I have no idea who you are or what you're talking about. My name isn't Candy."

"I didn't think it was."

Huh? "Then why did you just call me that?"

"Because that's the phony name you gave Robert in Chumley's Bar. A name as phony as the number you wrote down on that cocktail napkin."

The panic returned. Perhaps he was talking about Margot after all.

I saw you in some Center City bar all over some guy . . . Margot sure did get around, Mia thought, Norman Newman intruding in her thoughts.

She picked up her cup of coffee to feign nonchalance. "You must be confusing me with someone else," she said, trying to shake her arm from his grip. *Someone like my identical twin sister,* she added silently.

He tightened his hold on her. "You already tried that lie on me, remember? Right before you proved yourself a liar by kicking me and taking off."

Wait a minute. Margot had kicked this man? Because he'd been hurting her? Chasing her? Was *he* the reason that Margot had gone into hiding? Or perhaps this guy was one of her boyfriends? He was certainly the type. Six-feet-two, leanly muscular, and very good looking, with a shock of thick, chestnut brown hair and deep blue eyes, he was the kind of man Margot would go for. And the kind of man Mia wouldn't even think would look twice at her.

"You changed your clothes, I see," he said, his gaze raking her up and down. "Sweats and a paint-splattered T-shirt hardly seem your style. But as I told you earlier, I'd recognize you anywhere."

"I'm not who you think I am," Mia said wearily.

"Stop lying!" he growled. "For one damned second, stop your lies. I saw you in Chumley's last Saturday night with Robert. Right before he was killed. And you're going to tell me what happened."

Mia froze. *Killed?*

Someone had been killed?

Someone Margot had been involved with?

Was this what Margot had been referring to on the phone?

Oh God, oh God, oh God. Margot, what did you get yourself mixed up in?

He stared at her. "Even without all that make-up, it's you. I'll never forget your face. *Never.*"

Men rarely did forget Margot's face, Mia thought absently. But instead of gazing at her the way men usually did her sister, he looked as though he wanted to spit on her. He slowly sat down on the stool next to her, his hard thigh pressing hers against the wall. "I want answers, now," he repeated, his hand still on her forearm.

"I'm going to tell you again," she said. "You're confusing me with someone else. I've never seen you before in my life."

That was the truth. If she had seen this man before, she would not have forgotten. On the scale of men, Norman Newman was on one end, and this guy was on the other.

He raised an eyebrow. "You *saw* me a few hours ago, when you kicked me in the shin and took off. Maybe you'd like to see the welt that your spike heel left."

Why had Margot kicked him? Were they dating? Had they gotten into a fight? A lovers' quarrel? Did lovers kick each other and run off?

Despite the many questions she had, she wasn't going to tell him that she had a twin. Not until she knew what his relationship to Margot was.

And not until she knew why her sister had been frightened enough to leave town and go into hiding.

He sat so close to her she could smell the soap he used. "Last Saturday night, you were all over my brother in Chumley's. Okay, my brother was all over *you.* Twenty minutes later, he's dead in the parking lot." His grip tightened. "I want to know what happened."

The color had drained from Mia's face. "Your *brother—*"

"Don't play dumb, Can—whatever your name is."

"I'm . . . sorry about your loss," Mia said. Despite everything that was transpiring, the man had lost his brother. Even though she and Margot weren't close, if she lost her sister, she'd be as devastated as she'd be were they the best of friends.

Where are you, Margot? What did you do? Who is *this man?*

"All his money was still in his wallet," the man said quietly, his eyes downcast. "Robert still had his wedding ring, his expensive watch. You two got into a fight in the parking lot, and you stabbed him, right? He fought back, and you kept stabbing him. Was it self-defense? He probably had too much to drink, and you got into an argument. Is that what happened?"

Oh, God.

His dark blue eyes shone fiercely. "Or your boyfriend or husband came looking for you and caught you together in the parking lot and attacked Robert. Was that how it went down?"

Mia shrank away from him. She had never seen a man so angry. Never.

She glanced up at the teenagers behind the counter. Between the music blaring and a group of college students laughing in one corner, her conversation with this man couldn't be heard, and no one was paying them any attention. He could wrap his arms around her neck and strangle her, and no one would notice.

"Tell me what happened!" he growled again.

Mia swallowed. "I'm going to tell you for the last time. I'm not who you think I am."

The man's shoulders slumped. His hand still on her arm, he reached his other into his back pocket and pulled out a brown leather wallet. "Here. This is my nephew. He just turned two. He's now fatherless."

Mia could have sworn she saw tears well in his eyes. But then he blinked hard, and the cold desperation returned.

"His name is Robbie," he said so quietly that Mia wasn't sure she heard right. His hand loosened on her arm as he stared at the photograph.

Should I make a run for it? she wondered. *Scream bloody murder?* For all she knew, this guy was a psychopath and was making up everything.

I didn't do it, Mia. I swear . . . I have to go away . . .

He wasn't making it up. Mia would bet on it.

But what if *he* had killed his brother and was trying to frame Margot?

Don't be taken in by his good looks and expensive clothes, she told herself. *You were taken in by that once before.*

And those tears she thought she saw could have been staged.

Don't trust him, not for a second. Only the truth will get you the answers you seek, but be careful, Mia.

"My name is Mia," she said.

His head whipped up, and he stared at her. "Mia," he repeated.

"I'm going to be honest with you," she continued. "I have an identical twin sister—"

His hand tightened on her arm. "Stop it! Stop lying!"

"I'm not!" she shouted. She lowered her voice. "I'm telling you the truth. My sister called me about an hour ago and told me she didn't do it and that she had to go away for a while—"

"Didn't do what?" he asked frantically. "Didn't kill Robert? Is that what she was talking about?"

"I don't know! I don't know anything!"

"What else did she say?" he asked.

"Nothing. Margot was frantic and upset. The entire conversation lasted no more than thirty seconds. I jumped in my car and drove to Center City to see if I could catch her, but she was gone when I arrived at her apartment."

He was staring at her, clearly trying to determine if she was telling him the truth.

"My sister is not a killer," she added with conviction.

"Why should I believe you have a twin sister?" he asked. "How do I know you're not playing me? How do I know you're not this *Margot* and that you didn't just wash off the makeup and put on your gym clothes to try to fool me?"

Mia couldn't think of a single thing to say. She was so tired, and this situation was so complicated, so fraught with danger. Completely out of her league.

"I've already dealt with you once tonight," he snarled. "You nailed me hard in the leg and ran away. That makes you guilty. Otherwise, you would have stayed to talk to me."

"You're not exactly easy to talk to," Mia said angrily. "How would you like to be accused of murder, a murder you know *nothing* about."

"I have a reason to be upset," he said. "And I know exactly how it feels to be suspected of murder."

Mia gasped and stared at him. Who the hell was this man? What was she dealing with here?

"The police," he said wearily. "You saw what happened at Chumley's. I can understand why they're suspicious of me." He closed his eyes for a moment and hung his head, letting out a deep breath full of sorrow.

Why? Mia wondered. What happened at Chumley's? Why would the police suspect this man had murdered his own brother?

Mia reached for her own wallet and pulled out a photograph. "I'm not lying about having an identical twin sister. Here's a picture of the two of us. It's a few years old, but it's us."

The photo was actually five years old, taken during a rare get-together in which she and Margot had sat for a few shots in one of those black-and-white photo booths. Mia had asked Margot for help in choosing a wedding dress from a boutique in the mall, and Margot had surprisingly agreed. Usually, her sister didn't have time.

Mia bit her lip as the memory flooded her. Margot had flurried through the boutique, selecting a bunch of dresses for Mia to try on, and when Mia had come out of the fitting room in the first one, Margot, sitting on a little stool in front of the panel of mirrors, began to cry. *"Oh, Mia, you look so beautiful,"* she'd breathed. Mia had been shocked at first to see Margot so moved, but then the sisters had flown into each other's arms and hugged and cried, and it had been clear that they hadn't been crying tears of joy over the wedding details. They'd been crying for their losses, including the loss of each other.

Dress and veil chosen, they'd then headed for the food court for lunch and had passed the photo booth. Sitting for the photos had been Margot's idea. When the little black-and-white foursome of shots appeared in the slot, Margot had split them, taking two for herself and giving Mia the other two.

Mia and Margot had spent a few afternoons together since then; but Margot hadn't liked David, and the sisters had barely seen each other during the last five years. This past year, Mia had called her sister often, wanting to talk about the divorce, wanting to reconnect, wanting to open up about the differences that had always kept her and Margot from being close; but Margot had always been too busy, and Mia had finally stopped trying.

"So you weren't lying," the man said, snapping Mia out of her memories. She'd almost forgotten where she was for a moment. The man let out a deep breath and removed his hand from her arm. He gestured to Margot in the photo. "That's her and that's you," he said. "Right?"

He'd easily picked out Margot, glammed out as usual. Mia had been wearing an easy-to-remove button-down plaid shirt that day and her usual lack of makeup.

"Mia." He seemed to be trying out the name on his lips. He stared at the photo for a few more seconds, then handed it back. "And Margot. What's your sister's last name?"

"I don't think that's necessary information," Mia said, looking him in the eye.

He glanced at her. "Let's head over to the precinct. It's just a few blocks from here. We'll tell them about Margot's phone call and—"

Whoa. Whoa. "No police."

"Why not? If you're so sure she's innocent, she has no reason to be hiding, does she?"

Mia sucked in a breath. "I'm not betraying my sister before I know what's going on."

He shook his head and looked at her in exasperation. "My brother is *dead.* Do you understand that? *Dead.* I think that's a little more important right now."

"I'm very sorry about your brother," Mia said. "But I don't believe that my sister had anything to do with his death. She may have been in the wrong place at the wrong time and it looked bad to you, but I know she wasn't involved in his murder."

"What makes you so sure?" he asked.

"I know my sister," she said. But the moment the words were out of her mouth, she knew it was a lie. She didn't know Margot. Not at all.

"Well, I *don't* know her," he said. "I want to go to the police and tell them what happened today, that I found her and she ran. You probably can think of some place she'd go to hide."

"I'm not betraying my sister!" Mia yelled. "I've told you that!"

And even if she *would* betray Margot, she had no idea where her sister would go to hide. No idea at all.

"We have to go to the police," he said through gritted teeth. "I finally have some proof that she's connected to Robert's death. It's the only link I've got, dammit."

So the police didn't think Margot had anything to do with the murder? Then why did this man?

"I'm not going to the police," Mia said. "And that's final. Not until I'm sure she's safe, that she's not being set up—"

He raised an eyebrow, and the hard expression returned to his dark eyes. "If the two of you have nothing to hide, why are you afraid of talking to the cops?"

"Look," Mia said wearily. "Get this through your head—I don't know anything. I hadn't talked to my sister for a couple of weeks before tonight. I don't know why she's so afraid, why she felt the need to go into hiding. I assume because you accused her of murder the way you accused me when you thought I was her."

He was silent.

"My sister isn't a killer," Mia said quietly.

"So let's go to the police," he said again. "Let them find her and bring her back for questioning. If she's innocent, she's got nothing to worry about. Why should she be out there hiding and worrying when she could be safe at home?"

He was manipulating her. Once, Mia would have fallen prey to it, given him what he wanted. But Mia had been married to a master manipulator. She would never let anyone speak down to her again or try to twist the facts or lack thereof. She'd been a fool once, and she'd paid dearly. She wasn't going to play with her sister's life now.

"I want to find out what happened just as much as you do," Mia said. "Maybe we can put our heads together and do some investigating on our own, figure out how my sister met your brother, what their relationship was."

"How do I know I can trust you?" he asked. "How do I know you won't run the second I turn my back?"

She could tell he was a man who didn't trust anyone and never had. "Because I want to know why my sister is in hiding as much as you do. You want to find your brother's killer, and I want to clear my sister's name. We need to work together."

Those dark blue eyes stared at her. "Okay," he said. "Okay."

A blast of warm, muggy air hit Mia in the face as they left the coffee lounge. "Margot lives there," she said, pointing across the street at her sister's high-rise.

He glanced at her, then at the building. "I've been looking for your sister all week, and she's been right in there the whole time?" He let out a harsh laugh and shook his head. "I live three blocks from here, straight up Bridge Avenue."

"Well, now I know where you live, but I don't even know your name," she said.

"Matthew. Matthew Gray."

Mia nodded. "Mia Anderson. Anderson isn't my sister's last name, by the way."

He nodded. "I don't know you well, Mia Anderson, but I'm under no illusions that you're careless. You're staying at your sister's, I assume?"

Mia nodded. "Maybe she'll—"

"Call? Come back?" he finished for her.

Her gaze on the sidewalk, Mia let out a deep breath. "I was going to say 'come back.'"

"If she does, will you tell me?" he asked.

"I don't even know how to get in touch with you," Mia said.

He reached into his wallet and withdrew his business card. *Matthew Gray, President and CEO, Gray*

Enterprises. "My home phone number and cell number are on the back."

He gestured ahead for her to cross the street, and they walked in silence across Bridge Avenue to Margot's apartment building. "I'll see you upstairs," he said.

Mia had no idea if she could trust this man, if she *should* trust this man. But a small part of her did. In any case, if she was in any danger upstairs, Margot's eagle-eared neighbor would surely call management *and* the police.

She nodded, and they headed inside. As they waited for the elevator, an older couple gave Mia what was clearly a dirty look.

Your neighbors certainly don't like you, Margot, Mia thought. *Or approve of you.* She wondered if the couple figured Margot was returning home with yet another man.

What is your life like, Margot? Mia wondered. Suddenly, the wild city life that Margot led seemed lonely instead of glamorous. Mia would rather have busybody old Mrs. Wriggles talking her ear off and gossipy Jill Clark on the other side than have neighbors who looked down their noses with both jealousy and condemnation in their eyes.

How different our lives are, Mia thought. *Then again, our lives have always been vastly different.*

The elevator pinged open, and the two couples rode up in silence. Mia felt the eyes of the older woman on her. When the other couple got off on the sixth floor, Mia let out a breath she hadn't even known she was holding.

"I'll see you to the door," Matthew said.

Mia glanced at him, and he held her gaze. She nodded and led him to apartment 17K. She opened the door so it was slightly ajar, then turned to say good night.

"I'd like to get started on our investigation right away," Matthew said. "I don't quite know where to begin, but I'll give that some thought tonight. How about if I meet you here tomorrow morning at nine. If that works for you."

Mia nodded. "Nine tomorrow morning is fine—"

She froze at the sight of a large manila envelope under the door. "What's this?"

Matthew shrugged. "Open it."

Mia picked up the manila envelope. There was nothing written on the front or back. She slid a finger under the seal and pulled out a folder.

And gasped.

Inside the folder was a short typed note, a wad of cash, and two black-and-white five-by-seven photos.

Of Margot kissing a man in a crowded bar. Of the same man with his arm around her shoulder, his tongue darted in her ear.

"What is it?" he asked.

Mia was shaking. The folder dropped from her hands, and its contents fluttered to the floor. Matthew kneeled and picked up a photo.

And gasped himself.

His face white and his fingers trembling on the photograph of Margot kissing a man, Matthew straightened to his full height. "This man is my brother, Robert."

Mia stared at him, and the color drained from her own face.

Matthew read the note: *"Well done, Margot. Your fee is enclosed. Your services will be required again on July tenth at MacDougal's on Water Street. Ten P.M.*

Mia's knees gave out, and she dropped to the

floor. She tried to form words, but no sound came out of her mouth. Matthew stretched his arm out to her, offering her his hand. The expression on his face snapped her out of her meltdown.

"This doesn't mean anything!" she shouted. "Whoever sent this note is the killer!"

"Then what's the money for, Mia?" Matthew asked coldly. "That's fifteen hundred dollars. The pictures are proof that she was very likely the last person to see Robert alive, the note thanks your sister for a job well done, and the cash is her fee for murder."

"No!" Mia screamed. "No! You're wrong!"

The door to the apartment next door opened, and the woman who Mia had met earlier stomped out in her bathrobe. "I'm warning you, Margot. I hear one more peep out of your apartment and I'm calling the cops." And then she stepped back inside her apartment and slammed the door.

Matthew looked confused for a moment. "I guess I'm not the only one confusing you with your sister."

"Well, there's a first for everything," Mia said bitterly. Before Norman Newman's accusations earlier this evening, Mia hadn't been confused with Margot since sixth grade.

"What?" he asked.

"Nothing. Forget it." Mia stood and closed the door behind them. Her hands were shaking so hard she clasped them together to calm them. "My sister would never physically hurt anyone. I'd stake my life on that."

He stared at her, his expression unreadable, then handed her the folder. She looked at the contents again, the cash, the photo, the note.

"I think we should take all this to the police, Mia."

She dropped to her knees again and wrapped her arms around her. Tears stung the backs of her eyes.

Matthew knelt down next to her. She felt his arm around her. The heavy pressure felt good.

"It's okay, Mia," he said. "No police. At least for the time being. We'll get to the bottom of this ourselves, if we can."

Mia closed her eyes and let herself sag against him. Strangely, the warm, clean scent of him comforted her. She leaned closer, and her head dropped on his shoulder.

He flinched, and she pulled away, her cheeks burning. What had she been thinking? This stranger, this man she'd met under terrible circumstances not more than an hour ago, wanted to go to the police and have an APB put out on her sister. Mia was important to him only because she was the link to her sister. She'd have to remember that. They were both using each other.

He cleared his throat. "Will you be okay tonight?"

She could manage only a weak nod.

"You're sure?" he asked.

She nodded again. "I'll be fine."

"I'd better get going, then. I'll see you here at nine A.M. All right?" He searched her eyes. She could tell that he was trying to determine if she'd really show up, or if she'd disappear in the middle of the night.

"I'll be here."

And she would be. Because for the first time in her life, Mia Anderson was going to use someone, too.

* * *

Matthew lay in bed, staring up at the ceiling fan that provided the only relief from the sticky June heat. His air conditioner had conked out earlier in the week, but he'd been so focused on Robert's death that he hadn't even noticed how uncomfortable the still, warm air was.

His chest slick with sweat, Matthew grabbed the T-shirt he'd peeled off a couple of hours ago and mopped his face and torso with the cool cotton. He wondered if Mia was asleep or if she'd been tossing and turning for the past two hours as he'd done.

It was now three A.M., and he'd been unable to shake her from his thoughts since he'd gotten home at midnight. Was she telling him the truth? He'd find out. For now, it didn't matter, as long as she was there tomorrow when he arrived. He'd uncover what he needed if he had her help.

But help doing *what?* He'd been so focused on finding Candy—Margot—that he hadn't even given two thoughts to what he'd do once he'd *found* her. That she'd run from him earlier this evening told him she had reason to be scared, that she was involved in Robert's death in some way, however indirectly.

But what he and Mia had discovered slipped under Margot's door proved she was involved *very* directly.

Someone had photographed her and Robert during two romantic moments in a Center City nightclub. Why? What was the fifteen hundred for? And what exactly were her services? Was she a hooker?

Damn. He had so many questions and no answers.

Matthew flipped onto his stomach and let the breeze from the ceiling fan cool his back, thoughts of Mia running through his mind. He found it hard to believe that identical twin sisters could be so different, but Mia seemed the farthest thing from a hooker or someone who'd cozy up with a married man in a bar.

Then again, what did Matthew know about her? Nothing. All he did know was that his reaction to her when he saw her in the coffee lounge had been strangely very different from his reaction to Margot in the ice-cream parlor and on the street. He'd felt nothing but cold contempt for Margot, in Chumley's and earlier this evening, yet when he saw Mia in her old sweats and paint-splattered T-shirt, fresh-scrubbed, her hair in a ponytail, she'd seemed so vulnerable, so real. Like someone he could have a real conversation with. Nothing like the fake plastic bleached blonde from Chumley's.

Stop it, Gray, he warned himself. *Some soap and sweats doesn't change who a person is. The sweetest-looking people can be pure evil.*

He'd learned that a long time ago.

An image of Gwen Harriman popped into his mind, and instead of blinking her away the way he usually did, he let the memory of her face, the memory of their relationship, linger. It was good for him to remember. So he wouldn't be taken in again.

He'd never seen a more angelic-looking woman than Gwen Harriman. And despite his own rule never to get involved with a member of his own staff, he'd fallen hard for the beautiful twenty-two-year-old he'd hired as his secretary. Four years had passed since he'd fired her from his company and his life, but he felt the sting of betrayal as freshly as if it had all happened yesterday. Before she'd conned him, he'd thought he'd been proven wrong, that it *was* possible for him to fall in love, for him to consider marriage and family and a future filled with possibilities of the human spirit.

He'd been wrong. Gwen had shown him how wrong he'd been.

He hadn't made any mistakes since.

And he wasn't about to start with another angelic-faced woman who most likely hid a serpent's heart and poisonous bite.

No. He would not make that mistake again.

Especially not with the justice of his nephew's father on the line.

Chapter Five

At eight forty-five the next morning, Mia began pacing the expansive living room of Margot's apartment. There was lots of room to worry back and forth, given the lack of furniture. Margot had been living in this particular apartment for the past seven years, yet the place looked exactly as it had when Margot had invited Mia over when she'd first moved in.

A coffee-colored leather sofa, no pillows, a huge wood entertainment center with all the trimmings, and a wall of windows with no blinds or curtains made up the living room's decor. The only word Mia could think of to describe the room was *cold.* There was no color, no decorative touches, no artwork. No personal touches. Why wouldn't Margot want to make her home comfortable? Surely she couldn't find this austere apartment cozy?

Then again, as Mia had already acknowledged, she hardly knew her sister. The girl she'd once known had decorated her bedroom in the house they'd grown up in with crazy zebra stripes and hot pink, Margot's feather boa collection all over the fun, zany room. Her room had screamed "Margot," had screamed personality.

And now this. Margot's adult bedroom was no different from the living room. Beige, neat, and not a personal touch anywhere, save a photo of Margot, Mia, and their parents, the same one that Mia kept in her bathroom.

Last night, when Mia had spotted the photograph between an array of expensive perfumes and a jewelry box, she felt a small sense of relief for the first time in hours. The photo faced the bed; it was clearly the first thing Margot saw when she woke up in the morning and the last thing she looked at before falling asleep at night.

So perhaps I do know my sister, after all, Mia thought. No matter what the emotional or physical distance between them, she knew her sister's *heart.*

Margot wasn't a killer. And she wasn't mixed up in a murder. Mia had no idea what to make of the contents of that folder, but she would stake her life on one thing: Margot was being used as a pawn in someone else's game.

Mia simply had to convince Matthew Gray of that.

She'd thought of little else last night, as she'd tossed and turned for hours in Margot's huge king-size bed. The mystery of her sister's sudden flight, the mystery of Matthew's brother's death, had been too much for her to even think about alone. So instead she'd thought about the feel of Matthew's arm around her shoulder, her reaction to his nearness.

His reaction to *her.*

His flinch.

She'd forgotten herself in that moment last night, forgotten that a man wouldn't want Mia Anderson leaning on him, needing his comfort. She wasn't the kind of woman who inspired feelings in men, whether desire or protectiveness.

Stop it! she mentally yelled at herself. What the hell was she doing, standing here thinking like this? Her sister was in hiding, for God's sake. A man was dead. A child was without a father. And she was whining about being unattractive to men.

About being unattractive to Matthew Gray.

The doorbell rang, and Mia practically jumped out of her skin. She glanced at her watch. Eight fifty-nine A.M.

She took a deep breath and hurried to the door, peering through the peephole. There he was, looking as handsome as she remembered, if a bit rumpled and sleep-deprived. He hadn't shaved.

She opened the door, and his presence filled the doorway. As he stepped inside, the huge, empty apartment seemed small and almost claustrophobic.

"Good morning," he said.

"Morning."

He wore jeans, a white button-down shirt, and black shoes. Since Mia had left her own condo in a hurry last night, she'd had no choice but to select an outfit from Margot's closet. Which meant tight jeans and a slim-fitting T-shirt were her only option if she wanted to dress casually. Margot didn't own a single pair of jeans that weren't form-fitting, and her T-shirts were all teeny-tiny V necks. At least her sister owned a few pairs of sneakers—without heels or diamonds encrusted in the laces, too.

Mia noticed Matthew's gaze rove over her, and she knew it had nothing to do with her. She looked like Margot, even without makeup. The long, blond shiny hair, the sexy outfit. She was the same old lie she'd been for the past five years.

"Can I get you something, a cup of coffee?" she asked him. His nearness was overwhelming her, and she wanted to escape him for a few moments. "Margot doesn't keep much in the way of food, just some olives and a few bottles of wine, but she does have good coffee."

He was glancing around the apartment. "Yeah, sure," he said absently. "I could use some coffee. We can catch a bite a bit later."

Mia nodded and hurried into the kitchen. She hadn't even realized she was holding her breath until she let it out in one gush when the swinging doors came to a close behind her.

She measured the water and added the coffee and washed the measuring spoon until it gleamed. Then, to procrastinate just a bit longer, she washed it again. *You have to go back in there,* she told herself. *He's not in charge here. He doesn't make the rules. He doesn't dictate your life.*

He's not David Anderson, and you're not that voiceless woman with no self-esteem. Do not let him bully you.

A bit fortified, Mia took another deep breath and headed back inside the living room. Matthew was standing by the wall of windows, staring out at Center City. It was a gloomy, gray Saturday morning, not yet raining, but the clouds were threatening. At least the rain would help wash away some of the unseasonably warm weather, she thought dumbly, grateful to focus on something other than the situation at hand and why Matthew Gray was standing in her sister's living room with his intense eyes and suspicions.

"The coffee will be just a minute," she said, taking a seat at the edge of the sofa.

He turned toward her and nodded. "I think we need to figure out what the contents of the folder mean in terms of Margot's involvement with Robert, what the person who hired her *hired* her to do in the first place."

"Where should we begin?" she asked and instantly regretted the question. Why was she giving *him* the power to make decisions that affected *her* sister?

"Does she have a study or a desk in her bedroom?" Matthew said. "We could look through her papers, see if—"

"Wait just a minute," Mia interrupted. "I don't know about rifling through her personal papers—"

"How do you propose we find out what that folder was all about, then?" Matthew countered, those intense dark blue eyes trained on her. "Perhaps there are other folders, other photos, other notes."

Mia closed her eyes. Other photos . . . other notes . . . other evidence of Margot's required services, whatever the hell they were . . .

Calm down, girl. Don't get overwhelmed. Just think—and do what makes you *comfortable.*

Problem was, everything connected to this situation made her extremely *un*comfortable.

Matthew sat down in the center of the sofa. "Mia, I'm a businessman. I certainly wouldn't like it if someone went poking through *my* desk when I wasn't around. But my brother is dead, and your sister is in hiding. We have no choice."

Mia felt her every muscle clench. He was right. They didn't have a choice.

I'm sorry, Margot, but we're going to have to look through your personal things. I'm really sorry. I know how you hate people in your stuff.

That was the truth. Once, when Margot and Mia were fifteen, their mother had been worried that Margot was smoking marijuana (she was), and Mrs. Daniels had rifled through Margot's bedroom drawers for evidence. She'd even flipped through her journal to find out if Margot was writing about drugs. Margot had caught their mother red-handed reading her diary. She'd never seen her sister so angry as that day. Mia wasn't sure if Margot had been angry that her mother hadn't trusted her or that her mother had violated her personal belongings. She'd always figured it was a combination of both.

I did it for your own good, for your own protection, their mother had said. *And now that I know for sure you* are *smoking that funny stuff, you're going to a rehab center . . .*

The memory brought a gentle smile to Mia's lips. Margot, who'd smoked pot a few times with her friends and whatever boyfriends she had at the moment, had been so scared by what she'd seen during her "weekend rehab" that she'd never touched marijuana or any drugs again.

Mia had never been a believer in ends justifying means as a defense, but she did know that Matthew was right in this particular case.

"Margot has a desk in her bedroom," she told him. "It's locked, but I'm sure she keeps the key nearby."

He stood. At five-foot-seven, Mia always considered herself a tall woman, but Matthew towered over her.

Mia led the way into Margot's bedroom, uncomfortably aware of the king-size bed that dominated the room. "There," she said, pointing unnecessarily at the desk under the window. She went to the dresser and rifled through the jewelry box for the key. "Here." She handed the key to Matthew. "I'll go get us each a cup of coffee."

He nodded and set to work, and once again she was grateful for the chance to escape. Both from him and from what they might find in that desk.

What *had* Margot been hired to do? Mia wondered as she poured two cups of coffee and put what little milk Margot had in a creamer. Clearly the photos and the cash had something to do with each other, but what? Had she been paid to kiss Matthew's brother in a bar so that someone could take the pictures? Why?

Mia realized *she* had some questions for Matthew. About his brother, Robert. Hadn't Matthew said that Robert's wedding ring and watch hadn't been stolen? Why was a *married* man kissing her sister? Sticking his tongue in her ear? In a public place, no less.

Don't be naïve, she chided herself. *Your husband was a married man, and that didn't stop him from sticking his tongue and other parts of his body in women who were not his wife.*

White-hot anger burned in her stomach. How dare Matthew make Margot look like the bad one here! His own brother, a married man with a child at home, had been "all over" her sister in a bar. Perhaps Matthew should direct some of his anger toward his own cheating brother.

Whoa, there, Mia. A little judgmental, don't you think? You don't know the situation or Matthew's brother any more than he knows you or your sister. Find out the facts.

She couldn't help wondering what Robert Gray was all about. Perhaps the man had some enemies. Enemies who had nothing to do with Margot, nothing to do with a man and a woman sharing a few kisses and a few drinks in a bar.

Then what was the note and the cash all about? a small voice in her head demanded as she set the coffee, creamer, and a bowl of sugar on a tray and carried it into the bedroom. And what "services" of Margot's were "required on July tenth" at MacDougal's Bar?

The only "services" that Mia knew Margot offered were those of interior decorator. Though her sister's apartment wasn't the best example of her skills, Mia had seen Margot's work, well a few photographs, anyway. Margot was great at her job and quite passionate about decorating, albeit other people's spaces and not her own. So what "services" were required at ten P.M. at a bar on a Saturday night? And why did those "services" involve risqué photographs and cash?

"Key worked," Matthew said, and Mia looked over to where he sat on Margot's leather desk chair, rifling through the top desk drawer. "Paid bills, files for what looks like interior decorating clients— Mia, come look at this."

"What is it?" she asked, setting the tray on the dresser and hurrying over to him.

"A handwritten letter dated two months ago from someone named"—he turned the page and scanned the bottom of the letter—"Justin."

Justin? Margot had never mentioned a Justin.

Matthew swiveled in the chair to face Mia. "Listen to this." He held the one-page letter in front of him and read, "*Unless you give up this little side job of yours, Margot, it's over between us. I know that your interior decorating gigs don't pay very well, but what you're doing to supplement your income is creepy and sickening, and I can't deal with it anymore."*

"Creepy and sickening," Mia echoed numbly. "Does he say what the side job is?"

Matthew scanned the brief letter in silence. "No. Just that the time has come for her to make a choice. Him or the job."

"*What* job?" Mia wondered aloud. "What job entails meeting a man at a bar, kissing him, and having your photograph sent to you with a cash fee of fifteen hundred dollars?"

"I think we know *what* job," Matthew said softly. "Prostitute. Hooker. Looks to me like the person who sent the note and cash and pictures was simply paying her for satisfying her client—not that my brother ended up satisfied," he added darkly.

Mia's cheeks flamed. "My sister is not a prostitute!"

Matthew tilted his head and regarded her. "Then what?"

"I don't know! But I know she's not a prostitute."

"Mia, you've already hinted at the fact that you and your sister aren't very close. How do you know what she does in her spare time?"

She stared at the hardwood floor, unable to speak.

Matthew leaned back in the chair. "I think my brother arranged for a prostitute with a service, got Margot, flirted with her in Chumley's, and then things went sour when they were heading to his car to have sex either there or at a motel."

"Don't make me sick," Mia snapped.

"Don't be so naïve," he countered.

"Margot is *not* a prostitute."

"How do you know?" Matthew asked.

"I know."

"Like you know where she is right now?" he said. "Why she ran if she's not guilty of killing my brother?"

"Stop it!" Mia shouted, clamping her hands over her ears. "Just shut up!"

Matthew shot up and took her hands in his. He held them in front of him. "Mia, I'm sorry. I'm sorry. I'm just trying to find answers."

"Well, find *facts* first, and then throw around accusations. I could come up with a few scenarios myself for what might have happened to your brother—situations that don't involve my sister."

"Fair enough," he said, releasing her hands. "Fair enough."

Mia glanced at him, surprised by his quick compassion. He'd push, but he'd backed down when he crossed a line.

Some people never backed down; they pushed little by little until you were off a cliff.

Mia stretched out her hand for the letter and he gave it to her. She read the short note. "I wish there was more information. All he says is that he cares about her and that she has to choose."

"Well, we know what choice she made," Matthew said softly.

Mia looked up at him. "I suggest we pay this Justin a visit. I know we don't have much here to go on, but from his letter I get the sense that he's a decent person, someone who really did care about Margot."

"I agree," Matthew said. "And his return address is on the back of the envelope." He handed Mia the envelope. "Oak Ridge Road is only about a mile from here."

Mia dropped down on the edge of the bed and closed her eyes. She felt him step near even before she felt the depression of the mattress as he sat down next to her.

"I know this can't be easy for you, Mia," he said. "But between the two of us, we'll come up with the answers."

When she opened her eyes a moment later, he was back at the desk.

"Let's see what else we find, and then we'll head out to Justin Graves' place," he said, opening the second drawer.

Mia took a breath. What else *would* they find?

Matthew was almost grateful that they hadn't found anything else in Margot's desk. He didn't think Mia would be up for another terrible surprise. They had continued to search for an hour and had come up with nothing that might shed some light on what exactly Margot's "creepy" side job was—if it *wasn't* "high-priced call girl."

"My car's right there," Matthew said, pointing to the silver BMW he'd conveniently parked in front of City Bagels. Five minutes ago, he and Mia had ducked inside the small shop to get a quick breakfast of two bagels and cream cheese to go; she'd insisted on paying for her own, and he hadn't argued. Something had told him she needed to win a few battles.

As she slid inside the passenger side of his car,

Matthew couldn't help but notice the way her tight jeans molded to her shapely thighs and how flat her stomach was underneath the tight T-shirt.

"These are my sister's clothes," Mia said suddenly, and he quickly darted his gaze straight ahead. He'd been caught checking her out. "I don't usually wear such tight clothing, but—"

"You don't have to explain yourself to me, Mia," Matthew said. "And anyway, you look very nice."

"I'm sure you think so," she replied coldly.

What the hell is that supposed to mean? he wondered.

He dared a sideways glance at her, but she was staring straight ahead out the windshield. She pulled her bagel sandwich out of the bag and took a bite, which seemed his cue to drop the personal talk and start driving.

Forget trying to figure her out, Gray, he told himself. *You don't care anyway. You just need to find out what happened to Robert, and Mia is your ticket there.*

"We're lucky it's Saturday," he said to keep their conversation on track. "We might just catch Justin at home."

Mia glanced at him and nodded. She didn't say a word during the ten-minute drive to Oak Ridge Road. Matthew pulled up in front of a town house and noted the word *Graves* on the mailbox.

"This is it," he said.

Mia looked out the window, her expression tight.

"Look, Mia, whatever we find out, it'll be the truth, and that's what we're after, right? No matter how hard it might be to hear."

He didn't know why he felt the need to comfort her, but he did. Yes, he did know: they had to work together, and if she was going to fall apart and tremble and cry at every bad corner, they'd never get to the bottom of what had happened to Robert.

Mia's gaze dropped to her lap. Matthew could have sworn he saw her lip tremble. She placed her practically uneaten bagel back inside the bag.

"Let's go," he said, releasing the electric lock and opening his door.

But she didn't move. She sat staring at her lap, and now her lip was trembling in earnest.

"Mia—"

"You're right," she interrupted quickly. "The truth is always what matters. No matter how hard it is to hear."

And it usually *was* hard, Matthew thought grimly.

He got out of the car, hurried around to the passenger side, and opened Mia's door for her. She stepped out, and again, he was unable to stop himself from appreciating how lovely she truly was. Her long, straight, shiny blond hair was pulled back into a low ponytail, there wasn't a shred of makeup on her beautiful face, and her pale brown eyes—so like a doe's—sparkled despite the overcast gloom of the day. Her skin was smooth and creamy and her lips naturally red and full. The rest of her was almost too much to take in—firm, high breasts accentuated by the skin tight V-neck T-shirt and those mesmerizing, fit-her-perfectly jeans.

She was absolutely breathtaking, just as she'd been last night in her paint-splattered baggy T-shirt and sweats.

Ignore her, he ordered himself. *Focus on one of her nostrils or a hair of her eyebrow. Try not to look directly at her, especially not at her eyes.*

Yeah, that'll go over well while we're talking about something important.

Her effect on him had him worried. The last time he'd had this kind of reaction to a woman, he'd almost lost the corporation he'd built from the ground up. This time, he would risk nothing and lose nothing. It was that simple.

Mia is a means to an end, just as you are to her. You want to find your brother's killer; she wants to clear her sister's name. Whether you're working at cross purposes or not, you each need the other to get what you need. Don't forget that.

"Okay, let's do this," he said and started up the walkway to the three-story town house. Mia trailed after him.

As he rang the bell, he noticed that this was a private residence and not separate apartments as he'd originally thought. Justin Graves, whoever he was, clearly did well for himself.

Because he was a pimp to high-priced hookers? If Margot's fee was fifteen hundred, his cut had to be—

No. The direction his thoughts were taking wasn't worth his time. A pimp wouldn't want his meal ticket to *give up* the job, nor would he find said job "creepy and sickening." From the sound of Justin's letter, he was clearly in love with Margot and wanted the best for her, something she didn't seem to want for herself.

A tall, good-looking, thirty-something man in wire-rimmed glasses and green surgical scrubs opened the door. His expression darkened at the sight of Mia. "What are you doing here, Margot?" he asked, weariness evident in his voice.

Mia opened her mouth to speak, then closed it.

Matthew rushed to answer. "My name is Matthew Gray, and this is Mia Anderson, Margot's twin sister."

Justin's look of surprise faded. "Ah, yes, she mentioned an identical twin." Suddenly, his eyes clouded over. "Did something happen to Margot? Is she all right?"

"Why do you ask?" Matthew queried, his suspicions rising.

"I've known Margot for six months," Justin said, running a hand through his short blond hair. "In all that time, her twin sister never came knocking on my door at ten-thirty on a Saturday morning looking as though someone had died."

Someone did die, Matthew thought grimly.

"We're sorry to bother you," Mia rushed to say with a glance at Matthew, "but I have reason to be worried about Margot; and well, we found a letter you wrote to her, and we're hoping you could answer some questions for us."

Justin glanced from Mia to Matthew, nodded, and opened the door for them to enter. He led them into a beautifully decorated living room, masculine in its décor, yet inviting. A golden retriever lay sleeping in a patch of sunlight by the windows. "Recognize your sister's work?" Justin asked Mia as he gestured for them to sit down on the leather love seat.

Mia offered a weak smile and nodded, but Matthew could tell she was lying. She hadn't recognized her sister's style, and it clearly bothered her. Because she wanted to be closer than they were?

Better question was, if Margot had this kind of talent as an interior decorator, why was she taking money for having her ears licked by married men in bars?

"So why are you worried about Margot?" Justin asked, taking a seat in a chair across from them.

"My sister left town in a hurry, worrying for her safety," Mia said carefully. "I drove over to her apartment last night, hoping to catch her or find her, but I've had no luck. My friend Matthew here is helping me find out what scared Margot into leaving town."

"Well, that's not a case for Sherlock Holmes," Justin said, leaning back.

Matthew and Mia glanced at each other. "Because . . . ?" Matthew prompted.

"Well, if you found the letter I wrote her," Justin explained, "you know that I gave her an ultimatum—me or her side job. She chose the job. And the job comes with serious consequences—dangerous consequences."

"What exactly does my sister do?" Mia asked, her voice catching.

Justin let out a breath. "You don't know?"

Mia shook her head.

"She's a decoy," Justin finally said.

"A decoy?" Matthew asked. "You mean, like a police decoy?"

"Similar," Justin said, "except she doesn't work for the police. She works for whoever wants to set someone up to see if that person will take the bait."

"Wait a minute," Mia said. "I'm not following."

Matthew suddenly realized what Margot's little side job was. And it wasn't pretty.

"Let's say you want to find out if your fiancé can be trusted before you marry him," Justin said. "So you hire a very attractive female decoy to be in the same place at the same time as your fiancé and see if he'll go for her."

"*Go* for her?" Mia echoed.

"Take the bait," Matthew explained.

Justin nodded. "Exactly. Margot's job is to show up, say, at a bar or a party, all dolled up and sexy, and position herself near the target. If he doesn't make the first move, she will. A photographer or sometimes a videographer records the interaction between Margot and the man on tape."

Matthew looked at Mia. She was very pale and looked to be on the verge of tears. The revelation had obviously shaken her badly.

"May I use your rest room?" she asked Justin, her voice barely audible.

"Of course," Justin said. "Second door on the right."

Mia practically ran to the bathroom and shut the door.

"I had a similar reaction when I found out what she did to supplement her income," Justin said.

Matthew nodded, and both men were silent for a moment.

"So I gather you're a doctor?" Matthew asked, taking in Justin's green scrubs.

"Surgeon. Center City General. I know this'll make me sound like a jerk, but you can imagine how screwed up Margot's thinking is if she gave up a doctor who loves her for the life of a sleazy decoy. Independent or not, there are other ways to make money."

"A lot less dangerous ways," said Mia as she exited the bathroom and sat back down on the love seat.

"You okay?" Matthew asked her.

Mia looked at him and nodded, but he could tell she'd been crying. Those beautiful light brown doe eyes were full of sadness.

"Can you tell us anything about who hires her?"

Mia asked suddenly as though she wanted to cover her vulnerability. "Do you have any specific names?"

"No," Justin said. "Margot never talked about her work. And she'd never reveal the name of a client."

"So her clients were wives and fiancées and girlfriends?" Matthew asked.

"And rich daddies wanting to make sure their precious little girls weren't involved with lying cheats," Justin said.

"So her clients were male *and* female," Matthew put in.

Justin nodded. "Anyone with a suspicious mind. A bride-to-be's mother, a worried godfather, anyone."

"But are fiancées or wives the majority of her client base?" Mia asked.

"Honestly, I don't know," Justin replied. "She wouldn't tell me much about that part of her life, only that it was her night job and that her clients were both male and female."

"Was . . . was there ever—" Mia broke off and shook her head.

"I think what Mia wants to know is if there was sex involved," Matthew explained.

"That was the first thing I asked her," Justin said, "and she assured me she had never and would never go that far. A client had to be satisfied with getting the conversation or photos of kissing on tape. She refused to ever enter a car or a hotel or an apartment with the target."

"But she'd *leave* the setup location with a target?" Matthew asked.

"Yes," Justin confirmed. "If it was necessary to record the guy trying to set up a future date or to convince her to go to a hotel or his car for sex."

Matthew glanced at Mia; she was both pale and red-faced at the same time.

Justin glanced at his watch. "Look, I've got rounds in ten minutes and had better get to the hospital. If you have more questions, I'd be happy to answer them for you, but I really don't know more than I've told you."

"Just one more question," Mia said. "Can you tell us where you were last Saturday night?"

Matthew glanced at Mia in surprise. That had been his next question.

"I was on rounds from six P.M. to two in the morning," Justin responded. "Why? Is that when Margot took off?"

"Sort of," Matthew said, standing and extending a hand, which Justin shook. "Thanks for taking the time this morning to sit down with us. We really appreciate it."

Mia rose as well. "Did you really love Margot?" she asked Justin.

The man nodded. "I did."

With that, the three of them walked to the door in silence.

Chapter Six

"No," Matthew snapped. "Absolutely not."

"Why?" Mia demanded. "Why is it so inconceivable?"

"Robert's wife did *not* hire Margot," he replied coldly. "I know Laurie Gray, and there's no way she hired a decoy to see if Robert would cheat or not. End of subject."

Mia followed Matthew to a shady weathered bench on the promenade in Center City Park, anger boiling in her gut. How dare he! First he refused to even discuss the theory she raised, and then he demanded she drop it. Well, she wouldn't drop it. Just as he hadn't dropped *his* theory earlier—his *wrong* theory—that Margot was a prostitute.

"Matthew, we have to consider the idea," she insisted, sitting down next to him.

Without a word, he rolled up his shirtsleeves, dug noisily into the bag on his lap and pulled out the two cans of Coke and two submarine sandwiches they'd stopped for after leaving Justin's house a half hour ago. He handed Mia a Coke and a sub without looking at her.

Mia had learned a long time ago that being shut out didn't mean she had to shut up. He was going to listen to her whether he liked it or not. "Margot received photos of herself with Robert, a note thanking her for a job well done, and a wad of cash. Who else but Robert's wife would have a vested interest in finding out if he'd cheat or not?"

Silence. Matthew unwrapped his sandwich and took a bite. She waited for him to chew and swallow. Still he said nothing.

"Matthew?"

He bit into his sandwich again and stared out at the ocean. Mia rolled her eyes, leaned back against the bench and took a sip of her soda. She would give him five minutes' reprieve to eat in peace, and then she'd force the issue. Whether or not it gave him a stomachache.

She raised her face to the now bright blue sky, glad the sun had come out while they'd been at Justin's. It was almost noon, yet the temperature was in the low—instead of high—eighties for the first time this week, and the humidity was under fifty percent. The sun bounced off the gray-blue waters of the Atlantic and the mile-long promenade, which was packed with people enjoying a perfect summer Saturday afternoon: rollerbladers, dog walkers, couples walking hand in hand, families having picnics in the grassy area behind the benches. Mia wondered how many other couples out here were trying to solve a murder mystery. *I'll bet none,* she thought wearily.

Matthew and I are not a couple, she amended.

"You're missing a pretty good sub sandwich," Matthew said.

"I'm not hungry," she replied.

"Suit yourself."

I will, she responded mentally. *I sure won't be changing my opinions to suit* you.

Seems Margot didn't change her opinions to suit a man, either, Mia thought, Justin's words echoing again and again in her mind. Why *would* a woman give up a great guy who loved her for the life of a decoy?

My sister is a decoy. A woman paid to entice men into cheating.

Why would Margot do that? Mia wondered. The question had been plaguing her since they left Justin's. Where could such cynicism come from? Margot and Mia's parents had been happily married for twenty years before the car accident had claimed their lives. With the exception of a few typical clashes and teenage-provoked angst, their family life had been full of love. And Margot had had countless boyfriends, none of whom had cheated on her or even hurt her badly for that matter—at least as far as Mia knew. Had her sister been so scarred by their parents' deaths that she'd lost her faith?

"We should check out Justin's alibi," Matthew said suddenly. "Just because he's a doctor—just because he *says* he's a doctor—doesn't mean he's telling us the truth about anything."

Yes, we should, Mia realized. For the past half hour she'd been so focused on Robert's wife as the suspicious spouse—and so annoyed by Matthew's refusal to consider Laurie Gray as a suspect—that she hadn't even considered that Justin had his own motive for killing Robert: jealousy. But that didn't mean they shouldn't check out Laurie Gray's alibi, too.

Matthew turned toward her. "Maybe Justin spotted Margot with Robert in Chumley's, spied on them, flew into a jealous rage, and waited to ambush Robert in the parking lot."

"It's definitely plausible," Mia agreed, "but what about the pictures, the note, the cash? That proves Robert's murder wasn't random, but premeditated. He was set up."

"That's a good point," Matthew said. "And that would mean Justin, or whoever the killer is, *chose* Robert as a victim."

"Why?" they said in unison.

Matthew sighed. "We've got a hell of a lot more questions than answers."

Which means we can't rule out suspects just because you think they're not involved, Mia thought. *We're going to investigate Laurie Gray. Whether you can deal with it or not, Matthew.*

She glanced at him in time to see his tongue flick over his lips to catch a drop of mustard. She darted her gaze to the sandwich on her lap; she unwrapped it and took a bite more to have something to do than because she was truly hungry.

How could she be so aware of Matthew as a man? With all she had on her mind, with everything she would have to face and face up to, how could his very presence manage to have such an impact on her?

He's just a good-looking, masculine man, she told herself. *Any woman would find him attractive.*

Even a woman who has absolutely no interest in dating or romance.

Get your mind off Matthew and onto the case. Onto Margot.

"Dollar for your thoughts," Matthew said, turning to look at her.

His dark blue eyes met hers, and for a second, she envisioned herself in his arms, underneath him. . . .

She blinked, shocked at herself.

"Um, I was just thinking about Margot," Mia said, hoping her cheeks weren't as red as they felt. *Focus, Mia. Focus on what's important. And trust me, it's not your sex life—or lack thereof.* "I just can't understand why she would want to do such a thing—be a decoy. It makes no sense to me. Our parents were so happily married. They loved each other and us so much. There was no cheating, no suspicion. Just love and trust."

So how did you end up with a guy like David Anderson, who didn't understand the first thing about love or trust, let alone appreciate or respect those things? Don't be so quick to judge Margot, she admonished herself.

"You and I grew up in very different homes," Matthew said.

Mia glanced at him. "What was your—"

He stared out at the ocean. "Let's just stick to Margot's psyche, okay?"

"Okay, sorry," she said, taking a sip of soda. But once again, the focus was Margot, when they could very well be examining *Robert's* psyche, *Robert's* life.

"What's Robert's wife like?" Mia asked. "I gather that you think very highly of her."

Matthew nodded. "She's a wonderful person. Very kind, generous. A great mom."

"And you're one hundred percent sure that she couldn't have—"

"Forget it—" Matthew snapped. "Don't even bother going there."

"Matthew, I'm going to throw your own words back at you. We have to get to the truth, no matter how hard it is to hear."

"My sister-in-law didn't hire Margot."

"How do you know?" Mia asked, using his own tactics on him.

He stared at her, then stood up and placed his hands on the promenade railing, his back to her. "I don't know," he said. "But I'd bet just about anything on it."

"But, Matthew, your brother was clearly cheating on her," Mia said. "Maybe Laurie suspected that he was and wanted to find out for sure, so she hired Margot."

Mia could see the muscles tense up in his back. "Laurie didn't know and didn't suspect," Matthew said, turning around to face her. "Robert was sure of both."

Mia glanced at him. "So you knew your brother was cheating on his wife?"

"Look, it's complicated," Matthew said, running a hand through his hair. "Was I supposed to tell her?"

Mia let out a breath. "I don't know."

"That's what our fight was about," Matthew said softly, his eyes downcast. "I was passing by Chumley's last Saturday night, Robert's favorite bar, and I had a feeling I'd find him in there. And there he was, with his arm around your sister, his mouth on her neck, sitting so close to her he might as well have been on top of her."

Mia's heart went out to him. "Your last conversation with Robert was an argument?"

Matthew nodded and closed his eyes. "I saw him there with her, and I dragged him up out of his chair and over by the jukebox and asked him how he could pull this crap, how he could cheat on his wonderful wife, how he could cheat his own kid that way."

"What did he say?" Mia asked.

"He told me to mind my own business. That was my father's line, too," Matthew added. "As though the way my dad treated my mother, treated us kids, wasn't any of our concern."

"Oh, Matthew, I'm so sorry," Mia said softly, going to him. "I—"

"Forget it," he said, turning back to the water. "I know Laurie very well, and she's a very kind, sweet, trusting person. Robert told me he was sure she didn't know about his cheating, and if that's true, then she wouldn't have hired a decoy to set him up. Besides, she's very frugal. I highly doubt she'd spend fifteen hundred dollars on her suspicions."

Mia still wasn't taking Laurie Gray off her list of suspects so fast. Especially when there were only two people with motives—Justin Graves and Laurie Gray.

She sat back down on the bench and took a sip of her soda. "Well, then who else might have hired Margot to set up Robert?"

Matthew joined Mia on the bench, and the two were silent in thought for a few moments. They both stared out at the ocean, as though the answers could be found in the murky depths.

"I think we'd better search Margot's apartment again," Matthew said. "If she received that one folder, I'm sure there are others. Maybe there's a hidden compartment in her desk where she keeps them."

"Maybe that . . . job was her first one, her only one," Mia said in a rush, "and that's why she got so scared, because there she was, just paid to see if some married man would go for her, and he ends up murdered; so she got scared and ran . . ." Mia trailed off, realizing how stupid it sounded and how awful she sounded. *Some married man* was Matthew's brother, and she was talking about him as though he were a random stranger. She understood that Matthew wanted to think the best of his brother and his wife, despite the circumstances, just as she wanted to think the best of Margot.

Matthew's expression was stony. "From Justin's letter and what he had to say, it's clear that Robert *wasn't* her first job. I think you need to face up to what she did for a living, Mia. Just as I've had to face up to the fact that Robert was a womanizing bastard."

Mia bit her lip. She did need to face the truth that she didn't know her sister, just as she'd faced the truth about her husband, her marriage. There was nothing to be gained in life by hiding your head in the sand. She'd learned that the hard way.

Womanizing bastard. . . . Those were harsh words. Mia wondered what Matthew's relationship to his brother was—what their home life had been like. From what Matthew had said and had hinted at earlier, the Gray household had been the polar opposite of the Daniels house.

She had so many questions for him, but she knew now wasn't the time.

"Why don't we eat up, then head back to Margot's and do a thorough search," Matthew said.

Mia nodded and glanced down at the practically uneaten submarine sandwich on her lap. She tried to imagine ever having an appetite again—or the stomach for what they might find hidden among Margot's things.

They drove back to Margot's building in silence. Parked in silence. Rode the elevator in silence. And entered the apartment in silence.

Never had silence been so loud—or so uncompanionable.

Even without a word between them, Matthew couldn't remember ever being as aware of a woman as he was of Mia. Her presence. The smell of her shampoo. Her soap. Her—

As he followed her into the bedroom, he forced that last thought away before it could even complete itself.

Mia sat down on the edge of the bed, clasped her hands together, and stared at her shoes. A moment later, she sprung up and headed inside the walk-in closet near the windows.

He could tell she was nervous.

Because of what they'd find? Because she knew her sister was guilty and she was protecting Margot? Because she herself was "Candy"? Was Mia playing a role here?

No. If he could trust his instincts, which he'd honed after his education in betrayal at the hands of Gwen Harriman, Mia was the real thing. He had definitely met *Margot* in the ice-cream parlor, been kicked by *Margot* in the street. The sisters might look exactly alike, save the makeup, but they were very different women.

So different that Matthew was curious about Mia. Damned curious. There was so much he wanted to know about her, so much that didn't seem to make sense. Weren't identical twins supposed to be, well, identical? In character and personality as well as in looks? Granted, Matthew didn't know much about Margot; in fact, he knew hardly anything about the woman, but he did know she was a paid decoy—not a pretty job.

He got the sense that Mia couldn't even imagine such a profession existed.

But was anyone really that innocent? Perhaps a better word for it was *naïve.*

Who *was* Mia Anderson?

She was fiercely protective of her sister—that much he knew. Loyal. And yet at the same time, she certainly didn't know much about her own twin's life. Why? Perhaps because they *were* so different.

Why are you surprised that siblings can be nothing alike? Matthew asked himself. *You and Robert were always night and day,* he realized.

Not always, Matthew amended. After "the incident," as the Gray family had always called it, Robert had changed.

Just as Matthew had changed.

"Looks like just a ton of clothes and shoes in here," Mia said from inside the closet, and Matthew was grateful for the reprieve from his thoughts. "There are a lot of shelves with boxes. Probably just hats and shoes, but worth a look, I guess."

He nodded. "We shouldn't rule anywhere out. Even the hamper makes a good hiding place. I'll start with the desk. I'll try not to bust up the wood while looking for hidden compartments."

She popped her head out of the closet and regarded him, then nodded.

"Could you get me a butter knife or even a spoon?" he asked her. "Something I could use to jimmy open a compartment."

She nodded again and hurried out of the room.

When she returned with the knife, he couldn't help but notice how tired Mia looked, how vulnerable. Gentle shadows slightly darkened the area under her eyes, all the more noticeable because of her fair coloring.

Stop thinking about Mia and start thinking about the investigation, he chided himself.

She sat back down on the edge of the bed, and Matthew got to work on the desk. Anyone with such incriminating evidence had to have a hidden drawer, he thought as he knocked along the bottoms of the drawers for hollow areas. After all, you didn't simply throw away notes and photos that implicated you as part of something dirty, legal or otherwise. And Matthew hadn't found a paper shredder among Margot's possessions.

There had to be other notes, other photos. Other men whom Margot had been paid to entice.

As he searched, he was uncomfortably aware of Mia sitting on the bed, staring at the floor, hoping against hope that he wouldn't find anything else.

But he would. He knew it. And she did, too.

She pounced up again. "There's a stepstool in the kitchen. I'll just go get it and check the top shelves of the closet."

"Good idea," he said, and watched her hurry from the room. A moment later, she returned and set up shop in the closet.

A half hour later, though, Mia was looking a lot less nervous, and Matthew was feeling a lot less confident.

He'd found nothing. No hidden compartments. No folders. Nothing to do with the work of a decoy. No more folders. No more photos or notes. Nothing.

Dammit. He exhaled a breath.

"Matthew, look what I found," Mia called from inside the closet.

He headed inside and found her trying to steady herself on the stepstool while lifting a large metal box from a top shelf.

"Hey, careful," he said, steadying the stool. He reached up a hand to help her down, and when her warm palm touched his, when her slender, delicate fingers slightly clutched his own, his breath quickened.

Suddenly, all he could smell was traces of green apple shampoo and clean, fresh soap, and the scent that was uniquely Mia. He had an urge to pull her down into his arms, crush her against him. . . .

He was sweating.

"Matthew? Are you all right?" Mia asked. "You look a little flushed."

He blinked and shook his head. *Concentrate, Gray. Concentrate.*

"I'm fine," he told her. "Just a little stressed. Let's get you down from there. Hand me the box."

She did and climbed down, her nearness winning in the fight against his desire for her.

It's just physical, he assured himself. *Lust. Nothing more.*

"A locked metal box hidden away on a top closet shelf seems pretty promising," Mia said, averting her gaze. She looked at the wall, the floor, back to the wall.

Hmmm . . . Interesting. He'd thought the situation was what was making her nervous, but now, he wondered if he, too, had an impact on her.

If *he* made *her* sweat. . . .

She glanced up at him, those pale brown doe eyes full of so much, yet all of it unreadable. What was she thinking?

"There's a combination lock on the box," she said slowly.

He wondered if there was a combination to Mia. Something that would unlock her mystery.

Don't be a melodramatic idiot, he told himself. *If you want to know something, just ask her.*

Are you divorced? Separated? Seeing anyone?

"I have no idea what the combination could be," Mia said, staring at the box.

Neither do I, he thought, acutely aware of the rise and fall of her chest as she took each breath.

What the hell? he wondered.

Physical desire, he reminded himself. Simple lust. That was all.

It had been a long time, after all.

Forcing his attention away from the smooth, creamy expanse of skin the V of her T-shirt exposed, Matthew sat down on the bed and jiggled the lock. It was a steel combination lock built into the box, the kind you programmed yourself and the kind impossible to bust open.

Whatever was in this box was something Margot wanted protected from snoops.

"Let's try her birthday," he suggested.

"I know that, since it's my own," she said with a small smile. She sat down on Margot's desk chair. "August tenth."

"Eight ten," Matthew repeated, conscious that he was committing the date to memory as he set the numbers eight, one, and zero on the combination. He tried to pull up the latches. Nothing.

"What else?" he asked. "Any other special anniversaries in her life?"

"Well, she's never been married, no kids . . . ," Mia said. "I'm not sure if there are any special dates she'd choose."

"How about one of your parents' birthdays or their anniversary," Matthew said.

Mia brightened. "Yes, she'd probably choose their anniversary. It was September first."

"Was?" he asked without thinking.

"They were killed in a car accident when Margot and I were eighteen," Mia said softly. "Sometimes I can't believe eleven years have passed since I've seen them, since I've heard my mama's voice, seen my father's gap-toothed smile."

Matthew reached over and put his hand atop hers, which were folded on her lap. She flinched, and he pulled away his hand.

What the hell are you thinking? he asked himself for the second time in five minutes.

You don't make her nervous. She isn't attracted to you.

She probably hates your guts. For what you're putting her through. For your accusations. For your refusal to even discuss her theory about Laurie.

He doubted she'd appreciated that. After all, he'd slammed her sister's name through every kind of mud, and one question about a member of *his* family, and he'd all but walked away from her on the promenade earlier this afternoon.

He thought he was so defensive because of how tiny his family was. But clearly Mia had a tiny family herself. Her parents were gone, as his were. And she had a twin sister she couldn't be more distant from.

Perhaps they had more in common than he'd thought.

"I'm not sure what else to suggest," Mia said. "The only date I can recall Margot getting excited about was the day my divorce was finalized."

Ah. So she *was* divorced. Matthew felt an odd sense of relief and then the familiar desire to know more about her. What had happened to her marriage? Mia seemed the type to choose cautiously, yet given her age, she couldn't have been married very long, unless she'd wed at eighteen.

He couldn't imagine a man giving her up easily.

"Well, let's try that date," Matthew said, more to have something to say than because he thought for a second that someone would choose someone's divorce date as a combination to a lock.

And, if he was honest, so he'd know when she'd divorced without having to pry.

"December twentieth," she said.

"Were you separated for a while before that?" he asked, again without thinking.

She glanced out the window. "Yeah, for six months. He pretty much lived in the den, and then he moved out at the end."

Matthew nodded. "I didn't mean to pry."

"It's okay," she said, glancing at him, those doe eyes again full of an emotion he couldn't place. "My divorce was the best thing that ever happened to me."

He nodded again. "I wish my mother had believed in that way of thinking. Instead, she stayed married to my father, probably for my and my brother's sakes, and it was the worst thing she could have done. For herself and for us."

She held his gaze, her eyes now full of questions. Questions he had no intention of answering.

So change the subject, Matt. And keep it off your personal lives from now on. The two of you are working together to get to the bottom of Robert's death. Keep your mind—and other things—on the bottom line, man.

"December twentieth," he repeated, setting the numbers.

The lock popped open.

Mia's eyes widened, and her mouth dropped open.

"Guess your sister thought your divorce was the best thing that ever happened to you, too," Matthew remarked.

Mia bit her lip, then spun around in the desk chair and faced away from him.

Idiot, Matthew thought. *Why'd you go and say something like that?*

"Mia, look, I'm sorry. I didn't mean to be insensitive—"

She spun back around and faced him, a trace of tears under her eyes. "No, it's okay. I—it's just that . . ."

She trailed off and covered her face with her hands.

Matthew kneeled by her side. "Mia? What is it?"

"I . . . I just had no idea Margot cared so much," she said, her voice small and broken. "I didn't know I meant much in her life at all. We hardly spoke . . ."

He took her hands away from her face and held

them in his. "Then I guess if any good can come out of this, Mia, it's this. The good things we'll uncover."

She looked at him and nodded. "You're right," she said through a sniffle. "And I should be grateful I have a second chance to get to know my sister," she added. "Oh, Matthew, it must be so hard for you—"

"Let's see what's in the box," he interrupted, getting up and moving to the bed. Once again, she was encroaching upon an area he wasn't willing to talk about, wasn't willing to think about.

His brother was dead.

His only brother.

Matthew let out a deep breath and flipped open the top of the box.

He withdrew three pieces of white paper, to which were stapled three photos each.

Bingo.

"Three other notes," he said absently. "And three photos for each one."

Mia's gaze dropped to the floor. He could feel her disappointment, feel her fighting back tears.

"I need you to be strong, Mia," he told her. "Hard as it is. The truth is what we're after, that's all."

She closed her eyes and nodded, then stood and walked over to the bed. She sat down on the other side of the box. "What do the notes say?"

"The first one says basically the same thing as the one Margot received last night, just with a different date for her next assignment—'Good job. Your fee is enclosed . . .'"

The color drained from Mia's face, and Matthew didn't bother to read the rest. "I guess Margot attached the photos to the corresponding note when she received them after her assignment was completed."

Mia sighed. "Are the notes all in the same handwriting?"

"Yes," Matthew confirmed. "Each one is written in the same handwriting and the same as the one we found last night. They're definitely all written by the same person."

"So all the notes thank her for a job well done and direct her to another location on a certain date at a certain time?"

Matthew flipped through the brief notes, then nodded. "The first one is for four months ago, and it looks like there's been one note, one assignment for Margot, a month."

"The one she got last night is for two weeks from now," Mia commented.

"That definitely breaks the pattern," Matthew responded. "I wonder what it means, if anything."

"Oh, my God, Matthew," Mia said, her hand flying to her mouth. "Does this mean there's going to be another murder in two weeks?"

Matthew stared at her, his stomach turning over at the thought. "I don't know. And I don't know if it means there have been three other murders, either."

"Matthew, I think you need to be prepared to accept that the police might be right about Robert's death, that he was in the wrong place at the wrong time in the parking lot, got into a drunken brawl and—"

"Aren't you the one who said we shouldn't make up scenarios?" Matthew snapped.

She turned and stared out the window, her face set in stone.

"We can check the obituaries in the Center City *Gazette* online," Matthew said, unwilling to comfort her, unwilling to apologize every time he said something she didn't like. They weren't friends. They were two people trying to solve a murder. There was no place for sensitivity here. "Does Margot have a computer?"

She faced him. "I think she has a laptop," Mia said. "But I haven't seen one. She must have taken it with her."

"We can use mine, then," Matthew said. "I live just a half mile away from here."

Mia nodded, then stared out the window again.

Just what he needed. Mia Anderson in his apartment. In his bedroom.

He closed his eyes and let out a deep breath. This was going to be a very long night.

Chapter Seven

With the exception of a playpen and an overflowing toy chest in the living room, Mia wouldn't guess that *anyone* actually lived in Matthew's apartment. From the moment he'd unlocked the door to the huge one-bedroom co-op and ushered her inside, she'd been thinking that his place was a lot like Margot's.

Beige. Cold. No homey touches. No woman's touch, that was for sure.

The surprise was the playpen and the toys and all the photos of a beautiful baby boy.

"Your nephew—Robbie, isn't it?" Mia asked, looking at a particularly adorable photograph of the toddler in a Halloween costume.

Matthew glanced at the photo, and the feeling in the room completely changed. *He* completely changed. A warmth came over him, and for the first time since she'd met him, a smile appeared on his chiseled face.

He loved the boy, that was for sure.

Once again, Mia's heart went out to Matthew. It was impossible to stay too angry with him, despite all the snapping he liked to do, all the judgments he liked to jump to when he couldn't tolerate the same from her.

Scenarios? Here was one: it was entirely possible that Margot had had nothing to do with Matthew's brother's death. And if Matthew couldn't get his mind around that, then he wouldn't really be open to anything they uncovered.

At least Mia had an open mind. She was surprised to learn that about herself, actually. Maybe Margot had been involved with Robert's death, and maybe she hadn't. Maybe Margot's ex-boyfriend, Justin, had flown into a jealous rage and killed Robert, and maybe he hadn't.

Maybe, maybe, maybe.

That was all they had at the moment.

And now, looking at the photos of the sweet, young toddler, Mia realized that Robbie Gray was all Matthew had, period. That he needed more than *maybe.*

He'd lost his parents, and then his brother, his only sibling.

Mia wondered if there was a woman in his life.

"He's away at his grandparents' for a couple of weeks," Matthew said suddenly, his gaze on one of the photos. "I miss him like crazy."

Mia smiled gently. "He's such a beautiful child."

Matthew nodded. "No kids of your own?"

Kids. Mia had wanted to start a family when she and David had first gotten married, but he'd wanted to wait.

He hadn't wanted her to ruin her figure.

And then as time went on, Mia didn't feel their

marriage was stable enough, secure enough, to welcome a child. David, of course, had never raised the subject of children. *Why wreck your body and get all matronly before you're even thirty?* he'd said. *There's nothing sexy about mothers.*

Mia mentally cringed. She'd once loved the man who'd said those things.

"Let's get started on our research," Matthew said, reverting back to his stony demeanor.

Mia was glad. The last thing she needed was to feel for him, to wonder about him, to—

Care.

"Mia? You all right?"

She blinked.

He was staring at her quizzically. *Get it together, girl. Stay focused.*

She offered a smile and a nod, and he led the way into his bedroom.

Mia almost shivered when they entered the huge room. Beige again and cold. There were only three pieces of furniture—a king-size chrome bed, hastily made, a modern chrome-and-wood dresser, and a massive chrome-and-wood desk, which faced the window.

Matthew sat down at his desk chair and clicked on his computer. Mia stood and awkwardly crossed her arms over her chest, unwilling to sit down on his bed.

"Have a seat," he said, gesturing to the bed.

Mia felt her cheeks color. She sat.

"I'll do a search for recent deaths in Center City and the surrounding towns on those particular dates," Matthew said. He pulled the notes from the metal box out of his knapsack and glanced at them, then clicked at the keys.

Mia glanced at the photos lining the dresser. One of a man, a woman, and a baby—his brother's family, Mia assumed. Another of an older couple—most likely his parents. And two of Robbie.

None of women.

"Mia, look at this!" Matthew exclaimed, and she jumped up and leaned over his shoulder. "Three other men were killed in bar parking lots, one stabbed, one shot, one hit over the head several times with a lug wrench, and—"

And one stabbed several times in the back, Mia mentally finished for him.

"Are you all right?" she asked him.

He hesitated for just a second, then nodded once, his gaze not leaving the screen. "Four murders on the dates of Margot's assignments."

Mia gasped. The impact of what Matthew had found had suddenly hit her.

There had been three other murders.

Four altogether.

"Matthew, were those other murders at the locations where Margot was instructed to go?"

Matthew scanned the screen. "Yes. Although one was in an alleyway near the bar."

Mia's knees gave out, and she dropped fast to the floor. Matthew was beside her in a moment.

"Mia, are you all right? Do you need some water?"

She closed her eyes and nodded, and when he left her, she felt the loss of his presence so strongly.

Margot, what have you gotten yourself mixed up in? What is this all about?

Matthew hurried back into the room with a glass of water. "C'mon, let me help you to the bed. You should sit propped up against the headboard."

Mia felt so weak, so devoid of energy and thought,

that she let him lead her to his bed, let him help her sit down, let him lift her feet onto the bed. She felt his hands at the back of her head, making sure her head rested gently against the headboard.

"I'm just so scared for her," Mia said so quietly she barely heard the words herself. "I don't know what this all means."

He sat down next to her. "I'm going to throw your own words back at you, Mia. We can't jump to any conclusions or make up scenarios. Let's wait till we have *facts* before we make any leaps."

Mia nodded. "Just because it looks bad for her doesn't mean it necessarily is."

Matthew smiled, and Mia knew he didn't believe what she had just said. He was being kind again.

Dammit.

But she was grateful. She needed to hang on to something, even if it was flimsy.

She just had to remember one thing. Her sister, her identical twin sister, was not a killer. Mia knew that as surely as she knew herself.

So what the hell was going on? Why had Margot been sent to entice four men into cheating, only to have those four men end up dead?

Who had hired her?

Who had killed those men?

And what was Margot's connection to the four victims?

To the person who hired her?

"My head is throbbing," Mia said. "Do you have any aspirin?"

Matthew was gone and back with two tablets in five seconds. She took the pills with a long drink of water and leaned her head back against the headboard and closed her eyes.

"Are you okay to continue?" Matthew asked. "Or should I take you home?"

Mia opened her eyes. "I'm fine. Really, Matthew. The shock is wearing off a little, and now all I'm left with are questions. Lots of questions."

"Well, maybe we'll find some answers the more we dig," he said. He regarded her for a moment, then stood and sat back down at his desk and returned his attention to the computer. "This is interesting," he said, scrolling down the screen. "Two of the victims were robbed, and two weren't."

"That doesn't help us much," Mia said. "It doesn't set up a pattern."

Matthew expelled a breath and ran a hand through his hair. "Dammit. Who the hell hired Margot?"

"Maybe we should try to come up with a list of potential suspects," Mia said, swinging her legs over the edge of the bed to face Matthew. She felt a lot less vulnerable with her feet firmly on the floor.

Matthew grabbed a legal pad and pen. "Okay, let's start with Justin, Margot's ex. He hated what she did for a living, gave her an ultimatum, and she chose the job over him. Maybe he got angry enough, jealous enough, and snapped."

"But why would he send anonymous notes directing her to meet strange men?" Mia asked. "If he was so jealous, how could he stand it? What would be the point?"

"To get rid of the competition," Matthew supplied.

"The men."

He nodded.

"So he's angry at her, angry at the men he's never met for taking her away from him, for 'getting' her, so he hires her to meet them and then kills them?" Mia asked. "That sounds really far-fetched, doesn't it?"

"Especially because it doesn't explain why he would choose these four particular men," Matthew said.

Mia stared at him. "You're right. Why were these four men singled out?"

"Well, all we know is that someone hired Margot, a decoy, to specifically entice these men into cheating on a specific date at a specific time and—"

"Wait a minute," Mia interrupted. "*Do* we know that? The notes instructed Margot to go to a specific bar at a specific time, but none of the notes mentioned a specific *man* or gave any sort of physical description of a man to entice."

Matthew stared at her. "You're absolutely right. Photos of Margot with the man and the cash fee come *after* the note directing her to the assignment. And the notes say absolutely nothing about which man is the target."

"So how does she even know who to entice?" Mia asked. "I mean, how did she know that she was supposed to find out whether or not *Robert* would go for her or not?"

Matthew was silent. "I don't know. It doesn't make sense."

"Maybe we should look at the note writer as one of the widows," Mia said carefully. "A widow makes the most sense as a suspect, given that the person writing the note is hiring a decoy."

"But let's say Mrs. A wants to find out if her husband is cheating. She hires Margot, finds out the answer is yes because of the photos, flips out, and kills her husband, end of story. Why do three other men get killed?"

Mia shook her head. "This is making less sense the more we try to figure it out."

"Okay. Let's take the last note. Margot's supposed to show up at MacDougal's on July tenth at ten P.M. And do *what*? Meet *who*? Whoever chooses to pick her up?"

"That seems awfully random," Mia said.

"I know." Matthew shook his head.

"Well, we know the murders weren't random, drunken brawls because of the Margot connection," Mia said, "yet suddenly, the victims themselves seem to be chosen completely at random."

"Makes no sense." Matthew stared out the window, clearly frustrated.

"Let's both read the accounts of the victims' deaths," Mia suggested, "then compare thoughts. Maybe something will trigger an idea, somewhere to begin."

"Good idea." Matthew printed out two copies of each report and any additional information he could find on the victims.

Even with the information superhighway, there wasn't much information on the victims themselves. They seemed to be four regular Joes, four regular citizens. Two were businessmen, one owned a body shop, and one was an electrician. They were in their thirties and early forties. All were married and left behind widows; two of the men had children.

"Nothing seems to link the men together," Mia said.

"Just their marital status," Matthew commented, flipping a page. "They all lived in different towns, had different professions."

They both went back to the reports, reading them again and again, asking each other questions, dismissing this, discussing that.

Mia yawned and looked at her watch. Three hours had passed since they'd arrived at Matthew's. She closed her eyes, just needing to rest them for a few seconds.

But when she woke up, it was pitch-dark, save the illuminated computer screen. Mia had somehow kicked off her sneakers and curled up on Matthew's bed. Tired as she was, she wanted to burrow farther into the warm bed, get under the covers. But the sound of a man's breathing startled her and her eyes flew open.

Matthew was fast asleep in his desk chair.

God, but he was beautiful. The computer screen slightly lit up half his chiseled face and shone highlights on his dark, thick hair. His rolled-up shirtsleeves revealed tanned, strong forearms, lightly covered with dark hair.

He was tall and lean and muscular. And he had to be uncomfortable in that position.

Suddenly, he lurched out of the chair and practically flung himself on the bed, his eyes closed. He was still asleep.

And he was lying down right next to her.

He turned toward her and burrowed his face in the crook of her neck, his warm breath dancing along her collarbone. She could smell his soap, his musky aftershave, the masculinity of him. An arm snaked around her waist, then inched up, dangerously close to her breast.

Mia held her breath.

And then a thigh, a heavy, muscular thigh, clamped over hers as he inched even closer to her.

They were so close they could be making love.

What do I do? What do I do? What do I do?

She tried to gently wriggle her thigh out from under his, but it was no use. The same went for her waist, which was under his arm.

His eyes opened.

And then opened wide.

He bolted up, and so did she.

"How—" he began, two spots of color forming on his hard cheeks.

"I don't know," she said, her face flaming. "I guess we both fell asleep." Mia grabbed her sneakers and slipped her feet into them. "I'll just call a cab."

"Stay," Matthew said. "I mean, you can have the bed, and I'll take the couch."

"I—"

"It's"—he glanced at his watch—"three in the morning." He walked to his dresser and rummaged around in a drawer. "Here. A pair of sweats and a T-shirt that shrunk pretty bad the last time I tried to do my own laundry. They'll make comfortable pj's."

So I guess I'm staying, Mia thought.

Mia was in his bed.

That was Matthew's last thought when he'd bunked down on his uncomfortable sofa in the living room, and it was his first thought when he woke up a moment ago.

Mia, beautiful, sweet, headstrong Mia was in his bed.

No—she wasn't. Unless the sudden smell of bacon wafting from his kitchen could be attributed to a dream. The same dream that had found him lying in his bed next to her last night, so close that he could see himself reflected in the pupils of her eyes.

So close that all he'd had to do was move a quarter of an inch, and he'd be inside her.

He closed his eyes and savored the thought, until the sound of eggs cracking against a bowl assured him he wasn't dreaming.

Or maybe he was, since Mia was clearly in the kitchen, making breakfast. The last time a woman had cooked him breakfast in his own home was four presidents of the United States ago. Matthew smiled, fondly remembering his mother's cooking.

"Scrambled okay?" Mia asked, appearing in the doorway of the kitchen. She wore his apron around her waist and held a spatula in one hand and a frying pan in the other.

She looked absolutely beautiful in her jeans and T-shirt, her feet bare, her hair in a ponytail, her face fresh-scrubbed. She reminded him of sunshine.

"Scrambled's my favorite," he said, sitting up on the sofa and stretching. "Is that coffee I smell? I could really go for a strong cup."

"Coming right up," she said with a bright smile and disappeared back inside the kitchen.

Interesting. She was almost too friendly, too cheerful.

Matthew knew forced cheer when he saw it.

Ah. She was probably embarrassed about last

night, about the compromising position they'd found themselves in. Matthew wondered how long they'd lain that way, their arms and legs and breath entwined. All he knew for sure was that he'd been comfortable.

Which in itself was cause for alarm. Usually, unless there was sex involved, Matthew was always uncomfortable about lying in bed with a woman. *Snuggling* was a word that made him break out into hives. But last night, when he'd been in that delicious state between sleep and wakefulness, he'd been very, very comfortable.

He'd known that having her in his apartment would be trouble.

He'd been right.

"I'm going to take a quick shower," he called out.

"Okay. Breakfast will be ready in five minutes."

How domestic, he thought, wincing.

He shook his head to clear it, stood up and stretched, then headed into the bathroom. A hot shower was exactly what he needed. Add a cup of strong coffee, and he'd be fortified against Mia Anderson.

He stripped down and stood under the pulsing, hot water, his thoughts immediately turning erotic.

Mia, sleepy and naked under the hot spray of water.

Mia, her soft breasts pressed against his bare chest, her legs wrapped around his waist as he held her to him.

And buried himself inside her.

"Your eggs are getting cold," she called through the door with that same forced cheer.

It had the same effect as the water going cold.

"Be right out," he called back, quickly lathering up and shampooing his hair.

He hoped she wasn't a mind reader.

In a minute, he had a towel wrapped around his waist. But was he supposed to just waltz out of his bathroom this way? Was she in the living room, waiting for him to appear? Was he supposed to call out a warning that he was coming out?

What a gentleman would do aside, this was his apartment, and making Mia comfortable with him as a man wasn't one of his priorities. The less comfortable she was, in fact, the more comfortable he would be.

Towel wrapped around his waist, Matthew opened the bathroom door and headed out. Mia, walking from the kitchen to the dining room table set along the windows, a platter of scrambled eggs in one hand and bacon in the other, froze.

And stared.

He stared back.

For a moment, neither of them moved, and it was so quiet in the room that he could hear both their shallow breaths.

He could see the faintest outline of her nipples through the thin, white material of her T-shirt. And he was sure she could see the sudden effect that had on him, even through the thick towel.

"I . . . I'll just go get the coffee," she said haltingly. She quickly slid the two platters on the table and then rushed back into the kitchen.

Matthew couldn't help smiling.

Yeah, she was uncomfortable.

* * *

As Mia sipped her coffee and bit into her toast, she couldn't stop herself from seeing Matthew Gray naked. Well, next to naked. Matthew Gray in that small towel, his hard, muscular chest damp, his thick brown hair glistening, his intense blue eyes dark with . . . With what? Desire? Lust?

Mia knew all too well what a man's desire looked like. And she knew what it felt like to be the object of that desire.

She also knew what it felt like to be desired and not loved.

Desired and not even liked.

Desired for nothing more than the paint on her face and the revealing clothes on her body.

Her appetite gone, Mia turned to look out the window, at the amazing view onto Center City.

Her sister was out there somewhere, and what was she doing? Fantasizing about a man who had absolutely no idea who she was. Nor, she was sure, *would* he be interested in who she was.

Oh, Margot. Where are you? Are you hiding out close to home? Have you caught a bus or train somewhere?

Where are you, Margot?

"These eggs are delicious," Matthew said. "Thanks for cooking."

He'd completely cleaned his plate, which he'd loaded with eggs, bacon, and two helpings of toast. Her ex-husband had been a health fanatic who'd eat nothing but egg-white omelets and organic whole wheat cereal for breakfast; Mia had to admit that it gave her some pleasure to watch a man eat a hearty, manly breakfast.

"Thanks," she said. "So, I've been thinking about where to start today, and I suggest we check out

Justin's alibi. Make sure he really was on shift at the hospital the night Robert was killed."

"Good plan," Matthew said, sipping his coffee. "And if he clears, I think we should do some checking into the widows, especially the first in the time line."

Mia nodded. "How about if I head home, shower and change, and then meet you at the coffee lounge in"—she glanced at her watch—"an hour?"

"An hour, it is," Matthew said. "Come on, I'll drive you."

"No," she said quickly. "I'd really like to walk. I could use some fresh air."

And some distance from you. Right away.

"You sure?" he asked.

She nodded, and he led the way to the door. "I'll see you in an hour."

He opened the door, his gaze lingering on her face, and it was all she could do not to raise up on her toes and sink into a long, sexually charged kiss.

Oh, God. She really needed to get out of there.

Chapter Eight

When Mia realized she was sitting in the same spot at the coffee lounge as she had the night she'd met Matthew, it was too late to move.

He'd arrived.

He didn't look like a man who'd spent the night on a sofa too small for his six-foot two-inch muscular frame. He looked good. Too good. He wore faded jeans and a dark blue knit polo shirt that was almost the exact color of his eyes. To the morning crowd at the coffee lounge, he must have appeared just like anyone else, a good-looking guy out for some java and the paper on a Sunday morning. It was amazing how easy it was to make judgments about other people based on appearance—judgments that were as far from the truth as could be.

Mia was sure she appeared the same way to those who might have noticed her. She'd tried on just about everything in Margot's closet, hoping for one outfit that wasn't quite so snug fitting, but unless she wanted to wear a bathrobe, a pair of white Capri pants and a small, pale blue, V-necked T-shirt were her next best choices. Margot's collection of tiny tank tops, cropped T-shirts, and midriff-baring shirts and barely there miniskirts could win her a spot in the *Guinness Book of World Records.*

"Can I get you anything?" he asked, his expression unreadable. "I could use a shot of espresso."

"No, I'm fine, thanks," Mia said.

He looked into her eyes for a long moment as if to make sure she was telling the truth, then headed over to the counter.

A few moments later, he returned with a large take-out container, and they headed outside.

The day was warm and sunny. According to the radio in the coffee lounge, it was already eighty degrees and seventy percent humidity, and it was only nine-thirty in the morning.

Mia squinted up at Matthew in the sunlight. "So do we just walk into Center City General and ask if Justin Graves was working the night of June nineteenth?" she asked.

Matthew considered that. "Maybe we should call instead. I've got an idea that might work." He reached into his pants' pocket and pulled out a small cell phone. After getting the number of the hospital from information, he punched some digits on the phone and waited. "Hello, I'm calling from the law offices of Brown and Andrews, doing some fact checking. I'd like to find out if a certain resident was working the night of June nineteenth of this year. Can I get that information? Great—thanks. His name is Justin Graves. Yes, I'll hold." Matthew winked at Mia. The ruse was working. "He was on shift from six P.M. until two in the morning. Yes, thank you very much."

"Well, that rules Justin out," Mia said, staring at the ground.

"Mia, just because we're ruling people out doesn't make Margot any guiltier," he said, placing the phone back inside his pocket. "We don't know what happened that night."

He seemed as surprised by what he'd just said as she looked.

And he was right. Margot wasn't "guilty until proven otherwise"; there was a mystery to solve, and if he and Mia put their heads together, they could get to the bottom of it. They both had very high stakes in finding out what happened to Robert.

"Now what?" she asked. "Should we start investigating the widows?"

Matthew nodded. "I think that's our best starting place. I have the information from the web in my knapsack."

As he propped his knapsack on his knee and unzipped it, Mia found herself riveted by his thigh. The very thigh that had been clamped over hers last night.

"The first murder . . . ," he began, snapping her out of her inappropriate thoughts as he scanned the pages, "occurred on February twenty-first, in the parking lot of Good Times, a small nightclub in Bridgeville. That's a small city about a half hour away from here."

"Yes, I know it. I live next door in Baywater."

"Pretty town," he said. "Lived there long?"

Too long, Mia thought. "I moved there when I got married five years ago. I won the house in the divorce settlement, so . . ."

He nodded. "Well, if you need anything from home, today would be a great day to get it since we'll be so close by. According to this obituary for James Cole, he and his widow, Lisa Ann Cole, lived in Baywater."

"The names aren't familiar, but it is a big town," Mia said. "And yes, I would love to pack a bag from home. Get into my own clothes."

"Let's go, then," he said. "My car's parked just across the street."

He led her to the silver BMW, and in moments, they were on the highway, headed south toward Baywater.

"Why don't we head over to my house first," Mia suggested. "I can check the phone book for a listing for Lisa Ann Cole."

"Sounds good," he said. "And it'll give us a place to map out a strategy for how to approach her. How to approach all the widows."

"Including Laurie Gray?" she asked softly.

He took his eyes off the road for just a moment to glance at her. "Yes," he said after a moment's hesitation. "Including Laurie Gray."

She wondered if he had any idea how much his acquiescence meant to her. It assured her that they were on even ground, that all bets were on. That everyone, no matter how hard it was for either of them to believe or accept, could be a suspect.

As they drove in silence, Mia had the feeling he did know—and that he was adjusting to it himself.

More relaxed, Mia looked out the window at the

passing scenery, at each landmark that brought her closer to home.

Home. Baywater, New York, was hardly that. The large, suburban town had never quite felt like home, not after a lifetime spent in idyllic, rural Peach Haven, a forty-minute drive east from Baywater. The sleepy little town was full of white picket fences and azalea bushes and kind people who knew each other and helped each other. And it was where Mia and Margot and the Daniels had lived and loved until tragedy had intervened.

Until Margot had left for the city, and Mia had been taken in by David Anderson and his desire for a too modern house on an unfriendly block in a town she'd never felt comfortable in.

Baywater was a town where neighbors snooped and gossiped about each other, where keeping up with the Joneses was of paramount importance.

You're divorced now, she reminded herself. *The school year is over. You don't have to live in Baywater anymore. You can go anywhere you want.*

But where? Sometimes, it seemed to Mia that when you could go anywhere and do anything, you stayed exactly where you were. You got paralyzed by the choices.

By fear.

Or just by not knowing where to go and why it would be different than it was right where you were.

"You'll have to direct me to your house," Matthew said.

Mia blinked and looked out the window. She'd been so lost in her thoughts, she hadn't realized they'd gotten off the exit for Baywater.

"Just make a left up here, then your first right," Mia told him. "I'm the second house on the right."

As they neared her house, Mia saw someone—a man—knocking on the front door. He then leaned over the shrubbery to peer in the living room window, stepping on her impatiens. He almost fell into the bushes.

Was it the postman? No, it was Sunday.

Well, then who—

It was Norman Newman.

"Dammit!" she snapped.

"What is it?" Matthew asked, alarm in his voice. "Do you know this person?"

"I hate to say this, but he's a bit of a creep," Mia said. "We work together at the middle school, and he's been asking me out nonstop for months. He's the sort of guy who won't take no for an answer."

As Matthew pulled into the driveway, he stared at Norman, who suddenly turned around at the sound of the approaching car. Matthew quickly parked and stepped out. "Can I help you?" Matthew directed toward Norman.

Mia hurried out of the car herself. Matthew's expression was ice-cold, and Norman looked upset and nervous.

Norman narrowed his eyes at Matthew. "No, you most certainly cannot," he all but spit out. "I don't know you."

"Well then, what can *I* do for you, Norman?" Mia asked, her voice impatient.

Norman turned to Mia. "I was in your neighborhood visiting a sick friend, and I thought I'd drop by with some scones and coffee so that we could finish our discussion from the other evening. But"—he slid a glare at Matthew—"I see you're busy."

She sighed. "Norman, we finished our conversation," Mia said, crossing her arms over her chest in a defensive stance.

"Well, perhaps you're right, Mia," Norman said, "since I don't know what further proof I need that you lied." He fixed Matthew with a venomous stare.

Mia felt Matthew tense beside her. "Norman, I'm going to tell you again. The woman you saw in Center City last week wasn't me, but my twin sister. If you don't believe me, well, I'm sorry, then. The truth is all I can give you."

Norman slid his beady-eyed gaze from Matthew to Mia. "Good day, Mia."

"*Good day*, Norman," she said angrily, and he stared at her hard for a moment before turning on his heel and heading back down the walk.

"Gee, I'm surprised you keep turning him down for dates," Matthew commented, his voice edged with something that Mia couldn't quite name.

Mia reached into her purse for her house keys. "I used to think he was just a nice guy with a harmless crush. But lately, he's been a little too intense."

Matthew followed her up the three steps to the porch. "What was that all about, him seeing Margot in Center City and thinking it was you?"

Mia unlocked the front door. "Oh, he called the other night in a huff, sure I've been lying to him about not dating because he thought he saw me with a couple of different men in the city last week. I told him it was my twin he saw, but he accused me of lying."

Matthew's eyes widened. "So this guy Norman

hangs out in Center City bars," he said slowly, "and he thought that Margot, who he saw with other men, was *you*—a woman he wants to date."

Doorknob in hand, Mia froze. "Oh, my God."

"Let's head inside and talk this through," Matthew said.

But Mia couldn't move a muscle. Was this all her fault? Had she angered Norman so terribly that he'd snapped? Had he seen Margot with Robert last Saturday night and waited in the parking lot to confront them? Had Margot come into contact with Norman that night? Thought he was some psycho? Perhaps she'd gotten away from Norman, and then Norman had waited for Robert to come out of Chumley's—so that he could kill his supposed competition.

Oh, God.

This is all my fault, Mia thought, her legs trembling. *I'm the reason that Matthew's brother is dead. I'm the reason that my sister is scared out of her mind and hiding who knows where, worried sick.*

"Mia?"

Matthew caught her just as her knees buckled. He threw open the front door, then scooped an arm under her knees and another around her shoulders and lifted her into his arms.

The breath drained out of her, Mia turned her face to the street to gulp in a shot of air.

Norman Newman was standing in the middle of the street, staring at her with absolute hatred in his eyes.

A half hour later, the door to Mia's bedroom opened, and she finally emerged.

Matthew breathed a sigh of relief. After that episode with Norman whatever his name was, Mia had completely collapsed. He'd carried her into her bedroom and laid her down on her bed, and she'd immediately turned away from him, her eyes closed. She'd refused to talk to him, refused to answer even yes or no questions as to whether or not she was all right.

What the hell had happened?

One minute, they'd been about to discuss whether this Norman character could have freaked bad enough to—

Oh, man.

If Norman *had* snapped because he thought the woman he wanted was seeing other men—and lying to him about it—Mia's meltdown was very likely a result of blaming herself for his actions.

Damn. When was Matthew going to learn to think before he blurted?

As Mia walked into the living room, her expression was devoid of any emotion. Amid the colorful décor, the overstuffed red sofa and chair, the multicolored throw rug, the collection of candles on the mantel, Mia, in her white T-shirt, her face pale, looked even more wan, more delicate.

"Mia, I think you've had just about enough for one day. Why don't you just take it easy today? Relax here and not think about—"

"I'm fine, Matthew," she said, sitting down across from him on an overstuffed chair.

"You don't look fine," he said.

Her eyes welled with tears, and he mentally cursed himself. "I mean—"

"I know what you mean, Matthew," she said. "Look, I'm upset. To realize that Norman is a suspect—a major suspect—that I might be the reason for . . ."

"Mia, you're *not* the reason for anything anyone does," Matthew said. "Norman is responsible for his feelings and for his actions. Do you hear me?"

She looked up at him, bit her lip, and nodded. And then she burst into tears.

He was beside her in a second, kneeling down next to her chair. "Mia, what I'm saying is the truth. You're not responsible for someone else's actions, feelings, behavior—anything. That person is."

It had taken him years to come to believe that.

"But . . . if it wasn't for me, Norman wouldn't have—"

"Mia, first of all, we don't know that Norman *did* anything," Matthew pointed out. "And secondly, there's no such thing as 'if it wasn't for me.' Norman is responsible for what he does. Not you."

Mia leaned back in the chair and seemed to breathe a bit easier. Good. She had to believe in what he was saying. Or misplaced guilt and worry and fear would have a field day with her.

Matthew knew that all too well.

For years, he'd blamed himself for his parents' marital troubles. If only he'd been quieter, smarter, better at sports, better behaved, more like the neighbor's kid, maybe his father would have come home after work, instead of hanging out in bars, drinking and picking up women. Maybe if he hadn't snored as a kid, his father would have slept at home, instead of . . . somewhere else.

He'd learned that way of thinking from his mother, who'd blamed herself the same way. If only she'd been prettier, thinner, a better cook, a better housewife, more interesting, more this, more that. She'd worked herself to the bone to become what she thought would make her husband happy. But nothing had.

Nothing ever would.

Because you were never responsible for someone else's actions. That person was. It had been too late for his mother to learn that.

It wasn't too late for Mia.

"I'm really okay, Matthew," she said. "I'm not about to let Norman destroy me because of his jealousy—or because of what he might or might not have done. Anyway, I'll worry if I have reason to."

"That's the spirit, Mia," he said, covering her hand with his own.

She looked down at his hand atop hers. "Let me go put on my own clothes and splash some cold water on my face, and I'll join you in a few minutes."

He missed the warm softness of her hand as she got up and headed back into her bedroom. She was a strong woman, stronger than she realized.

She returned to the living room in white pants and a pale pink T-shirt, her hair loosely twisted in a bun at the back of her head with some sort of short stick. She looked like a woman, like summer.

God, she was beautiful.

"I just want you to know I appreciate the perspective check," she said, sitting back down on the overstuffed chair. "I feel a lot better."

"Good," he said. "I'm glad to hear that. Do you feel comfortable talking about this Norman character and how he might fit in, or would you rather skip him for the time being and concentrate on the widows?"

"Let's talk about Norman," Mia said. "As long as I keep my mind on what's important—the truth and not my own worries—I'll be fine."

And so over two more cups of coffee, Mia filled him in on everything to do with Norman Newman and his bad habit of not taking no for an answer.

"I think we should trail Norman tonight," Matthew suggested. "See if he heads over to Center City. I want to watch him for a while; then we'll let him see you with me, and we'll see how he reacts, what he does."

Mia paled. "But, Matthew, that could put you in danger."

"I'm about six inches taller and a lot more muscular than that weeble," Matthew said. "You don't have to worry about me, Mia. Besides, he can't ambush me when I'm looking out for him."

She took a deep breath. "I don't like it, but all right."

"See, we didn't have to spend much time talking about that jerk, after all."

"He makes me so angry!" she said, sparks in her eyes. "How dare he keep coming around when I've told him I don't date."

"Some people have big trouble with the word *no,*" Matthew said darkly. "It's nothing to take lightly."

"It's so strange—lately, I've resorted to what I consider downright rudeness to keep him at bay, but even a bad attitude on my part doesn't deter him. He just keeps coming back."

"Because it's not really about you," Matthew said.

"He doesn't hear you or see you. He only knows what he wants. It's a sickness."

Mia was quiet, and Matthew wondered if he'd said the wrong thing again.

"That sounds a little too familiar," Mia finally said. "I had a husband like that."

Matthew looked away, wanting to give her some privacy, yet also wanting to know more. Why had she married a man "like that"?

For the same reason your mother married a man like your father, Matthew was thinking. Letitia Gray had fancied herself in love at a time in her life when she'd been weak and desperately in need of love and support. And Matthew's father's strength—his false bravado and big mouth and overconfidence—seemed qualities to admire.

His mother had always said that the marriage wasn't a mistake, that after all, she got to have two beautiful children. Matthew had taken some comfort in her comfort in that.

"Let's move on to the first of the widows, Lisa Ann Cole," Matthew said.

She glanced at him for a long moment, then got up and went into another room and returned with a heavy phone book. She flipped through some pages. "Here she is, Lisa Ann Cole, 253 Berry Street. That's on the other side of Baywater, one of the cross streets for the library."

"I think we should tell her and the others the truth," Matthew said, "that we're looking into my brother's death and checking into other unsolved murders that occurred during the past six months."

Mia nodded. "Our visit isn't going to be easy on

the widows. Let's be as gentle with our questions as possible."

"But let's not forget that one of them could very well be a cold-blooded killer," Matthew reminded her. "We should also be very careful and very sly."

Mia paled again.

Chapter Nine

"That no good son of a bitch! He can rot in his grave for all I care."

As the widow Cole ranted on about her late husband, Mia tried to adopt a neutral expression. It wasn't easy.

"I was going to divorce the jerk anyway," Lisa Ann Cole continued as she handed Mia and Matthew each a cup of coffee. "Sugar?" she asked, holding out the bowl with a bright smile.

Mia shot a quick glance at Matthew; if he was as shocked as she was, you would never know it.

"He got his just deserts," Lisa Ann trilled as she dropped a cube of sugar into her own cup. "That ass was cheating on me for years. Why I didn't throw his sorry butt out of here when I first found out is beyond me." She shook her head, then continued on about how much weight her husband had gained and how surprised she was that he'd managed to cheat on her with any woman, given his "roly-poly" stomach. "I mean, you should see that thing swaying in the breeze under his stained tank tops."

"Um, Mrs. Cole—" Mia began.

"Please, call me Lisa Ann," the woman said, readjusting the polka-dot scarf around her neck. "I'm thinking of going by Lisann—just one word. Sounds almost foreign, doesn't it? Exotic."

Mia smiled tightly. "Lisa—Lisann, could you tell us about the night that your husband—that you lost your husband?"

The widow leaned back against the sofa and sipped her coffee. In her early thirties, Lisa Ann Cole was attractive in a harsh way. Her pretty blue eyes were rimmed with black kohl and a lot of mascara, and her blusher and lipstick were quite bright. Thin and angular, she favored animal prints for her clothes and furnishings. Her blouse was leopard print, and so were the pillows and throw on the sofa. So were her high-heeled pumps.

"Well," Lisa Ann said, putting down her coffee cup. She reached into her purse and reapplied a coat of lipstick. "The police came over around nine o'clock or so that night back in February. Sat me down and told me they'd found Jimmy dead in the parking lot of a bar out in Center City."

"Can you remember any of the details they might have shared with you?" Matthew asked.

The widow leaned forward and smiled flirtatiously at Matthew. Mia mentally rolled her eyes. From the moment they'd arrived, the widow had all but draped herself at Matthew's feet. She'd directed all her niceties to him: *Would you like a cup of coffee, Matt? You don't mind if I call you Matt, do you, honey? Matthew is so formal. My James's mother always called him James, but the minute I met him, I called him Jimmy. Would you like a piece of pound cake, Matty? Some cookies? They're just store bought, but you can't bake better than Entemann's can.* Giggle. Twirl of beads at her neck. Lick of the lips.

It wasn't that Mia didn't get it. Matthew was one handsome man. Exceptionally handsome, actually.

So was she jealous? Of what? Of another woman fawning and fussing over him? That made no sense.

"There really weren't too many details," Lisa Ann said. "Jimmy had just left the bar, one of his usuals in the city, and he'd been heading toward his car in the parking lot when he got jumped. Hit over the head several times with a heavy object, a lug wrench, most likely. Poor Jimmy. The cops said he probably didn't even know what hit him." She brightened for a moment. "Hey, that's almost funny, ain't it?"

Mia suddenly felt very sorry for Lisa Ann Cole. The woman put on a great act, but inside, there was a very sad, very troubled heart beating.

"Lisann," Matthew said, "do you recall if your husband was robbed?"

"Nah, I got all the stuff that had been in his wallet. He had sixty bucks and a bunch of credit cards. His cheap watch that no one would want. And his wedding ring, which I guess wasn't worth much, but still, it's fourteen-karat gold."

"Lisann, we really appreciate your taking the time to talk to us," Matthew said.

The widow smiled and leaned forward again, offering Matthew a view of her freckled cleavage. "Sure thing, sweetie. I'm sorry about your brother."

Matthew stood and Mia shot up, too.

"Yes, thank you very much, Lisann," Mia said, extending her hand. The widow grasped it with both of her hands, then walked her guests to the door.

"Oh, you know what was always interesting to me about that night?" Lisann said at the door.

"What's that?" Matthew asked.

"His wedding ring," Lisann said. She reached into her cleavage and pulled out a gold wedding ring on a long chain around her neck. "Jimmy never wore his wedding ring. I mean, never. Not for years. He always kept it in his wallet. I used to get on him about it when we first got married, then got sick of hearing myself yell without getting any results."

Mia glanced at Matthew. She could tell he was as eager for what the widow was about to say as she was.

"Strangest thing," Lisann said, eyeing the ring. "The night he was killed, the police said he was wearing his wedding ring. Right there on the third finger of his left hand. Ain't that interesting?"

"Yes, it certainly is," Matthew said. "Very interesting."

Lisa Ann seemed lost in her thoughts. "He never wore it, but there it was on his finger."

"I think it means he wore his ring more than you think he did," Mia offered the widow. "When he was away from home and missing you."

The widow's face broke into a shy smile. "Huh. You really think so? That's something, ain't it?"

"Yes," Mia said. "It's something."

And with that, Mia and Matthew showed themselves out, Lisa Ann Cole holding open the door, her expression full of wonder.

* * *

"He was everything you could want in a husband," Ashley Davidson said, dabbing at her eyes with a tissue. "So kind, so loyal. And such a good daddy to his two baby girls."

Matthew wasn't sure if a man could be a good father and a cheating husband at the same time, but *loyal* was definitely not an adjective to describe Ray Davidson. The photos of Davidson and Margot had been the most intimate, the most revealing. They'd been taken in the parking lot of Good Times, a popular bar in Center City. Davidson and Margot, passionately kissing, his hands all over her ass. In another photo, you could see Davidson's slimy tongue in Margot's ear.

You could also see Margot's smile.

It wasn't the smile of an actress at work. It was the smile of a woman enjoying herself, getting off. It made Matthew sick to his stomach. Mia had said nothing of the photos of Margot with Davidson and the other victims; she'd turned away, her eyes closed.

Mia was loyal to Margot; Ray Davidson was loyal to his wife.

Or so they both thought. *How easy it is to deceive people*, Matthew thought, his stomach churning as Mrs. Davidson openly wept for her husband, gone since March.

"Mrs. Davidson, we're both so sorry for your loss," Mia said, leaning forward and clasping the woman's hands. "And we're so sorry for intruding. We didn't mean to add to your grief." Mia stood, and Matthew jumped, too.

"Oh, no," the woman said. "Please stay. Yes, I'm still grieving for Ray. I always will. But it helps to talk about him. After the first few weeks, people stopped coming by, stopping asking me how I was doing. I guess folks don't know what to say."

Mia nodded and sat back down. Matthew did as well. "I know. I remember it being like that when my parents died," Mia said. "Just when the shock started wearing off and I needed support the most, there wasn't much to be found."

"Yes, yes! That's exactly how it is for me!" Mrs. Davidson said.

"Why don't you tell us about your marriage, Mrs. Davidson," Mia said. "Sounds like you and Ray were very happy."

The woman smiled. "Oh, yes. So happy. Ray was on the road a lot—he was a salesman—but when he was home, he was so devoted to his family."

Matthew's stomach turned over. "I wish my own family life was as wonderful as yours," he said. "There was an awful lot of fighting in my house growing up. My parents were always at each other's throats."

"That's terrible," the widow said, shaking her head. "Ray and I barely argued. Friends thought I was too lenient with him, but I wanted him to be happy."

"Lenient?" Mia prompted. "About what?"

Mrs. Davidson shifted in her chair. "Oh, well, about his going out on Saturday nights. He and some of his friends from the bowling league would drive down to Center City and go to some sports bars on Saturday nights after their games."

"And that didn't bother you?" Matthew asked. "That he was taking time away from his family?"

The woman's expression fell a bit. "Well, I suppose it did, since he was away from home so often as it was. But he always spent Sundays with me and the girls."

Mia smiled warmly. "How long were you married?"

"Seventeen years," the widow said. "We got married when we were only both nineteen."

"That's a beautiful ring," Mia said. "Your wedding ring?"

Matthew could have kissed her. She was leading the conversation perfectly.

"Yes," the woman said, holding it up for Mia to see. "Ray had it made special for me. He bought us his and hers rings, and we vowed we'd never take them off when we got married."

"And I'll bet neither of you did, right?" Matthew asked.

The widow's eyes filled with tears. "You know what? When the police found Ray in the parking lot of that bar, he'd been robbed clean. But his wedding ring wasn't taken. And it's twenty-four-karat gold with a diamond on it."

Matthew glanced at Mia.

"I think he must have pleaded with his killer to take everything but to leave the ring for me," the widow said. "I can see Ray doing that. His wallet, his watch, gold cuff links—all taken. But the ring was on his finger like it always was. That did give me some comfort."

Because you killed him? Matthew wondered. *Because you knew he was cheating, got your proof, murdered him, and made sure he met his maker with his wedding ring on?*

"How are your girls doing?" Mia asked.

"They get a little stronger each day," the woman said. "They miss him terribly, though."

"So the police haven't been able to come up with any leads?" Matthew asked. "Nothing?"

The woman shook her head. "They think he was simply in the wrong place at the wrong time. Ray dressed so well, he liked very expensive clothes, so the police figured he looked like a good target for a robbery victim. One gun shot, and my husband was gone."

Mia shook her head. "I am so sorry."

Matthew stood up. "We really have taken up too much of your time, Mrs. Davidson. Thank you so much for speaking with us."

The widow nodded. "I doubt they'll ever catch Ray's killer. I do hope you have better luck."

"Thank you," Matthew said. "Catching my brother's killer is the most important thing in the world to me, but it's looking like his death will go unsolved."

"Mrs. Davidson, did you do any investigating on your own?" Mia asked. "Try to find clues?"

"Oh, goodness no," the woman said. "I left that to the police. I had two girls to see to. And I wouldn't have known the first place to start."

Theresa Healy was not as forthcoming as Lisa Ann Cole or Ashley Davidson.

"I said, what the hell are you coming around bothering me for?" the woman snapped from behind her screen door.

Mia shot a glance at Matthew, who stood next to her on the step to the two-family house. "We're so sorry to intrude, Mrs. Healy, but—"

The widow frowned. "That's not my name. I never went by Healy."

"Ms. . . ?" Matthew prompted.

"It's none of your goddamned business what my name is," the woman growled. "Look, I don't see what your brother's death has to do with my husband's."

"We don't know either," Mia said, hoping the woman didn't slam the door in their faces. "We just figured that if we looked into other unsolved homicides in the area, maybe we'd find some sort of pattern. Something that would help us find out who killed Matthew's brother."

"I'm not interested in your brother," the woman said. "And I'm not interested in finding out who killed Carl, either."

Mia tried to keep her mouth from dropping open. "May I ask why?"

"He pissed off a lot of people," Theresa said. "He gambled, played poker, bet on horses. He owed people money. I don't need to be looking over my shoulder, wondering if whoever killed him is going to come after me to get paid."

"Are you worried about that?" Matthew asked.

"I rent this stinkbox," the woman said. "And I get paid minimum wage at the diner I waitress at. There's forty-six dollars in my checking account right now. Anyone comes after me is going to be very disappointed."

"So your husband didn't leave you with an insurance policy?" Mia asked.

The woman laughed. "That cheapskate? He drank his insurance premiums, and he spent everything else on gambling. He even lost his wedding ring in a poker game. He tried to steal mine to gamble with, but I caught the bastard and beat the crap out of him."

Matthew and Mia glanced at each other. "So he didn't have a wedding ring?"

"Not his original one," she answered. "But he always wore a cheap one. Said if anyone ever bothered him, he could plead for his life by talking about his pregnant wife and kids at home."

Mia paled. "You were pregnant at the time of his death?"

The woman laughed. "It was just a story he made up, thinking the loan sharks and bookies would go easier on him if they thought he had a pregnant wife at home. Whoever killed him didn't even bother to take that pathetic charm-machine wedding ring. The cops gave it back to me. I tossed it in the river with his ashes. Whatever."

Whatever, Matthew thought. He wanted to reach inside the screen door and shake the woman until she got a mind and a heart.

"Mrs.—Theresa," Mia began, "the news report of your husband's death noted he was robbed of his wallet in an alleyway in Center City. Is that right?"

"Yeah, that's what they said. Robbery. They found Carl in the alley of his favorite drinking hole. I figure whoever offed him was pissed that he was spending his money on booze and not paying up. And that he didn't have any money on him or a bank account worth nothing."

"But isn't it odd," Matthew began, "that the killer would steal his wallet and leave his gold wedding ring?"

"I don't think it's odd," Theresa said. "The killer was most likely a bookie wanting his money. Any bookie knows a five-dollar fake gold ring when he sees one. They took his wallet most likely so that the police couldn't identify Carl and link him back to his enemies."

"So how *was* he identified?" Mia asked, not totally sure she wanted to know.

"Tattoo on his left butt cheek from some drunken party years ago. Had his first initial and last name."

"And—" Matthew began.

"Look, I have to get to work," Theresa interrupted and closed the door.

Mia and Matthew stared at each other. They both shook their heads in unison.

"My brain is mush," Mia said.

Matthew let out a deep breath. "Mine, too. Let's get the hell out of here. Man, if I vowed never to get married before, I make the vow three times over now."

Mia glanced at him. "Matthew, just because—"

Matthew turned and headed down the steps. "No, Mia. *Just because* is all there is."

Was he kidding with this stuff? "When I was upset about Norman's actions, *just because* didn't hold water. But it does when it affects you?"

"This is different," Matthew said through gritted teeth.

Mia followed him down the path to his car. "Why, because it's *you?*" she asked.

"Yes, that's exactly why."

"Fine," she said.

"Fine," he echoed.

She rolled her eyes at him, and he rolled them right back at her.

"I'll tell you what," he began. "How about I make us a decent dinner and we sit down and wade through what we learned today. I need a couple of hours to unwind and process; then I'll hit the supermarket. How does that sound?"

"Great," Mia said as she slid into the passenger seat of Matthew's car.

Just great.

She leaned back against the plush upholstery and closed her eyes. But the faces of the three widows started juxtaposing themselves on top of one another, tears from one, pride from another, bitterness from the third. She wondered what they'd get from Laurie Gray.

If Matthew ever let them interview her, that was.

Interesting. For a man who didn't think too highly of marriage, he sure seemed to respect the sanctity of Laurie's Gray's marriage—even if it was a lie.

There was so much to Matthew Gray. So much that scared her, so much that intrigued her.

Forget it. She just heard him say that he'd never marry. Mia wondered if she even wanted to get involved with a man who wouldn't make a commitment.

I'm already involved, a small voice whispered inside her head. *Way over my head.*

By the time Matthew unlocked the door to his apartment and kicked off his shoes, it was almost six o'clock in the evening. Mia had gone to her sister's apartment to unpack her bag and check the machine for calls from Margot. She was due to arrive at Matthew's at six-thirty for dinner.

Which Matthew was preparing at the moment. Nothing special, just a couple of steaks and baked potatoes and some asparagus. His groceries bought and halfway down the block from the supermarket, he'd gone back for salad fixings. He'd done the same for a bottle of wine.

He was putting a little too much thought into this dinner.

But after the morning Mia had had and the afternoon they'd both had, she could use a relaxing home-cooked meal—and so could he, even if he was making it himself.

As Matthew pricked the potatoes and slid them in the oven, he thought about Lisa Ann Cole, Ashley Davidson, and Theresa Healy. One who was desperate to know her husband loved her, one who was devastated over his loss, one who couldn't give two figs.

But tears didn't necessarily mean innocence, just as Mrs. Cole's and Theresa's harsh words for their husbands didn't mean guilt. All three women had been unable to provide much more information than what had been in the news reports and obituaries—except for the very interesting bits about the wedding rings.

Each man had been found wearing a wedding ring, despite the fact that two of the men had been robbed of everything else in their possessions.

Matthew pondered that as he cooked. If the police had wondered why two victims of homicide and robbery were spared their wedding rings, Theresa Healy's explanation would certainly solve one of them.

Matthew shook his head. Maybe there was no link. Maybe the wedding ring angle meant absolutely nothing. Lisa Ann Cole's husband never wore his ring, yet there it was on his finger when *he'd* been found. And Davidson and Healy, both robbed of their wallets, watches, and anything else in their possession, were found with their wedding rings on *their* fingers.

What the hell? What did it mean?

The doorbell rang, and Matthew was almost grateful for the reprieve from his thoughts. He was so tired of asking questions that had no answers.

Mia looked absolutely beautiful. She wore billowy, silky black pants, a matching tank top that buttoned up the back, and low-heeled strappy sandals. He could barely take his eyes off her. Suddenly, he couldn't remember any of the widows' names, let alone why he thought wedding rings had anything to do with the case.

She smelled faintly of perfume. And green apples. And soap.

Say something, you idiot, he chided himself. "Wine?" he asked, grabbing the bottle from the counter.

"Thank you," she said. "I'd love some."

Matthew uncorked and poured two glasses. He handed her one and lifted his own glass to her. "A toast?"

Mia tilted her head and waited. He had no idea what he was going to say.

"To . . . working together," he said. "Though I wouldn't mind forgetting about the case for just a little while. I tried to relax earlier, but I couldn't stop thinking about the widows."

"Me, too," Mia said. "Well, then, to working together," she repeated with a smile, "and to relaxing for just a half hour or so."

"I'll drink to that," he said, and they clinked.

Mia sniffed the air. "Something smells delicious," she said. "Umm, is that steak? And baked potatoes?"

"And asparagus," he added.

The delight on her face made his trips back to the supermarket worth every second.

"My ex-husband never cooked a meal in his life," she said with a laugh. "He wouldn't even pour a bowl of cereal on his own."

Matthew couldn't remember having heard Mia's laugh before. It was really a beautiful sound. He was glad she was relaxing enough to do so—and that she could talk about her marriage in a light-hearted way. He'd gotten the sense that she'd suffered a great deal.

"Well, it was either learn how to cook some basics or spend a fortune on take-out and delivery," Matthew said. "Plus, it's nice to cook for someone else."

She glanced at him and then shot her gaze to the floor. Ah, the shyness had returned. Matthew smiled inwardly.

"Have a seat, and no, you cannot do anything to help but grace the table with your presence and beauty," he said.

Her lovely face broke into a smile, and she sat down and unfolded the napkin on her lap. In moments, Matthew had served their meal and had taken a seat beside her.

"Thank you, Matthew," she said, those pale brown doe eyes sparkling. "Everything looks absolutely delicious."

"Yes, it does," he said, unable to stop looking at her.

"Ummm . . . ," she murmured appreciatively with her first bite of steak. "This is so good!"

Matthew smiled, and they clinked their wine-glasses again, then dug in. They kept the conversation light, about Baywater and Center City and the surrounding towns they'd visited today. Nothing too personal that might make him lose his appetite.

When they finished their meal, Matthew moved their wine bottle and glasses into the living room and set up a bowl of fresh fruit and some lemon sorbet on the coffee table.

"I'm impressed, Mr. Gray," Mia said. "Sorbet and everything."

Matthew sat down next to Mia on the sofa. "Something told me you would like it."

"I do," she said with a smile. "And lemon is my favorite flavor."

Matthew felt a bit too good about all this. He wondered if he had a goofy smile on his face.

"So I've been thinking about something all day," Mia said, sipping her wine. "Davidson and Healy were both robbed, yet not of their wedding rings. Why?"

"Yes, I've been wondering about that, too, for the past hour," Matthew said, running a hand through his hair. "Especially because Davidson's was real gold and encrusted with a diamond."

"I can understand why the killer left Healy with his, I guess," Mia said.

Matthew nodded. "And then James Cole never wore his ring, yet he was found dead with his ring on his finger."

Mia spooned a bite of sorbet. "My brain is turning to mush again."

"Let's go over it again," Matthew said, leaning forward. "Yesterday, we'd realized that the only thing that links these four guys is the fact that they were all married and that they all were photographed in compromising positions in bars with Margot," Matthew said, popping a piece of strawberry into his mouth. "Now we find out that one who shouldn't have had his wedding ring on his finger was wearing it and that two who were robbed were not robbed of their rings. The wedding rings are of paramount importance, but I can't see the *why.*"

"I think the wedding rings point a finger back at a widow as suspect, don't you?" Mia asked. "I mean, the person behind hiring Margot is out to see if these men would cheat. They all did. And even though two were robbed, all four men were wearing their rings. As if the killer wanted to do right by the marriage."

Matthew stared at her. "You're absolutely right, Mia. There is something there."

"What I still don't get is why any of the widows would hire Margot to entice the other husbands," Mia said, leaning back against the sofa. "Why would, say, Lisa Ann Cole care if Theresa Davidson's husband cheated on her? None of the widows even know each other."

That was true. Matthew had asked each widow if she'd heard of the others, and the answer had been no. He'd been careful to watch for the slightest change in expression or body language, and the three widows hadn't flinched a bit.

He had a vague feeling that none of them was involved in the death of her or anyone else's husband. And he knew, without a shadow of a doubt, that Laurie Gray was as innocent. He didn't know about Norman Newman, but the wedding ring connection didn't seem to point to him at all.

"What about Robert?" Mia asked. "He was wearing his wedding ring when he was found, right?"

"Right, but there's nothing to indicate that he—"

"What?" Mia asked.

"Wait a minute," Matthew said, his mouth dropping open. "Wait. A. Minute."

Mia turned to him, eyes wide.

"When I burst in on Robert and Margot in Chumley's and dragged Robert over to the jukebox, he *hadn't* been wearing his ring. I noticed that. It was one of the reasons why I'd gotten so angry at him."

"But he'd been wearing it when he was found in the parking lot?"

"Yes, I saw it on his hand when I identified him in the morgue," Matthew confirmed.

"So now there are two men who weren't wearing their rings before they were killed yet were *found* wearing their rings," Mia said.

"What the hell is going on?" Matthew asked. "What's the connection with the rings? Who killed these men?"

"And who is the killer's target on July tenth at MacDougal's?" Mia asked softly, shaking her head.

Matthew stared at her. "I'm at a total loss."

"Maybe we should go to the police, Matthew," Mia said. "We have very good reason to believe that someone is going to be in grave danger of losing his life in two weeks. We have to tell the police what we know."

"And risk incriminating your sister?" he asked, eyebrow raised.

Mia took a deep breath. "I know Margot is innocent. I also know that I could be saving a man's life by coming forward."

"Let's keep on track," Matthew said. "We've got two weeks before we have to start worrying about this psycho's next victim. Two weeks to uncover the killer before he or she can strike again."

Mia nodded and put down her practically untouched bowl of sorbet. Clearly, her appetite, like Matthew's, was gone.

"And we've got a suspect to trail tonight," Matthew said, the image of that weasly loser Norman Newman intruding in his mind.

Mia let out a deep breath.

Chapter Ten

Mia was surprised that so many people were out and about in the city on a Sunday night. Granted, it was still early, only eight o'clock, but at this hour on a Sunday, Mia would be curled up in an armchair with a good book or at her desk grading tests and ready to hit the sheets by ten.

Then again, she'd never been much—anything, actually—of a party girl. Never had done the bar circuit in her single days or gone to nightclubs, which Margot had always enjoyed. Mia had always wondered about the quality of men she'd meet in a bar—and then she'd gone and met and married the worst of men right next door. Several of Mia's fellow teachers at Baywater Middle School had met their boyfriends and husbands in bars or nightclubs, and they were quite happy, quite in love with wonderful men.

She wondered if Matthew spent time in singles bars. He lived right in the middle of all this energy and madness, so he must enjoy all that living in the city had to offer.

She glanced over at him. He'd changed into black pants and a gray knit polo shirt. And he'd shaved, too. Every now and then, Mia would get just a hint of his aftershave, a spicy—

Oh, my God.

"Matthew!" she whispered, grabbing his arm. "There he is. There's Norman."

He followed her gaze across the street. Norman Newman, carrying a brown leather briefcase, was stopping at every bar window and peering inside.

Is he looking for me? Mia wondered, panic filling her stomach. "Why is he carrying a briefcase on a Sunday night when school's over for the year?" she asked, her voice cracking. "He wasn't even working for the last two weeks—he's been taking care of his sick mother. And he got out of his summer school assignment because of it, so—"

"Mia," Matthew said, turning to her, his blue eyes intense on hers. "He can't hurt you. And he can't hurt me. Okay? You don't have to worry about this creep."

She managed to nod. In silence they watched Norman head down the street, covering the top of his eyes with his hands as he looked into the windows of bars and restaurants that lined the busy boulevard.

"He's definitely looking for something," Matthew commented. "Maybe for friends, or maybe to see if a place looks inviting to him—"

"Or maybe for me," Mia added dryly.

"Let's trail him," Matthew said. "We'll stay a bit behind like we are, on this side of the street. When he goes in somewhere, we'll go in, too. At some point, we'll let him see us."

Mia swallowed.

She felt Matthew take her hand, clasp it in his. Startled, she glanced up at him, but he was staring straight ahead.

He was playing a role, Mia realized. Just in case Norman should suddenly turn around and walk their way, he wanted Norman to see them holding hands. He was encouraging Norman's anger. To see what it would lead to.

But still, Matthew's strong, warm hand felt so good against hers. She felt safe.

After five minutes of staring in windows, Norman backed up a few steps and headed inside Red Hots, a popular bar known for their buffalo wings.

"Let's go," Matthew said, leading her across the street.

Mia paused in front of the entrance.

"All right?" he asked.

She nodded, and they headed inside, still holding hands.

Norman was sitting at the bar, facing away from the door. He was perusing a menu. His briefcase was sitting on the ledge under his feet.

Matthew leaned close. "Let's head toward the back where it's crowded and watch him for a while," he suggested over the blare of the jukebox. "Let's watch who he watches, who he talks to."

Mia nodded, and they headed to the back, taking a seat behind a large group of people that still afforded them a bit of a view of Norman's profile. Norman was wearing his "special assembly" clothes, outfits up a notch from the usual "business casual" dress code of Baywater Middle School. He'd taken pains to comb his wiry brown hair, which was usually flopping in different directions—and not in an endearing way.

A few minutes later, an order of buffalo wings was placed in front of Norman, and he stuffed two in his mouth at once. He also ordered what looked like a ginger ale.

Two women came in and sat down next to Norman. One smiled at him, but he ignored her and instead gnawed on a wing as though he hadn't eaten in days.

Matthew raised an eyebrow. "Interesting. A nice-looking woman smiles at him, and he's more interested in his food?"

Mia didn't know what to say. Did Norman like her so much that he wasn't interested in other women at all?

Norman either stared at his food or at the television above the bar, which was airing a baseball game. So perhaps he'd only come in to watch the game and have some wings. Maybe he'd been peering in windows for television sets.

Mia breathed a sigh of relief. Norman wasn't a suspect. He was just an annoying and socially inept man.

"Mia," Matthew whispered, nudging her forearm. "Check this out."

Mia followed Matthew's gaze to Norman, who had set his briefcase on top of the bar. He was pulling something out, a large book.

"It's the Baywater Middle School yearbook," Mia told Matthew.

"Looks like he has it bookmarked to a specific

page," Matthew said, craning his neck a bit to see around a particularly tall man. "Yes, he's flipped right to it. He just seems to be staring at it."

Mia shook her head and sipped her club soda. "I can't imagine why he'd want to look at the yearbook only a few days after school ended, even if he did miss the last two weeks. No teacher gets that nostalgic that fast."

"I have the feeling that school provided his only social outlet," Matthew said. "Most likely, he really misses it."

Mia shrugged. "You're probably right."

"Let's move a bit closer, get a better view," Matthew said. "There's still enough people between us and the bar that he won't see us unless he turns around."

They quietly stood with their drinks and moved to a table closer to the bar. Norman didn't look up from the yearbook.

The woman who'd smiled at Norman knocked into her beer mug with her elbow, sloshing some of her beer on the bar, and Norman suddenly jumped up, the yearbook in his hands, a vein popping out on his temple.

"Be more careful!" Norman snapped. "You almost ruined my book!"

"Sor-ry," the woman snapped back, rolling her eyes as she mopped up liquid with a wad of napkins.

Norman inspected the area in front of him to make sure it was dry, then sat back down and stood the yearbook up in front of him. Mia could now see the page at which he was looking.

Baywater Middle School's Faculty. He was staring at the first page, which featured teachers whose last names began with the letters A–C. Six photos.

But Norman had blacked out every photo with a heavy-duty magic marker—every photo except for one.

Except for Mia Anderson's.

Mia squeezed her eyes shut.

"He's obsessed," Matthew said darkly. "I don't like this one bit."

"I *hate* it," Mia responded quietly.

The woman next to Norman leaned over and looked at the yearbook. "Pretty," she commented, her gaze on the page. "Your girlfriend?"

Norman eyed the woman as though she'd interrupted an important conversation, then returned his gaze to the yearbook. "Yes. She is."

The woman raised an eyebrow. "Too bad she's sitting right over there with another guy, then. Look, they're holding hands. Ooh, she's cheating," the woman trilled in singsong.

Norman's head swiveled so fast that Mia was sure he'd sprained his neck. His gaze locked with hers, then took in Matthew and their hands entwined on top of the table.

Norman's face turned beet red, and the same vein popped out in his temple. He slammed the yearbook shut.

The woman next to him burst out in a giggle, and Norman jumped up, threw the yearbook in his briefcase, then reached into his wallet and pulled out a ten-dollar bill, which he tossed on top of the bar. He fixed Mia with a withering glare, then stalked out.

"C'mon, let's follow him," Matthew said, reaching for his wallet and getting up.

"Matthew, I just want to go home," Mia said. "I've had more than enough espionage for one night—one weekend. One *lifetime*, for that matter."

He sat back down and pulled his chair close to hers. "Mia, listen to me. I know this is hard to deal with, but we've just seen evidence, our first real evidence, that a suspect is truly unhinged. We need to follow him for his own safety and for everyone else's. If he's a killer, then—"

Mia's hands shook. "Okay," she interrupted. "Just stop talking."

But when they hurried out of the bar, Norman Newman was nowhere to be seen.

"You're either staying with me, or I'm staying with you," Matthew told Mia.

While he let her digest that piece of information, Matthew took one last look up and down the boulevard. For the last hour, they'd circled the main drag of Center City twice, gone into several bars and nightclubs, but they hadn't spotted Norman.

He sure hoped the guy wasn't watching *them.*

"I suggest we stay at Margot's," Matthew said. "There's a good chance that Norman has followed Margot there, thinking it was you, thinking it's your weekend place in the city. If he knows where *we* are, it makes it easier for us to find *him.*"

Mia let out a deep breath. "All right."

They headed to Margot's building in silence. Mia seemed lost in thought, and Matthew was preoccupied with keeping an eye out for Norman Newman.

"I know it's creepy," Matthew said as they reached the high-rise. "The whole situation with Norman. But I want you to know you don't have to worry about him. I won't let anything happen to you. I promise."

She glanced up at him, those doe eyes full of trepidation. She only nodded, then returned her gaze to the sidewalk.

When they entered the apartment, Mia ran to check the answering machine for calls from Margot, but she was disappointed once again.

"Where could she be?" Mia asked rhetorically as she walked to the wall of windows and crossed her arms over her chest. She stared out at the night. "Margot, where *are* you?"

Matthew walked up behind her, tempted to put his arms around her, to rub her shoulders, to hold her. But he didn't. "She'll come home when she's ready. For now, we need to believe that she's safe."

Mia continued to stare out at the night. "Do you still think she's the one?" she asked quietly. "Do you think she killed your brother—and the others?"

"I really don't know what to think anymore," Matthew said. "C'mon, Mia—let's sit down on the sofa and kick off our shoes. It's been a very long day."

After a moment, he saw her shoulders relax. Her arms dropped down to her sides.

"Wait a minute," Mia said, whirling around to face him. "I just realized something about Norman Newman. He can't be a suspect!"

"Why?"

Mia's eyes were flashing. "Because if he thinks

Margot is *me*, why would he hire her as a decoy? There's no connection between Norman and hiring Margot!"

Matthew realized she was desperate to take Norman off the list to ease her mind. "Mia, we have to remember that the folder that arrived the other day didn't have a name on it, nor did the note. It wasn't addressed to Margot Daniels. The manila envelope was simply slipped under the door. For all we know, Norman thinks being a decoy is *your* side job and that this is *your* base of operation."

Mia bit her lip and seemed to consider that. "But if that's true, how would he even have found out about the decoy thing?"

Matthew shrugged. "How does anyone? I have no idea, but *someone* has been hiring her. And I've heard of decoys for as long as I can remember."

"And so he'd hire her—me—to watch me with other men—why? So he can get good and riled up and furious, then kill the men?"

Again, Matthew shrugged. "It's a possibility, Mia."

She dropped down on the sofa and let out a deep breath. "The whole thing is revolting. Absolutely revolting. I still can't understand why my sister would have gotten herself involved in that kind of business. It makes no sense to me at all."

"It would make a lot more sense for someone from my family," Matthew said darkly, running a hand through his hair. He sat down next to her, kicked off his shoes, and put his feet up on the coffee table.

Mia stared at him. "Why?"

"Because my father cheated on my mother constantly."

The moment the words were out of his mouth,

Matthew felt the familiar taste of bile. He pictured his father, graying, pot-bellied, smelling of beer, his shirts stained with junk food, his expression either a smirk or a scowl. And then he pictured his mother, his sweet, kind mother, who'd tried so hard and thought she was a failure.

"Did your mom know?" Mia asked.

"She knew," Matthew said flatly.

"Because she hired a decoy to test him?"

Matthew laughed bitterly. "No. She didn't need to."

"How . . . How did she find out?" Mia asked.

Matthew leaned back against the sofa and stared up at the ceiling. "My father paraded his women right in front of her."

Mia sat up straight. "What?"

"He even brought them home." His mother had deserved so much better. So much more than her bastard of a husband. Why hadn't she left when she first found out about the infidelities? How could you know you were being cheated on, disrespected on every level, violated, and not pack up and leave?

Because it's never that simple. And that was the answer.

Shades of gray, his mother had always said when Matthew demanded answers. *Just like our name. Remember that, Matthew. Nothing is black or white.*

But things *were* black and white, just as there were facts and assumptions. There was a right and a wrong, period. Gray was nothing but rationalizations.

"He brought them *home?*" Mia repeated, her voice incredulous.

"My parents had been sleeping in separate bedrooms for a few years," Matthew said. "My father said my mother snored like a giant. Made her feel awful about it. So he had his own bedroom."

"And he brought women to your mother's *house*?"

He was glad that she found it hard to believe. It should be hard to believe. No matter how many women had come and gone through his father's bedroom, Matthew had never gotten used to it, never thought it was the way people lived.

"Oh, Matthew. I don't even know what to say."

"There's nothing to say. It's sickening. Why get married in the first place if you're going to cheat on your spouse? Vows are supposed to mean something, but they don't, apparently."

Mia nodded. "They are supposed to mean something. They *do* mean something. They mean everything. I guess I like to think that the one who ends up cheating meant the vows when he or she spoke them."

"Well, that's optimistic of you," Matthew said, "but I don't buy it."

"Why?" she asked.

"My father cheated on my mother on their wedding night," Matthew said. At Mia's open mouth, he nodded slowly. "Yup. On their wedding night. He told me—when I was around twelve or so. Boasted about it to his sons. How do you like that?"

Mia shook her head. "That's awful."

"You ask how your sister ended up becoming a decoy? I'd like to know how my brother ended up a cheating bastard just like our old man. After seeing how it affected our family, what it did to my mother—after that incident—" Matthew stopped abruptly and stared at the ceiling.

"Incident?" Mia echoed.

Matthew could hear the shouting, smell the liquor

emanating from his father's bedroom, smell his mother's desperation and anguish, hear the police sirens as though it were all happening right now instead of almost twenty years ago. He expelled a harsh breath. "My mom came home one night to find my father naked in bed with a woman. Though it wasn't the first time, she snapped."

"Snapped?" she asked hesitantly.

Snapped was an understatement.

"My mother was a nurse," Matthew said, "and she'd been working the graveyard shift to make extra money. That night, she'd lost a young patient she cared very much about, and when she got home and found my father and the woman, that was it. Something inside her just broke."

"What . . . happened?"

Matthew closed his eyes. "She screamed bloody murder at the sight of them, but my father told her to shut the hell up and close the door, give him some 'goddam privacy.'" Matthew opened his eyes and stared at the floor. "So my mother did as he asked, then walked into the garage, got the gun my father kept in there—"

At Mia's gasp, her hand flying to her mouth, Matthew paused.

"Maybe I shouldn't tell you this," he said.

"No, please, Matthew. Continue."

The memories flooded his mind so fast, yet all he felt was numb. "She held the gun in her hands, opened the bedroom door and stood in the doorway, pointing the gun straight at my father's chest. My brother and I came home from a party at the moment she'd cocked the trigger—"

Mia gasped. "Don't tell me you witnessed this scene yourself!"

Matthew nodded. "Sure did. I was thirteen. Robert was seventeen."

"Thirteen years old," Mia repeated. "I can't begin to imagine how scared you must have been."

You don't know the half of it, Matthew thought. He could still remember the fear, the paralysis, the way the hairs had stood up on his nape, the way he'd shivered and felt burning hot at the same time. "My brother and I were so shocked we couldn't speak, couldn't move. Finally, Robert was saying, 'Mom, put down the gun.' He said it over and over and over."

"And did she?"

Matthew shook his head. "No. She kept it pointed at my father. Finally, she started trembling and burst into tears. Robert and I were afraid to move. Eventually, my father reached over to the nightstand for the phone and called the police." Matthew paused as images from that night overwhelmed him. He closed his eyes for a moment.

"What was the woman doing?" Mia asked.

"Screaming her head off," Matthew said. "She kept saying, 'Do something, do something' to my father." He leaned forward and dropped his elbows on his knees, letting his head dangle.

"Matthew, we can change the subject," Mia said, her voice soft. "There's no need for you to relive this."

"I never talk about that night," he told her, raising his head to face Mia. "Never. Not with Robert, not with anyone. I've never talked about it since it happened."

So why the hell did I just tell her about the worst night of my life? Matthew wondered. *Why tonight? Why her? Why at all?*

Mia's hand flew to her heart. "Thank you for sharing it with me, Matthew. I'm so glad you're able to."

He looked away. "Must not be easy to hear."

"It's not, but I want to hear it. Go on, Matthew. What happened then?"

He heard the sirens, distant and then closer and then so close they rang in his ears. "The police arrived. My mother was still in that same spot, standing in the doorway, crying hysterically, pointing the gun at my father, his floozy screaming bloody hell."

Mia was quiet, waiting for him to continue.

"My brother and I watched as a team of cops surrounded my mother with weapons pointed at her. It was probably the worst part of the entire night for Robert and me."

He felt Mia shiver next to him. "The cops arrested my mother and took her away in the squad car. My father didn't press charges, so my mother was released. She had to spend some time in counseling, but she still came home every day, cooking breakfast and dinner for my father, washing his damned clothes and his semen-stained sheets as though nothing had happened."

For a few moments, neither of them spoke.

"I guess she must have been broken," Mia said gently.

Matthew nodded. "Yes, that's exactly what happened to her. The spirit, the life, caring about anything was just crushed out of her. And then there was the car accident . . ."

"The car accident?" Mia prompted with trepidation in her voice.

Matthew slumped back against the sofa, the life

force drained out of him. "The police were unable to determine if she ran into the tree on purpose or if she lost control of the car. It was raining that night, but my mother drove in rain at night all the time. It was the summer I graduated from high school."

"Oh, Matthew," Mia said, her voice catching. "I'm so, so sorry."

The pity he heard in her voice strengthened him, brought back the bitterness. "My father had a woman in his bed the night of my mother's funeral and until his sorry life ended five years ago," Matthew said.

Mia reached for his hand, and though his first thought was to pull it away, he didn't.

He let himself have her warmth and softness for a moment, then leaned back against the sofa and slipped his hand from hers. "I vowed that night, the night my mother was taken away by the police, never to get married. Never to be in the position to hurt anyone—a wife, kids. Anyone."

"Matthew, I know we talked about this earlier, but to deny yourself a family because of someone else's—"

"Like father, like son," he said.

"But just because Robert—"

"*Just because* again? Well, I wasn't wrong, was I?" he reminded her. "My brother ended up exactly like our old man. And I'm protecting myself and any woman unlucky enough to fall for me from that fate."

She didn't say anything for a moment. "My father was a wonderful man. I guess I got lucky. Loyal and faithful to my mother for twenty-one years until a car accident took their lives."

Matthew turned to face her. She seemed on the verge of tears. "I'm glad to know there are some good guys out there," he told her gently.

"I thought all men were good—like my dad and my grandfathers," Mia said. "What a naïve idiot I was! It never occurred to me that my own husband would cheat on—" She paused, two spots of color forming on her cheeks.

Interesting. From how she talked about marriage and vows, he assumed infidelity hadn't been among her marital problems. He wondered how she remained optimistic about love when she'd had firsthand experience with betrayal. It made no sense.

She turned away, and he realized she was embarrassed that she'd admitted what she did. "Mia, what your husband did doesn't reflect on you. It's nothing to be embarrassed about."

"I think I'll always be embarrassed about it," she said, her voice small. "About not being enough. I wasn't enough for him."

Did she really believe that? "Mia, I don't know your ex, but I do know this: It's never about the spouse. It's about the cheater. Something lacking, missing in them that has nothing to do with how hard you work at the marriage."

She bit her lip, and it was all he could do not to pull her into his arms and kiss away the imprint of her teeth marks.

She burst into tears.

"Mia?" He kneeled down beside her and took her hands away from her face. "Mia, it's okay."

He looked down at her hands, so small and delicate and pale, and he kissed them, first one, then the other.

She didn't move. She didn't even flinch.

And then he put an arm around her neck and rubbed gently. He felt her sag against him, and that was it.

He pulled her into his arms and kissed her, his mouth tender on hers at first and then hard. He could feel her soft breasts against his chest, could feel his manhood pressing into her stomach.

She hesitated for just a moment, then arched her back, and he picked her up and laid her down on the sofa and covered her body with his own, careful not to rest his weight too heavily on top of her. He trailed kisses across her sweet face, down her neck. He reached behind her to unbutton her top, and he removed it in quick order.

The sight of her breasts, so soft and creamy beneath two scraps of black lace, stopped his breath. With his teeth, he moved aside the lace cup and tickled her rosy nipple with his tongue, raising it to a peak. He gave the same treatment to the other and was rewarded with a hoarse moan from Mia.

She arched up into him again, and he pulled off his shirt, then pressed against her so hard he was afraid he was hurting her. But the expression on her face assured him she wasn't feeling any pain at all.

He put her hand against his erection, and she hesitated for just a moment, then let him lead her in a hard stroke up and down the length of him.

Their mouths fused, Matthew moved on top of her, showing her just how it would feel once he removed the rest of their clothes.

"Oh, Matthew," she breathed.

He looked at her then, her eyes closed, her expression so full of desire—and something else . . .

Something that made him go numb.

There was hope on her face. Sweet, innocent hope.

Matthew rolled off her and sat up, running a hand through his hair.

"Matthew?"

He said nothing.

"Matthew? Is something wrong?" she asked, confusion in her eyes.

He couldn't face her. "Look, it's late. Why don't you head on in to the bedroom and I'll bunk right here."

She stared at him, but he still wouldn't look at her.

He rolled up his shirt in a ball to make a pillow, then lay down on the sofa and closed his eyes.

And closed the subject.

He heard the tiniest sob escape her lips before she hurried away.

Chapter Eleven

Mia wondered if he was awake yet, if he'd found her note.

She'd woken up at the crack of dawn after tossing and turning all night, memories of the previous evening bombarding her the moment she opened her eyes.

She'd had to get out of there, to get away from him. And so she'd showered and dressed quickly, then tiptoed past his sleeping form on the sofa and out the door.

She'd breathed the moment she hit the air outside.

And burst into yet another round of tears.

Mia had known exactly where to go. The one place that never failed to give comfort, never failed to give her answers: her parents' gravesides.

At six A.M. on a Monday, the cemetery was empty, save a caretaker walking through the grass. The flowers she'd placed on top of her parents' tombstones were just beginning to wilt, and Mia wished she'd brought a fresh bouquet.

She sat down between the two graves and pulled her knees to her chest. "Oh, Mama, Daddy. I know you know what's going on, and I know you must be worried; but everything's going to be okay. I know it will."

A blue jay settled on her mother's tombstone and whistled, and Mia felt her heart lift just a little.

"You see, Mama? Everything will be okay. Matthew and I are working together to figure out what's going on—"

Matthew and I.

There was no "Matthew and I" and there would never be, and Mia had better wrap her mind around that fact here and now.

He'd found her lacking.

Just like her husband had.

At least she'd learned that it didn't matter how blond or thin or gussied up you got. If a man didn't want you, didn't love you, he wouldn't love you if you looked like a Playboy bunny or the Wicked Witch of the West. And if he did want you, did love you, then he'd love you no matter what you looked like.

Which meant it was her, something in her, something about her, that turned off men who caught her heart.

Caught my heart, Mia repeated mentally. Was that true?

No. Last night simply got out of hand. They'd opened up to each other, and one thing had led to another. She'd been so touched when he told her that he'd never shared that terrible story with anyone but her. She'd thought it meant something, that he felt close to her—

But he didn't. Not emotionally, anyway. Luckily for the two of them, Matthew had had the wherewithal to pour a bucket of cold water on them before things went too far.

And they would have, she knew.

She'd never wanted a man more than she'd wanted Matthew last night, to feel that tall, strong, muscular body of his on top of hers, to feel all that intensity inside her.

And before she would know what hit her, she'd be in love with a man who didn't love her back.

A man who had one thing on his mind: solving his brother's murder. Mia knew she was simply a means to an end for Matthew.

She'd best not forget it again. He certainly hadn't.

Suddenly Mia was glad she hadn't had the opportunity to dye back her hair and cut it chin length. She wanted to remember that looking like her sister, looking like a "babe," as her ex-husband had called it, had resulted in nothing but a loss of her self-esteem and identity—

Oh, my God.

Her *identity.*

As the blue jay flew up and away, Mia realized she knew exactly how to solve Robert Gray's murder and clear her sister's name.

"What the hell is wrong with you?"

Matthew was furious. *Furious.*

"I've been pacing every inch of this apartment for the last two hours," he barked.

"I didn't realize you were my keeper," Mia said,

dropping her keys back in her pocket. "Are you going to let me in now that I'm back?"

The woman in the apartment next door suddenly stepped out in the hallway. "Will you two shut up!" she screamed. "It's eight in the morning! And you're making my dog bark like crazy! I am so sick of you, Margot! I'm complaining to the board first thing in the morning!" With that, Margot's charming neighbor slammed the door.

Matthew stepped aside, and Mia barged inside the apartment.

"Maybe you've forgotten a creepy little stalker named Norman who likes to carry around yearbooks with everyone's photo blotted out but yours," Matthew said coldly. "Maybe you've forgotten that he thinks you're his girlfriend. Maybe you've forgotten—"

"I'm capable of taking care of myself, Matthew," Mia interrupted, her voice cold as ice. She dropped down on the sofa and crossed her arms over her chest. "As you can see, I'm back here in one piece."

"That's not the point," Matthew said. "The point is that there's a guy out there who may or may not be a killer and who definitely seems to be under the impression that you're his girlfriend. After last night, he probably thinks you're cheating on him."

Her face paled, and he felt a bit of victory. Which immediately made him label himself a jerk. But at least he'd gotten through to her how serious this was. She couldn't just up and leave because her feelings got hurt—

Oh, damn.

He'd been so freaked out by finding her gone, so wrapped up in the thought of Norman getting his psycho hands on her, that he hadn't even stopped to think about why she'd gone out in the first place.

You idiot.

How he could have forgotten last night for a second was beyond him.

From the moment she'd rushed inside the bedroom last night, he'd been unable to stop thinking about her. The feel of her, the scent of her, the everything of her.

If he hadn't been able to control himself, they would have made love.

And this morning's conversation would have been very different.

Interesting, though, Matthew thought, *that the mood is the same. Anger. Disappointment.*

Had they made love, he would have made some excuse to leave this morning just like your typical jerk who couldn't deal with commitment or intimacy or a real relationship.

Well, he couldn't.

And Mia would have been hurt and angry and confused.

Much like she was now that he'd stopped them from making love.

Stopped them from making a mistake with way too many consequences. At least now they could move past this and stay focused on the case.

But first he'd have to deal with what happened last night. Deal with it and be done with it. He sat beside her.

"Look, Mia, about last night—"

"Let's not waste precious time talking about something that needs no discussion," Mia interrupted. "Last night was a mistake. I was upset and not thinking straight, and you were. Thank God one of us was."

It was a mistake.

Yes, it was. That she'd said so, that she thought so, should have made him feel much more comfortable. But instead, his stomach rolled.

"Anyway, the reason I left this morning was because I started formulating a plan for catching the killer, and—"

"Wait a minute," Matthew interrupted, furrowing his eyebrows. "*What?*"

"A plan came to me, and I wanted to walk around with it. That's what I've been doing for the past two hours."

"A plan to catch the killer," he repeated a little too sarcastically.

"That's right, Matthew. I do have a brain, too, or did *you* forget that?"

"Mia, this isn't a children's game at your school. This is life and death."

"How dare you?" she snapped. "Who the hell do you think you are?"

"I think I'm someone who cares about—"

He caught himself just in time. "About getting to the bottom of my brother's murder and your sister's flight. About finding the truth. I don't have time to listen to plans that won't help me seek justice for Robert."

"You arrogant jerk," Mia said. "Well, I'll tell you what. You don't have to listen to my plan. I'll just put it into motion on July tenth and handle it myself. The plan doesn't require you or your help in any way."

"July tenth" he repeated. "What are you talking about?"

"I thought you didn't want to hear it. I thought you didn't want to listen to children's games."

"Mia, if you've cooked up some dangerous scheme that'll get you hurt, I need to know so I can stop you."

"You really are a jerk."

She stormed into the bedroom and slammed the door.

Matthew realized that was the second time in twelve hours that he'd provoked her to that. Had she really left this morning to formulate a plan, or to escape him and what had happened last night? Had she been plotting on her own as a means to shut him out as he'd shut her out?

Once again, he had questions and no answers. He was getting really tired of that.

He let out a deep breath, got up, and threw open the door.

"Get out," she snapped. She sat at Margot's desk and faced away from him.

"I want to know what you're planning."

"As I said, Matthew, it doesn't concern you. In fact, I'm quite comfortable with proceeding on my own from here. So why don't you just leave?"

She turned around then and shot him a glare that told him she meant every word she said.

"Maybe I will," Matthew said. "Just to teach you a lesson."

"How many times will I have to call you an arrogant jerk in one morning?" Mia asked. "Just get out."

"Fine," he snapped.

"Fine."

"Fine," he said louder.

"Fine," she yelled.

The dog next door started barking, and suddenly, someone was pounding on the wall that Margot's bedroom shared with the apartment next door.

"Now look what you did," Mia said, lowering her voice. "You're going to get my sister evicted. She'll come home, thanks to my plan, and she'll have no home to come home to!"

He stared at her for a moment. "Look, let's just both get out of here, get some fresh air. You can tell me your idea."

"Gee, thanks," she said.

"I'm sorry, okay? I'm serious. I want to hear it."

She lifted her chin. "If you're not going to treat me like an equal partner in this—in this . . . *whatever* it is we're doing working together, then forget it, Matthew."

Man, but she was exasperating. "Okay. You've got a deal."

"Fine," she said.

"Fine."

"I'd like the last word," she said. "For once."

"Fine."

They both tried, but neither could resist a smile.

"No way," Matthew said. "Absolutely not."

"Like I said, my plan doesn't require you—or your approval—Matthew."

"Mia, listen to me. It's too dangerous. Way too dangerous. There's no way in hell I'm letting you do that."

Mia took a deep breath and stared out at the Atlantic Ocean. The truce they'd formed five minutes ago was certainly short-lived. From the moment they'd left Margot's and walked the few blocks down to the promenade with a couple of bacon-and-egg sandwiches and large coffees, her back had been up about telling Matthew the details of her idea. And before she'd even had a chance to flesh it out for him, he'd interrupted with his absolutely nots.

Yes, her plan was dangerous. But if she didn't think she could handle it, she wouldn't have raised it.

And what gave him the gall to even think he could tell her what she could and couldn't do? The man was more than impossible. More than infuriating.

"Letting me?" Mia asked. "Last time I looked I was a grown woman."

"A grown woman who must watch a lot of television," Matthew said. "This isn't an episode of *Law and Order*, Mia. It's real life."

Mia sighed. "Matthew, on July tenth, Margot is expected to show up at MacDougal's Bar and entice someone into cheating. Someone who is going to end up dead if the pattern holds. And I'm going to stop that from happening."

"By getting killed instead?" Matthew asked.

"By being very careful."

"Mia, you're not dressing up as Margot and taking her place on July tenth to see what goes down. There's no way in hell I'm letting you do that."

There it was again. *Letting you do that.* Did he really think he could stop her?

Her plan was a good one, the only one that would work, and it seemed very simple. Margot had received instructions to show up at a certain bar on a certain night at a certain time, and Mia was going to take her place. Since there were no instructions other than where and when, Mia figured she'd just wait and watch and see what happened. Who approached her, perhaps. And when the killer made his or her move, Mia would be ready.

As ready as she could be for a murderer, that was.

Suddenly, her stomach turned over and then twisted into a knot.

"Mia, we have no idea what the details of that night are supposed to be or who we're dealing with," Matthew said, pulling his coffee out of the bag. "We'd be going in blind."

"We?" she asked, eyebrow raised. "So you're with me on this?"

A vein was working in Matthew's temple. "Let me think it over, figure out how we could possibly do this and guarantee your safety at the same time."

"Matthew, I don't think we can *guarantee* my safety," Mia said. She took a sip of coffee. "There are no guarantees with anything in life. The only guarantee with my plan is that I'll know I did everything I could to lure your brother's killer out of the woodwork. Even if it's a failure, I'll know I tried to help when I had the power to do so."

He looked into her eyes, his expression unreadable, and she wondered what he was thinking.

He stood up, walked to the railing and stared out at the ocean, then turned back around and sat down. "We've got five suspects. Norman Newman and the four widows. Let's exhaust the possibilities that one of them is our killer before we send you in to do your sister's dirty work—"

"Please don't talk about my sister that way," Mia

snapped. "We don't know what led Margot into that line of work or why she chose to keep doing it."

"We know it was important enough for her to give up love for it," Matthew commented. "She made a job—a sleazy job—more important than her relationship with a man she loved, a man who loved her."

"First of all, we don't know that Margot loved Justin," Mia pointed out. "We don't know anything about her or her situation."

She hated how true that was. How could two sisters who'd lost their parents at such a young age become so distant from each other? Instead of reaching out for each other, they'd gone their separate ways, looking to fill the void elsewhere instead of with each other.

It was crystal clear that they were both still looking.

"So, partner, how does my compromise sound?" Matthew asked, his blue eyes locked with hers.

Was he charming her? Manipulating her? She couldn't tell. Damn.

"I know what an equal partnership is, Matthew," Mia said. "Don't call me partner if you don't mean it. Don't try to manipulate me into doing things your way. I won't stand for it."

He looked at her, then glanced out at the ocean for a long while. Finally he turned back to her and held her gaze. "Equal partners. I'll even shake on it."

When his large hand enveloped hers, she felt the jolt from the nape of her neck to her toes.

"Let's concentrate on the widows today," Matthew

said. "I'm a little sick of Norman Newman at the moment."

"More than fine with me," Mia agreed, unwrapping her sandwich. She took a bite, savoring the crispy bacon. "Matthew, you said we had five suspects—Norman and the four widows. Are you saying you're really willing to investigate your sister-in-law?"

He took a slug of his coffee. "I don't know. I only know there are four widows of the four victims and that she's one of them."

Mia wanted to grab his hand and put it to her heart, tell him she understood how hard it was. But she couldn't. He wouldn't let her.

"Laurie left a message on my answering machine letting me know that she's coming back early from a visit to her parents," Matthew continued. "She said she needs to be in the home she shared with Robert, not running away from the memories they built. She's going to leave the baby with her folks for the rest of the week, to give her some time to grieve without affecting Robbie."

"I can understand that. She sounds like a strong woman," Mia offered.

"If, of course, she didn't kill Robert and the other men," Matthew said flatly.

"But based on what you know of her, you highly doubt she was involved in any way?"

"Ninety-nine percent, I'm sure," Matthew said. "But I need to be smart about this. I learned a long time ago that people can often not be what they seem. And that whether out of desperation or depression—whatever—people can be reduced to doing just about anything."

Mia wondered if he was thinking about his mother. She'd bet on it.

"What do you think is our best way of approaching the investigation of Laurie Gray?" Mia asked.

"She invited me for dinner tomorrow night," Matthew said. "Why don't I tell her I'll be bringing a guest? Over dinner, we'll ask some questions in a very careful manner."

"Who will you tell her I am?" Mia asked.

"A friend of mine," Matthew said. "It's the truth, isn't it?"

They locked eyes, and she nodded. But she was thinking that friends didn't go around doing what they were doing last night.

Right here, right now, Mia Anderson was taking a bubble bath.

The thought that one thin bathroom door separated him from her naked body was almost too much to bear. Much like turning her away last night had almost been his undoing.

He lay on Margot's uncomfortable leather beige sofa, so like his own, and wondered whether Mia wore her hair up or down in the tub.

Whether those silky blond tresses were streaming over those soft, creamy breasts.

His zipper straining against his erection, Matthew imagined himself in the tub with her, lathering her with soap, their bodies slick against each other. . . .

Damn, he wanted her.

"Matthew?"

Please join me in the tub and wash my incredible body from head to toe. . . .

Very curious, he got up and hurried to the bathroom door. "Yes?" he called through it.

"I was just thinking about something Margot and I used to do when we were kids," she said, her voice light. "The two of us loved bubble baths. While one of us was in the tub, the other would sit outside the bathroom door and wait her turn, and we'd talk and talk and talk. I guess knowing you're out there in the living room made me think of it."

Matthew had to control himself from flinging open the door, stripping off his clothes, and joining her. "My mom had to bribe my brother and me to take our baths," he told her.

Mia laughed. "Not me and Margot. We did all our best talking with the bathroom door just slightly ajar and one of us sitting outside. It was easy to talk through tough kid stuff when you couldn't see the other person's face."

Matthew tried to imagine himself and Robert talking about anything as kids, let alone making a ritual out of it. "You and Margot were clearly close once. What happened?"

Mia didn't answer for a moment. "Puberty mostly," she said. "Margot became the most popular girl in school, and I became the most invisible. Actually, I take that back—people knew who I was because they were shocked that I was Margot Daniels' twin sister."

"Shocked? Uh, didn't you look exactly alike then, too?" Matthew asked.

"Hardly," Mia said. "It was more like I was the 'before' and she was the 'after' in a makeover session."

"Okay, now you've lost me," he said. "You'll have

to explain to me how identical twins can look so different. "But first, how about if I crack open the door so we can hear each other a bit better. It'll be like old times."

"That would be nice," she said.

He opened the door just slightly and slid back down on his butt against the wall just outside.

"To answer your question," she said, "one becomes adept at cosmetics and blow-dryers and mall shopping for stylish clothes and flirting, and the other is a flop at it all."

"A flop? Or just not interested in that kind of stuff?"

"I guess I wasn't interested," she confirmed. "I preferred to spend my money on books or music than on cosmetics and clothes. That didn't make me too popular with the boys."

"I find it hard to believe that you didn't have teenaged boys salivating over you."

"Trust me—not a one. Not too hard to believe when your sister looks like every boy's dream. Like I said, I always looked like the 'before.' What was interesting was that it really seemed to bother the girls at school."

"The girls? Why?"

"They just couldn't believe that I'd choose to look like a plain Jane when I could look like Margot so effortlessly. It bothered them that I seemed to shun popularity, shun what I could have."

"God, I wish people would just leave other people alone," Matthew said. "Even when you grow out of adolescence, there's still so much crap, so much of people trying to make you live up to their expectations."

"I know. I found that out when I got married.

My ex wanted a certain type of woman, and he created her."

"What do you mean?" Matthew asked. If she was a plain Jane in junior high and high school, she'd certainly blossomed into a swan at some point. The woman was drop-dead gorgeous.

"I mean that he wanted me to look a certain way, and I wanted to make him happy, so I changed how I looked."

"Are you trying to tell me you're not a natural blonde?" he asked, laughing.

"Exactly."

"I'd bet anything that you'd look amazing as a brunette," Matthew said.

"My ex-husband didn't think so."

"Mia, if you don't mind my saying so, your ex-husband sounds like a guy who didn't know what he had."

She was quiet for a few moments. "Did you go through a lot of that—people wanting you to live up to their expectations of you?"

"Well, I guess with women," he said, not sure he wanted to be on this track.

Then again, perhaps it was a good way to make her realize that he didn't have commitment in his blood.

"Oh?" she asked.

"I'd get into relationships, and the girls and later women would have all these expectations of me, even though I made clear that I wasn't looking for a relationship, wasn't looking to get serious. They'd get serious, call me a jerk, and that would be that."

"You're not trying to cry 'misunderstood,' are you?" she accused in a teasing tone.

"Not misunderstood. Not *listened to.* I'd say it's

the biggest problem between men and women. Not listening. When someone says they're not interested in commitment, the other person should believe it."

She was quiet for a moment. "I do have to agree with you about listening. If only I'd listened to what my ex-husband was saying when we first met, I would never have gone on a second date with him. But I heard what I wanted—or I ignored what sounded wrong to me."

Now they were both quiet.

"Matthew, I'm about ready to get out of this tub before I shrivel up like a prune, but I forgot to bring in my robe," she said. "Would you mind getting it for me? It's right on the bed."

"Sure, no problem," he said and headed off to fetch it.

Pink terry cloth had never looked so sexy. Her full-length robe lay on the bed she'd slept in last night, and he was tempted for a moment to lie down and just inhale the scent of her.

Get a grip, buddy, he told himself.

He grabbed the robe and headed back to the bathroom door. "Uh, Mia, I've got it. Should I come in?"

The door opened a bit more, and a delicate arm poked through.

"Here," he said and handed it to her—or tried to. The robe caught on the doorknob, and she ended up swinging the door wide open.

She stood naked before him, her hair damp around her shoulders. She gasped and stared at him. He stared back. At everything there was to see.

He unbuttoned his shirt, slowly at first to see if

she'd tell him to go to hell or at least to stop, but she didn't, and then he practically ripped it off his chest. His pants followed the shirt in a heap on the floor.

She still said nothing.

He walked toward her and pulled her into his arms and kissed her hard, so hard that they banged against the wall. This time there was no hesitancy on her part. She met his passion with equal fervor.

"Oh, Matthew," she breathed into his ear, and his entire body shuddered.

He picked her up in his arms and pressed his lips to her mouth, his tongue probing inside the sweet softness of her. He trailed kisses along her neck, in her ear, across her collarbone. He let his tongue flick over her breasts, and as he licked and suckled the rosy tips, he carried her out of the bathroom and laid her on the thick, soft carpet in the living room.

And then she surprised him.

She pushed him down onto his back and lay on her side against him, running her hands and mouth over his chest. And then she took him in her hand and brought him to the edge.

"Mia," he breathed in her ear. "I have to have you."

She shifted until she was lying on top of him, her legs straddling his own. As much as he wanted to look at every inch of her, he had to squeeze his eyes shut for a moment to keep control.

And then she slid down on top of the length of him, slowly . . . slowly . . . and then faster, harder.

"Oh, Mia," he whispered, trailing kisses along her neck, across her breasts.

His hands roamed her entire body as she shook

and trembled and writhed on top of him, and then he couldn't take another moment. He flipped her over so that she was on her back and he was on top of her, and then he teased her, the tip of his manhood toying with the soft, sweet entrance to her femininity.

"Matthew, please," she moaned. "Please . . ."

He flicked his tongue over her nipples, lightly biting the rosy peaks until they were hard, and her husky moan almost undid him. He savored every inch of her warm, smooth body, his mouth and hands everywhere at once.

And when he couldn't take another moment, he entered her gently.

She groaned low in her throat, her eyes closed, and he thrust harder, then withdrew until his manhood was almost completely outside of her. Her eyes flew open, and she arched up.

Their gazes locked, he teased the sweet entrance to her femininity with the tip of his erection, and she arched her back again, her head moving from side to side.

"Matthew . . . ," she whispered brokenly, a smile toying at her lips.

"Yes?" he breathed into her ear, his tongue darting in and out, then down her neck and across her breasts. He took her nipple in his mouth again and suckled the rosebuds until they hardened, while slipping his manhood inside her inch by inch.

"Matthew . . . ," she whispered hoarsely.

He thrust into her hard, and she met him, their mouths locking against each other, their tongues exploring, their hands slipping and sliding everywhere they could reach.

They rocked together in perfect rhythm until he heard her moan over and over and then gasp, her expression blissful, and then his own world exploded.

He kissed her softly on the lips, then rolled onto his back and closed his eyes. "That. Was. Amazing."

"Mmmm," she breathed next to him. "Amazing."

And then he picked her up in his arms and carried her into the bedroom and slid her under the satin duvet comforter. In the dimmest recesses of his mind, he thought of kissing her good night and heading to his bunk on the sofa, but there was no way he could bear being that far away from her.

He slid under the comforter and wrapped his arms around her.

Chapter Twelve

Mia knew he was gone even before she opened her eyes.

She rolled over in bed on her side and stretched her arm over the empty spot where Matthew had been. It was still warm.

She closed her eyes and inhaled the scent of him, masculine, soapy, clean. She could still feel the imprint of his lips, his mouth, all over her body.

No matter what they'd both said or would say, no matter how either of them felt, last night hadn't been a mistake. Mia had never experienced anything like it, not in five years of marriage, not even when she'd still been in love with her ex-husband.

She'd had no idea that lovemaking could be that way, could feel that way, could take her places inside herself that would set her free.

Which was why she wasn't upset, wasn't crying, wasn't beside herself with disappointment. David Anderson had called her frigid, boring. But last night, Mia knew she'd been anything but.

She was enough. She had been enough.

A smile formed on her lips as the warmth spread through her stomach and traveled downward and upward.

Last night hadn't been a mistake.

Matthew, judging from his early morning absence, didn't agree.

I will not fall in love with a man who doesn't want a relationship, she told herself. *I won't, won't, won't.*

The problem was, she already had.

She flung off the covers and trudged into the bathroom. His clothes were gone from the floor.

It wasn't that she expected his clothes to be there. She didn't know what she expected. Matthew to be lying next to her, his arm heavy over her stomach, his soft breath against her neck?

Mia felt the sting of tears at the backs of her eyes. *Don't cry, don't cry, don't cry,* she ordered herself. *He told you he's not interested in commitment. You just had an entire conversation last night about listening.*

You chose not to listen.

And now you're going to pay the consequences.

Mia closed her eyes and willed herself to stop thinking about him. For a very long time she'd prayed that David Anderson would love her, would accept her for who she was. She'd learned that it only mattered that *she* loved and accepted *herself.* So why was she hoping against hope that Matthew would change his feelings?

Don't do this to yourself, Mia. Don't go there. Don't want something you'll never have.

But she did want. She wanted very much.

As the tears flowed down her face, Mia stepped into the shower and let the hot spray wash away the taste and feel of Matthew Gray on her body.

Let go of what you can't have, Mia. Don't grieve for what was never yours to begin with.

But hadn't it been hers last night? For just a little while?

No. That had been sex. That was all it had been to Matthew. Sex. Nothing more, nothing less.

The tears stopped, and anger began edging its way inside her. By the time she stepped out of the shower, she was ready to stand on her own again.

Mia stared hard at herself in the mirror. *I'd bet anything you'd look great as a brunette . . .*

Yeah. Right. Even the sexy blond look couldn't keep Matthew around the morning after.

She forced away that line of thinking. She had to remember that a man's interest had nothing to do with how dolled up a woman got, but how much he actually liked her, loved her.

And Matthew Gray did not love her.

Because if he did, he'd be here.

So what do you have to do? she wondered. *What does it take? And why does it keep eluding me?*

Get yourself dressed and go out and help bring your sister back home, Mia told herself. *Stop moping around this empty apartment, waiting for someone else to make decisions for you.*

Five minutes later, Mia was dressed and out the door. If Matthew came back and didn't like it that she was gone, well, that was just too damned bad.

At nine in the morning, the air was sticky and warm as usual. Mia slipped her thin cardigan off her shoulders and tied it around her waist.

She had no idea where to go, what to do.

"Hello, Mia."

She turned to her left to find herself staring into the cold, beady eyes of Norman Newman.

"I hoped I'd run into you," he said. "*Alone.*"

A knot of fear formed in Mia's stomach. Had he been hanging around since she saw him last, waiting for her? "Oh, gosh, is it nine o'clock already?" she asked, making a show of glancing at her watch. "I'm running late, Norman. Can we talk another time?"

He narrowed his eyes at her. "I'm *sure* you have time for a cup of coffee, Mia."

She darted her gaze up and down the block, hoping that Matthew would magically appear. But he was nowhere to be seen.

Nor was a police officer.

"I'd really like to discuss what happened the other night," Norman said. "Our little *misunderstanding* in the bar. I was quite embarrassed."

Mia had no idea what to say. Was she talking to a complete psychopath? Or was he simply the annoying and creepy Norman Newman she'd always known from Baywater Middle School? *Would* he hurt her?

Had he hurt four men—fatally?

"Mia? I'm just asking for a half hour of your time to discuss the other night. After all the time we've known each other, is that really too much to ask?"

Mia forced the semblance of a smile. A half-hour cup of coffee would allow her to slyly interrogate him about his whereabouts on the nights of the murders. As long as they were in a public place, whether a street or a coffee lounge, she'd be safe.

"Okay, Norman," she said, "a cup of coffee sounds nice."

His face lit up in surprised delight. "Wonderful."

"How about right across the street," she said, gesturing at the coffee lounge where she and Matthew had met for the first time.

"Oh, no, Mia," Norman said. "That place won't do at all. Their coffee is terrible."

Mia felt the color drain from her cheeks. "I like it fine," she said. "And besides, it's right here."

"I know a much better place," Norman said, staring at her. "It's quite close by. Just a few blocks from here."

Against her better judgment, Mia nodded and let Norman Newman take her arm and lead her away.

Matthew wondered what Mia was doing right then. Pacing the apartment? Cursing him out? Crying?

Maybe you're giving yourself way too much credit, he told himself. *Maybe she's glad you were gone when she woke up. Maybe she regrets last night, too.*

From the way she'd responded to him, though, he found that hard to believe. Her passion had come from her heart, her soul. And that had been the problem. He'd never experienced that kind of want from a woman. Last night, it had translated into the most passionate sex he'd ever had.

But this morning, it had unnerved him.

He'd woken up to find her nestled right beside him, her arm across his chest, her expression so sweet, so trusting.

And he'd had to get out of there.

Dammit, he'd told her last night when she'd

been in the bathtub that he wasn't interested in commitment. If she couldn't deal with that, she shouldn't have let last night happen.

So maybe she could deal with it. Maybe she wanted what he wanted.

What *did* he want?

No ties. No commitments.

Gwen Harriman's beautiful face floated into his mind. Twenty-two, with sweet blue eyes and baby blond hair, she'd come across as the picture of innocence. And she'd played the role of love-struck secretary to the hilt.

But she'd been a spy for his competition, the girlfriend of his competition, and in the end, she'd stolen documents that could have bankrupted him had he not acted quickly and ruthlessly in return.

She'd shocked him, something he didn't think anyone could do after what he'd gone through that terrible night with his mother and the gun.

Betrayal, in the worst way.

He'd let her get inside when he'd vowed no woman would ever do that, and he'd been screwed royally.

He was not going to allow that to happen again.

Not when for all he knew, Mia Anderson was playing some kind of sick game with her twin sister. Or perhaps she was simply just using him to clear her sister's name.

How the hell did he know if she'd disappear the moment she had what she wanted?

So what *did* she want? She wanted her sister's name cleared. She wanted her sister home. And if Norman Newman was the person they were after, she wanted her guilt assuaged with justice.

You're reaching, he knew. *You'll do anything to justify walking away this morning. Walking away from any sort of involvement other than professional.*

Matthew took a deep breath. All around him, couples walked along the promenade on their way to work, holding hands, holding briefcases, holding dog leashes.

That'll never be me, he reminded himself. *I will never allow myself to be stupid again. Never allow myself to become my father.*

And the way to ensure that was to avoid getting tangled up with Mia Anderson.

He got up and stretched, his limbs achy from staying in one position for two hours. It was time to go back to Margot's and deal with Mia.

With every step, Mia felt more and more uncomfortable. For someone who wanted to talk to her, Norman was being awfully silent. In fact, he hadn't said one word since they began walking ten minutes ago.

Ten minutes of utter silence, save their heels clicking on the sidewalk, was very unnerving, especially because they'd entered Center City's industrial area. A bit too desolate for Mia's comfort with a lot of construction sites, the north part of town wasn't an area she'd ever frequented.

"Norman, I thought you said this coffee lounge was a few blocks from where we were," Mia said.

"I meant a few *avenues*," Norman responded, his beady blue eyes raking over her for just a moment. "Ah, here we are."

Mia glanced up at the Center City North Motel. A neon sign in the window advertised an all-night coffee shop. This wasn't exactly what she had in mind.

"Is this a favorite coffee shop?" she asked, trying to keep the nervousness out of her voice.

"They have the best coffee in Center City. You wouldn't know it from looking at the place . . ."

Mia stared at the run-down brick building. They would be entering a public place that surely had plenty of staff and at least a few patrons. She would be fine.

You want to rule out Norman Newman as a suspect, here's your chance, she reminded herself.

She forced a smile, and Norman smiled back.

She felt his hand at her waist as they entered the motel, and she tried not to flinch.

The small motel was clean, if shabby. The only person in the lobby was a clerk, a middle-aged woman behind a short counter. She sat reading a paperback novel and popping chocolates from a box into her mouth. She didn't look up when they entered.

"The coffee shop is this way," Norman said, leading her to a narrow hallway.

Mia smiled tightly, hoping her expression didn't betray her. At the far end of the hallway, she saw a peeling sign: *Restaurant.*

Halfway down the hall, Norman stopped short. Mia practically bumped into his back. "Oh, darn. I just realized I left my wallet in my room," he said. "It's right here, one-oh-four."

Mia felt sick. "Um, why don't I meet you in the—"

Norman had his key out and the door to his room opened before Mia could finish her sentence.

And before she could scream, he took her arm and pulled her inside.

* * *

Where the hell was Mia?

Matthew paced Margot's apartment, then tore through the rooms for the second time looking for a note, looking for anything that might indicate where she'd gone. Dammit! Hadn't he gotten through to her how dangerous it was for her to walk around Center City alone?

"Where are you, Mia?" he shouted in the empty apartment. *Where would she go?* he wondered.

He hoped she didn't feel she had something to prove. That ridiculous plan of hers—using herself as bait, pretending to be Margot to catch the killer—that was the plan of a woman who felt she had something to prove. It was beyond dangerous, crazy.

Was she out there setting herself up as bait to lure Norman Newman into talking? Into confessing?

No, she wouldn't be crazy enough to attempt that alone. Would she?

If she felt alone, she might, he answered himself.

He tore out of the apartment.

Norman stood in front of the door, his arms crossed. "I don't bite, for heaven's sake," he said, his expression suddenly turning . . . romantic.

Mia felt sick to her stomach. She was trapped with him in his motel room, and no one knew where she was. Bile rose in her throat. "Norman, I . . . I would prefer we talked in the coffee shop. I'm quite thirsty and a bit hungry. I could really go for an order of French toast with maple syrup." She'd tried to inject a lighthearted tone into her voice, but she knew she sounded unnatural. "Doesn't that sound good to you?"

"What sounds good to me, Mia," he began, his gaze moving from her eyes to her breasts and lingering there before traveling back up again, "is a little private time with you. I've been unable to accomplish that all year. And now here you are." Suddenly, a bulge formed behind the zipper of his tan slacks.

Stay calm, stay calm, she ordered herself. *Just stay calm and think, girl!* "The coffee shop probably isn't very crowded, Norman," she said, forcing a tight smile. "Why don't we head over. Boy, could I go for a strong cup of coffee."

"I have coffee here," he said, his gaze roving over her breasts again.

Mia crossed her arms over her chest, grateful that she'd brought over some clothes yesterday from her own apartment. She wore a pale blue T-shirt and jeans, neither tight. Had she been wearing an outfit of Margot's, she would have felt even more uncomfortable than she already did.

"The motel provides individual serving sizes of decaf and regular, plus nondairy creamer and sugar. Little plastic cups, too," he added with a smile.

Think, Mia. Think. Calm down and think.

She dropped her arms to her sides to appear less nervous. "Um, Norman, some regular coffee with cream and sugar sounds wonderful. Why don't you go make us a cup each while I freshen up in the bathroom. That walk over in this humidity left me a bit sticky."

Smile, Mia, she told herself. *Offer him a smile.*

He stared into her eyes, and she forced a warm

smile. His gaze moved back down to her breasts and stayed there. "All right, Mia. You are looking a bit flushed from the heat. "It's that door to the left."

Mia glanced at the open door. She could see a window. *Thank God!* she thought, hope soaring. *Oh, thank God.* "I'll be just a minute or two," she said, turning to give him a smile.

"And I'll have your coffee waiting," he said, licking his lips. "Go ahead in. I like to watch you walk. You have quite a sexy sway, if you don't think me too bold in saying so."

She forced a giggle. "Well, a little bold," she said, the bile rising higher. "Okay, I'll be out in a jiffy."

Once inside the tiny bathroom, Mia closed her eyes, sank against the back of the door, and let out the breath she'd been holding. She opened her eyes and looked for a lock on the door. No such luck.

She quickly moved to the window.

She was fumbling frantically with the stiff latch when she heard the bathroom door crash open and she felt Norman Newman's hot breath on her neck and his arms pulling her back, away from the window.

Mia was trapped with him in the bathroom. He stood blocking the door.

"Yes, Mia, it *is* awfully hot in here, isn't it?" he said. "I can understand why you'd want to open the window, but since we're on the ground floor, I'm a bit wary of intruders. We are in the city. This *isn't* Baywater."

Mia swallowed.

"In fact, I think I'd be a lot more comfortable if I removed this long-sleeved shirt," he said, his gaze roving over her body. His eyes lingered at her crotch, and it was all Mia could do not to throw up.

His gaze didn't move as he removed his shirt.

Just when Matthew thought that looking for Mia was like looking for "Candy" all over again, he spotted a familiar flash of long blond hair on the hill that led to the industrial part of Center City. She was only about two blocks north, but this part of the city was teaming with commuters on their way out of the Center City Station and the bus depot, and seeing past the hordes of people for another flash of hair wasn't easy.

He saw the flash of blond again. Yes! It had to be Mia! She was walking with a man shorter than herself, a bit stocky, with wiry brown hair.

Jesus. It was that creep Norman Newman.

Dammit. Was she walking with him willingly? Or had he exerted some sort of force?

Dammit!

"Mia!" he shouted up the hill at the exact moment a train from the suburbs roared into Center City Station.

As he ran to catch up with them, he strained past the hordes of people to see her, but he'd lost them.

Dammit! Where the hell had they gone?

Out of breath, Matthew ran faster, looking in every direction at once. He caught the flash of blond and blue T-shirt enter the Center City North Motel. Newman held open the door, then followed.

Dammit! What the hell was she doing? Why would she go in there with him? He had to have a gun or a knife on her!

By the time he entered the motel, there was no one in the lobby but a clerk reading a novel.

"Excuse me," he shouted to the woman behind the counter. "A woman and a man just came in here. Do you know where they went?"

The woman nodded toward a hallway. "Coffee shop, I figure. Or the guy's room."

Matthew's stomach roiled. He ran down the hall to the coffee shop. Three people sat at the counter eating breakfast. No sign of Mia or Norman.

He raced back to the lobby. "Ma'am, what room's the guy in?"

"You the husband?" she asked, looking up with interest.

"This is an emergency," he said. "The woman could be in danger. What room?" he shouted.

"One-oh-four," she said. "Don't bust up nothing!" she called after him.

Matthew tore down the hall and pressed his ear against the door.

Silence.

He knocked. "Mia? Mia, are you in there?"

Silence.

Except for the sound of splintering glass.

That's it, he told himself and kicked open the door.

"Hey! What's going on down there?" he heard the clerk yell. "I told ya not to bust up nothing! Don't make me call the cops!"

The small room was empty. Matthew pulled open one door—a closet. He tried to push open another, but it was either locked or someone was wedged against it.

"Mia! Mia, are you in there?" Nothing again. His heart racing, Matthew called out, "Mia, stand away from the door; I'm kicking it in!"

The door gave easily. Mia was crouched in the corner, her hands protecting her face. A window was wide open, the glass by the latch shattered jaggedly.

Norman was gone.

"Mia! Are you all right? Did he hurt you? Did that bastard put his hands on you?"

Her face drained of color, Mia opened her mouth, but no sound came out.

"Come on, let's get the hell out of here," Matthew said, gently lifting her up. With his arm supporting her, he led her from the room.

"I called the cops," the clerk said, her eyes on the paperback. "You'd better pay up for that door."

"You can charge the scum who rented that room," Matthew hissed at the woman.

"Uh-huh," said the clerk. "Bob Smith. Like I'm sure that's his name."

Matthew wasn't surprised that Norman had registered under an assumed name. The man clearly had a lot to hide and a lot to answer for.

"Let's get a taxi," Matthew said to Mia. "There's one right there."

"Hey! You'd better wait for the cops!" the clerk said.

But Matthew already had Mia in the taxi. It sped away just as a police car pulled up to the motel.

Matthew relaxed. He had Mia back. That was all that mattered.

* * *

As Matthew gently lay Mia down on the couch in his apartment, she lost it. She burst into tears and covered her face with her hands.

Matthew knelt in front of her. "Mia, you're safe now. It's all right."

"I was so scared. I've never been so scared in my life."

Anger, sharp and hot, coiled in his gut. That damned bastard! Just wait till Matthew got his hands on that twerp. "He can't hurt you now. And that bastard will never come near you again, not if I'm alive."

"I was so afraid he was going to—" Mia let out a sob and turned her face away from Matthew. "If you hadn't come when you did, there's no telling what might have happened."

Red-hot rage coursed through Matthew's veins. *Calm down for her sake,* he ordered himself. *She needs you now—not your anger.* "Mia, it's all over. He will never come near you again. I'll make sure of it. In fact, when you're up to it, I want us to go down to the police station to press charges against Newman and to get a restraining order. Kidnapping will put him away for a long time."

"I didn't even get to ask him any questions," she said, her voice breaking. "That's why I agreed to go have coffee with him. I thought I could get him to confess, but before I knew what was happening, he pulled me into his room . . ."

She trailed off, unable to repeat what had happened in that stuffy, smelly motel room. He hadn't touched her, other than to pull her away from the window when he'd first come after her in the bathroom, but the way he'd looked at her—the way he'd taken off his shirt—

Mia's hand flew to her mouth, and she shot up off the couch and into Matthew's bathroom. She kneeled on the cool tile in front of the toilet and threw up.

"Mia, are you okay? Can I get you some water?"

"Thanks," she managed with what little voice she had left.

She heard his footsteps tapping away and sagged against the toilet bowl. *Get up, Mia. Get up and take care of yourself. No one else is going to do it for you. And the last thing you need is Matthew Gray seeing you this broken down.*

Bracing against the toilet bowl, Mia pushed herself up and took a deep breath. She walked to the sink and checked her reflection in the mirror. She looked exactly as she felt. Terrible.

Mia splashed some cold water on her face and felt a bit refreshed. She squeezed a dab of toothpaste onto her index finger and did the best she could with her makeshift toothbrush. Then she exited the bathroom. The less time she spent in bathrooms for a while, the better she'd feel.

Matthew was sitting on the sofa, a tall glass of water and some saltines on a plate on the coffee table in front of him. "You okay?"

She nodded and sat down. "I just had quite a scare there, but I'm fine. I'll be fine in a little while. The shock is wearing off a bit."

"Mia, you've got to promise me that you won't go off alone again," Matthew said. "Promise me."

"Maybe you should practice what you preach," she said and instantly regretted it. She hadn't meant to say that.

He looked at her, and she saw the guilt in his eyes.

Great. Just what she wanted to inspire in a man—guilt.

"Well, it's a bit different for me," Matthew said, handing her the glass of water.

"Oh? Why is that? Because you're a man and therefore can take care of yourself?"

"That's right," he said. "It's not a chauvinistic attitude; it's just the truth in this case."

His arrogance knew no bounds. "So, what you're saying is that Norman couldn't have jumped you with a knife or pulled a gun on you and done you some very great harm?"

He glanced at her uneasily. Dammit! How could she be so insensitive? He must be thinking that his brother had met with a very similar fate, whether at Norman's hand or someone else's.

"If you're referring to my brother," he said, "let's not forget that he was legally drunk when he was . . ."

He trailed off, and Mia suddenly felt very small. "Matthew, I'm sorry, I—"

"Forget it," he said. "Let's just get off the subject, okay? In fact, why don't you take a couple of hours to just rest up, and then we'll head off to my sister-in-law's for dinner, if you're still up for that."

Mia nodded. "I have to say, Norman has sure crawled to the top of my list for suspects."

"Mine, too," Matthew said. "We'll stop by the police station and file a report on him before we head out to Laurie's house. We can find out if there's been any progress on the cops' end of the investigation, but I'm sure they filed the case away right after they realized they had no leads."

"No, Matthew," Mia said. "No police." She thought of her sister, hiding somewhere, all alone, scared out of her mind. If Norman was the killer, then Mia was responsible. She trembled. "No police, Matthew. Not yet. Please."

He looked at her, into her eyes, then nodded.

"We'll get to the bottom of what happened, Matthew," she said, needing to assure him.

"I know we will," he responded flatly.

And then we'll go our separate ways, she mentally finished for him.

She knew that was what he was thinking.

Chapter Thirteen

As twilight settled over Center City, Matthew pulled onto the highway, Mia quiet in the passenger seat of his BMW. She hadn't said much for the past few hours, but he certainly couldn't blame her. She'd been through quite an ordeal with that creep Norman Newman.

He glanced at her; she was sagged back against the seat, her face turned toward the window. She looked as frustrated as he was.

She's been through quite an ordeal with you, too, he reminded himself. Their conversation about last night—well, about this morning—hadn't gone well. She'd nipped it in the bud, and there was no way he was going to press the subject.

He knew, more than ever, that he had to keep his emotional distance, had to resist her physically. When he'd spotted her on the street with that psycho, even before he knew she was in terrible danger, he'd been overcome with feelings he wasn't willing to think too deeply about now.

Distance. It was all about emotional distance. He was good at that.

Of course, Mia looked absolutely beautiful. She was good at *that.* She wore a feminine lavender-colored sundress, low-heeled sandals, and her hair was loose around her shoulders.

Just remember Gwen Harriman, he told himself. *She looked sweet and innocent, too.*

It wasn't that he thought Mia would suddenly become a monster, show her true colors, and stab him in the back. And then the heart. It didn't matter to him whether she could or couldn't be trusted. That was beside the point.

The point was keeping himself from getting involved.

"Mia, I know you're emotionally exhausted," Matthew said, "so just relax at dinner. I'll ask some pointed questions, and we'll see where it leads."

"I think we've found our killer," Mia said, still facing out the window. "Norman has made it clear that he's dangerous and way unhinged."

"He's definitely that," Matthew said, "but we can't be sure he's the one. It adds up, but we've still got to rule out all our possibilities before we decide to hone in on one person."

"It won't be easy for you to question Laurie, will it?" she asked, turning toward him. "Even though you'll be discreet, I know it'll be hard on you."

Matthew took a deep breath and nodded. "My gut tells me she's innocent, that she had no idea Robert was cheating and therefore wouldn't even think of hiring a decoy. But, she's one of the four widows, and whether or not I've got a personal connection to her and can vouch for her character doesn't mean she shouldn't be investigated."

"It's too bad little Robbie won't be there," Mia said. "I would have loved to meet him."

"He's a great little kid," Matthew said, his heart lightening a bit.

Mia smiled gently and turned her attention back to the window. He was grateful she'd brought up his nephew. The mention of Robbie's name reminded him that finding Robert's killer was the only thing that should be on Matthew's mind. Not women and their feelings.

That included Laurie Gray's.

Steeled to what he had to do, Matthew was relieved that traffic was light so he could get to Laurie's house and get this questioning over with. If he was careful, which he would be, she would have no idea that she was being questioned.

And if he was right, if he could trust his instincts, he and Mia would leave with the assurance that Laurie could be crossed off their list.

"We're here," Matthew said to Mia as he pulled off the highway. "The house is just up this street."

Mia sat up straight. "Ready?"

He nodded and pulled into the Gray driveway. He hadn't been back to this house since the day of Robbie's postponed birthday party. Through the bay window on the front of the white colonial, he could see Laurie at a distance in the kitchen, carrying what looked like a roast of some sort.

She was a normal woman, making dinner for her guests. She wasn't a cold-blooded killer.

Don't let me be proven wrong, he prayed to the fates of the universe. *I don't think I could take it.*

As they exited the car, Laurie stepped onto the porch and waved. "Hi there. Hope the traffic wasn't too heavy."

"None to speak of," Matthew said as he and Mia joined her. "This is my friend, Mia Anderson. Mia, my sister-in-law, Laurie Gray."

The two women exchanged hellos and handshakes, and they all headed inside the house.

"Please, have a seat and make yourselves comfortable," Laurie said. "I'll just go and open up this lovely bottle of wine. You really didn't have to bring anything."

"It was our pleasure," Mia said, and Laurie smiled at her.

Matthew and Mia settled on the sofa in the living room. Laurie returned with a tray with three wineglasses and the bottle of white wine. She sat in an overstuffed chair across from them.

"I'm so sorry about your husband," Mia said.

"Thank you," Laurie responded. "Sometimes I forget that he's gone, that he's never coming back. I didn't see too much of him as it was; but he always came home eventually, so I keep expecting him to walk in the door . . ."

Didn't see too much of him as it was? Matthew echoed mentally. *What does that mean?* "Robert was quite the workaholic," he said, nodding.

"Matthew, you don't need to use euphemisms around me," Laurie said. "I'm not a little girl."

Matthew was puzzled. "Euphemisms? What do you mean?"

"Honey, we know Robert Gray was no workaholic," Laurie said with a warm chuckle as she stood up. "Let me check on the roast. Why don't you two go sit down in the dining room. I'll be serving in a few minutes."

Mia eyed Matthew. "Can I help?" she asked Laurie.

"Absolutely not," Laurie said. "You two just sit and relax. I need to keep busy."

As Laurie disappeared into the kitchen, Matthew felt Mia's gaze, but he couldn't face her. He couldn't be wrong about Laurie. He couldn't.

No workaholic. . . . Did that mean she knew he'd been long cheating on her? Had she hired a decoy to find out for sure?

And had she snapped when she saw her husband with another woman?

No. It made no sense. Three men were killed before Robert. Three men with no connection to Robert or to Laurie.

Dammit! What the hell was the connection, then?

"That's a beautiful vase," Mia said, pointing to the delicate ceramic piece on the mantel.

Matthew knew she was keeping him on track, making sure they kept their expressions and conversation light. "They got that on their honeymoon in Italy," he said.

And that was when he realized that something was missing from the mantel: Robert and Laurie's wedding photo. It had always sat dead center. Now it was gone, and in its place was a glass vase of tulips.

Why had Laurie taken away the wedding photo?

"Let's go sit down in the dining room," Mia said.

He looked at her, and he caught the concern in her gaze. He nodded and led the way. They took a seat across from each other.

Laurie served a roast beef with potatoes and asparagus. They ate while making small talk about the surrounding towns, local schools, a new department store that had opened up, and Robbie.

"Matthew talks about his nephew all the time,"

Mia said. "He showed me a photo. Robbie's so adorable."

"He sure is," Laurie said. "And sweet as can be. He just turned two, but there's no 'terrible' anywhere. I hope it lasts. Hey, how about I serve that delicious-looking apple pie you brought, Mia. I love apple pie."

"Matthew told me so," Mia said with a smile. "I love apple pie, too."

In moments, Laurie served pie and coffee, and they all dug in; but Matthew's appetite was gone.

"Laurie, are you really holding up okay?" Matthew asked. "It's me here. You don't need to put on a strong front. You know that, right?"

Laurie sighed. "Matthew, honey, I know you care, but honestly, you coddle me. I'm doing fine. I cry, I grieve, but I have to be strong for Robbie. That's what keeps me going."

Matthew hated himself for what he was about to say, for the lie on both counts, but he had to—for Robert. "I only hope that when it's my time to settle down, I'll have a great marriage like you and Robert had."

Laurie raised an eyebrow. "Wow, Mia, he must really be smitten with you. I've never heard the words settle down come out of Matthew Gray's mouth."

Mia blushed and Laurie laughed.

"Ah, it feels good to laugh," Laurie said. "I haven't laughed once since . . . since that night."

Matthew gave Laurie's hand a warm squeeze. "I meant what I said, Laurie. I know I've never seemed like the marrying kind, but if I do get married, I can only hope I have a marriage like you and Robert had."

A strange expression passed over Laurie's face; Matthew couldn't quite put an emotion to it.

Laurie stared at her pie. "Well, we don't want our pie to get cold. There's nothing like warm apple pie."

And the subject of marriage, good or bad, had been closed.

From the moment Matthew and Mia had left Laurie Gray's house fifteen minutes ago, the expression on Matthew's face told Mia to hold her tongue—at least for a little while.

Laurie Gray had, with very little provocation, become a prime suspect. She'd more than alluded to knowing that her husband was cheating on her, which meant she could have hired Margot. Wanting tangible proof, she—

"Wait a minute!" Mia shouted.

Matthew whipped his head to face her. "What's wrong?" he asked, alarm in his voice.

"I just realized something," she said slowly, thinking through the thread that had just popped into her mind. How had they missed this before? "Matthew, if Laurie Gray had hired Margot, if *any* of the widows had hired Margot, they would have freaked upon seeing *me!* Laurie especially."

Matthew's mouth dropped open, and he flicked on his blinker and inched over into the right lane and then pulled up onto the shoulder to a stop. He turned to face her. "You're absolutely right. They would have thought you *were* Margot. Not one of the widows blinked when they met you. Not one."

"Unless the four of them are really great actresses," Mia said, "but I doubt that."

"I don't know, Mia," he said. "Maybe we shouldn't be too quick not to give any of them too much credit. Whoever is behind the crimes got away with four murders. He or she is clever. That much we know for sure. Hiding a reaction so as not to get trapped sounds like something a clever killer could accomplish."

"I guess you're right," Mia said. "And I guess that puts us back to where we started. With five suspects."

Matthew ran a hand through his hair, let out a deep breath, and then pulled back onto the highway.

"Matthew? Are you okay about what happened back there with Laurie?"

The subject of marriage and family seemed to have put Matthew in a deep funk, and when the conversation had turned to Robbie after dessert, the flow of talk had been kept light. Mia wondered if Matthew had put an end to the questioning because the topic of adultery, of secrets and lies, was making him sick, or because he couldn't deal with the fact that his sister-in-law did have a motive for murder.

"Not really," he said. "Not only do I have to admit that she's a suspect like the rest, but it blows my gut instinct out of the water. I thought they had a solid marriage. I thought Laurie was happy."

"His cheating had to put some distance between them, no matter how well Robert hid it," Mia put in. "His guilty conscience, the lies he had to make up, the lies she had to rationalize in order to keep harmony, to keep her marriage—that must have taken quite a toll."

"Yes, I'm sure it did," he said, his voice devoid of

emotion. "I guess I didn't want to face the truth. I guess I wanted to think they had a chance, unlike my parents. With a perfect, healthy, beautiful son like Robbie, I wanted to believe that their family life was magical. But it wasn't. Man, am I a chump."

Mia rested her hand on his shoulder. "Oh, Matthew. I'm sorry."

He flinched, and she pulled her hand away, grateful he couldn't see the way her cheeks flamed with embarrassment. She kept making the mistake of thinking their intimate conversations meant intimacy between them. But they were simply working together, that was all. He'd said from the beginning that he was after the truth and would do anything to get to it. Searching his soul was clearly something he was willing to do to find the answers.

It had nothing to do with her. And the sooner she remembered that, the less hurt she'd be.

Problem was, that didn't quite make sense.

It had been nearly two weeks since Norman Newman disappeared into the anonymity of Center City, nearly two weeks since Laurie Gray had proven herself a key suspect, and almost three weeks since the death of Robert Gray. And Matthew was no closer to solving his brother's murder than he'd been at the start.

Dammit! he thought, staring at the suspect grid he and Mia had created. Norman Newman, Lisa Ann Cole, Laurie Gray, Theresa Healy, Ashley Davidson. Five people. Five possible motives. No evidence. No connection.

There *had* to be a connection between the four victims. Yet no matter how long and carefully

Matthew went over all the possibilities, he couldn't find what tied the four men together besides the fact that they were married and lived within thirty or so miles of each other. He was convinced that once he found the connection, he'd find the killer.

Matthew took a slug of his cola for the caffeine boost and glanced at Mia, who sat on the sofa in his living room, reading over the brief articles on each murder and the obituaries.

As she stretched her arms over her head and yawned, her breasts rose and fell, and he was momentarily captivated.

He realized it had also been nearly two weeks since they'd made love.

Made love.

Funny he should think of it in those terms instead of *had sex*, the wording he preferred.

For the past two weeks, they'd been very polite with each other. Discussing the case, keeping their personal lives out of it. They'd been staying at Matthew's apartment, Matthew on the uncomfortable couch and Mia in his very large for one person bed.

The thought of her sleeping in his bed every night had been almost unbearable. Every single night he had the urge to rush inside and join her, show her the effect she had on him.

Physically, that was.

Emotionally, he had shut down. Keeping his mouth shut helped; instead of talking about Robert or how it felt to know that his brother and sister-in-law hadn't had a good marriage after all, Matthew talked about facts and motives. When they weren't working, they either made small talk or were silent.

"I'm not getting anywhere with the grid—again,"

Matthew said, his frustration evident in his voice. "I know there's a connection here, but hell if I can see it."

"I know," Mia said. "I've been wracking my brain trying to find the connection between the victims, and there's absolutely nothing."

Matthew sighed. "Except for the fact that they were all married, all lived relatively nearby, and all frequented bars in their towns or Center City—like a million other men."

Mia was silent for a moment. "Matthew, July tenth is three days away. Unless we do something, we're going to lose the opportunity to catch a cold-blooded murderer."

"I know that," Matthew said. "Why do you think I've been working around the clock to figure out who it is?"

"I think we need to put my plan into action," she said.

"No."

"Matthew, we have no choice," Mia said, her voice strong and steady.

"We do have a choice—it's called not being stupid. Do you realize that you could get hurt? Killed?"

"Do you realize that my sister might never come home and that your brother's killer might never be caught?" she countered, eyebrow raised.

Do you realize that this time, I might not be able to come to your rescue? he thought, a wave of nausea coursing through him. The idea of being helpless against a force he couldn't control was something Matthew couldn't tolerate. There was no way he would allow Mia to put herself into danger.

"The *possible* ends do not justify the means. The answer is no," he said, his voice cold and flat.

"I think you're forgetting something, Matthew," Mia said. "I don't need your permission. I have the means to put the plan into action without your help. I'm the one who looks exactly like the decoy the killer has hired."

He stared at her, his anger boiling in his gut.

"If I don't play the part of Margot on the night of the tenth at MacDougal's Bar, we'll lose our chance to trap this psycho, Matthew. I won't let fear stop me."

"Fine," he said. "If fear or logic won't stop you, *I'll* stop you."

"How do you propose to do that?" she said. "Lock me in the closet?"

"I'll figure something out."

"Matthew—"

"The subject is closed, Mia. Closed."

"Matth—"

He turned away and flopped onto the couch full-length and closed his eyes.

He felt her silence and her anger. And then she stormed up and stalked to the door. "Mia," he said, shooting up. "Where are you going?"

"Somewhere where I'm treated with respect," she said. "Which means away from you."

"Mia—" He grabbed her arm.

She wrenched away from him. "I'm going back to Margot's to plan for the night of the tenth. Like I said, I don't need you to do this. Goodbye, Matthew."

She put her hand on the doorknob, and Matthew covered it with his own. "Please, Mia."

"No. You won't discuss it, not even ways to handle the plan as safely as possible."

The breath sagged out of him, and his head dropped. "What if there is no safe way, Mia. I can't handle the thought of sending you into jeopardy, with me helpless to protect you . . ."

He felt her gaze on him. She placed her palm against his cheek. "Matthew, you're not a thirteen-year-old boy scared and helpless against his parents' problems. You can control this situation. *We* can control it—together."

"We can't even find a way to conduct this investigation without making each other angry. How are we going to control a third party?"

He'd surprised her, he could tell. She tilted her head and regarded him. "You make me angry when you withdraw, Matthew. When something between us gets too hot to handle."

"I just know I don't like the way things have been between us the past week. We're like strangers tiptoeing around each other."

"I thought that *was* how you wanted it."

He shook his head. "I thought so, too, but I hate it."

"Are you saying you want—"

"I don't know what I want. I don't want anything. I just know what I don't want."

Mia sighed. "Well, I do want something, Matthew. I want it all. I've betrayed myself in the past, and I won't do it again. I won't give myself less than I deserve. Not anymore."

"I can't give you it all, Mia. I can make love to you, I can work closely with you, I can even talk through this crazy plan of yours. But I can't give you any more than that."

"I thought you said you hate the way things have been between us," she said. "Clearly, you want it that way."

He had no idea what to say anymore.

She turned away from the door and headed toward the bedroom. "I'm going to sleep, Matthew. I've had just about enough for one night."

"You won't sneak out if I fall asleep?" he asked.

"I promise that I won't."

He nodded. "I'm sorry, Mia."

"So am I," she said before closing the bedroom door behind her.

Mia had been tossing and turning for hours, the things Matthew had said playing over and over in her mind like a tape recorder.

I can't . . . I won't . . .

I hate the way things have been between us . . .

Helpless against things I can't control . . .

That was what it was, she realized. The crux of the problem between them. He couldn't stand the idea of not being able to control what happened to him. And that meant he was in for a very lonely life.

Mia sighed and flopped onto her stomach.

But you don't want a lonely life, she told herself. *You're willing to let destiny and fate have their hands in your happiness. You're willing to give something your all.*

If you want it that bad.

Did she want Matthew that bad? Bad enough to risk rejection, risk her heart, risk that he might never be able to open up to her?

Yes, because you love him.

Mia bolted upright, her mouth open.

I'm in love with Matthew Gray.

Mia glanced at the clock on the bedside table. It was midnight.

Do it, Mia. Just do it.

She took off her T-shirt, worried her lower lip, then put the shirt right back on.

Go to him. Completely naked, completely bare. You're telling him something.

Mia took off the shirt, then slipped off her sweats and socks. Naked, she padded over to the mirror over the dresser and looked at her reflection.

I'm just a woman in love with a man and offering him who I am.

Mia walked slowly to the door. She paused for just a moment, closed her eyes, then left the room.

The windows were open, and the night breeze stirred the curtains. Mia breathed deeply of it, letting the warm air ruffle through her hair. She glanced at the sofa; Matthew lay across it, a white sheet pulled up to just below his stomach.

His chest was bare. She wondered if he was completely naked, too. He moved just a fraction, and the sheet slipped lower, revealing a line of fine dark hair just below his belly button and disappearing under the sheet. He groaned slightly, and his hand also disappeared under the sheet for just a moment.

Mia gasped. Was he dreaming of her?

She went to him and knelt before the couch. Slowly leaning over, she pressed her lips gently to his.

His eyes closed and his breathing shallow, Matthew wrapped his arms around her and returned the kiss, his lips forcing open her mouth and his tongue probing. Mia sank into the kiss, and he pulled her onto the couch on top of him. The weight of her breasts pressed against his chest, Mia gave everything to the kiss.

She felt his hips move, and she matched his upward thrusts with downward ones. She slid and slipped against the sheet that separated them until Matthew moaned and dipped his head low to take one of her breasts into his mouth. As his tongue teased her rosy nipple into a hard peak, Mia groaned and writhed against him. He gave the same pleasure to her other breast, then trailed hot, wet kisses in her cleavage. Mia raised herself up on her arms, and he continued the kisses under her breasts and across her stomach.

As Mia writhed against him, groaning low in her throat, the sheet suddenly slipped lower, revealing his manhood. He was as naked as she was. And from the rock-hard length of his arousal, Mia had no doubt that he was as ready as she was.

She poised herself on top of him, his erection teasing at the entrance to her femininity. "Look at me, Matthew," she breathed into his ear.

He opened his eyes and seemed to drink in the sight of her; then his eyes widened, and he slid back on the couch, bolting upright. "What the—"

Mia felt her cheeks flame, and she grabbed the lower half of the sheet to cover herself. "I—"

"Oh, God, I thought I was dreaming. I thought I was having the most amazing dream of my life," Matthew said, his expression stricken.

"You weren't dreaming," she said softly, and then holding his gaze steady, she let the sheet drop from her breasts.

"Mia . . ."

She stretched out over him and placed two fingers gently on his lips. "Just make love to me, Matthew."

"I think you should go back to your bedroom, Mia," he said flatly.

It was as effective as a bucket of cold water dumped on her head. Humiliated, Mia stared at him for a moment, then grabbed the sheet, wrapped it around her naked body, and ran, tears streaming down her face, into the bedroom.

Chapter Fourteen

Matthew awoke to the sounds of cabinets slamming and dishes clinking hard in the kitchen.

Good, he thought. At least she was still here and hadn't taken off in the middle of the night as he'd feared. He'd been so afraid she'd run out again that for three or maybe four hours, he'd kept his eyes open and trained on the bedroom door until he was sure she must have been fast asleep.

He breathed a sigh of relief.

Relief. That was a funny word. He'd also spent the night praying for relief against the rock-hard erection she'd left him with. Correction: he'd *made* her leave him with.

God, how he'd wanted her. Sending her away had been the hardest thing he'd ever done, and possibly the least selfish. *Please let that count for something in this life,* he thought. With one thrust, he could have taken her, had the most amazing night of sexual fulfillment of his life, and then retreated back behind the wall he'd already told her wasn't about to come down. He wouldn't have been wrong to take what she had offered him last night. She knew the deal; they'd spoken about it just hours earlier. She'd come to him well aware of the compromise she'd have to make.

And she'd chosen to make it.

But there was no way in hell he was going to let her do that, whether or not he had the right to make that decision for her.

You're reaching again, Matt, he told himself. *You didn't send her away for her sake; you did it for your sake. Because you can't handle it. Can't handle her. Can't handle how you feel about her.*

That thought startled him. How *did* he feel about Mia Anderson?

Before he had a chance to ponder that question, she slammed her way out of the kitchen, a pot of coffee in one hand and a plate heaped with toast in the other. She did not look happy.

"Let's get one thing out of the way right now," she said, not looking at him. "I don't want to talk about what happened last night. I just want to go on with my life. In fact, I'd like to just get on with planning the night of the tenth. If you're with me, that is."

So, he was getting away with not having to talk about last night. "Mia, I—"

She glared at him. "If you're about to bring up what happened last night or if you're about to tell me you're not letting me put my plan into action, I suggest you think of something else to say, Matthew." She slammed the plate of toast on the dining room table. She was a bit more gentle with the coffee. In silence he watched her stalk back into the kitchen and return with a tray containing mugs, cream, and sugar. She slammed that down on the table, too, then poured herself a cup of coffee and sat down. "Okay," she said, picking up a pad and pen from the table. "On the night of the tenth, the killer is expecting Margot to arrive at Mac—"

"Mia, stop it," he said.

"I believe I already told you that I'm going to play the part of Margot whether you like it not," Mia said coldly. "Either you're with me or you're not. If you're not, I'd be happy to go work at Margot's apartment and leave you to waste both our time by wracking your brain for evidence and connections we've been unable to find."

"Your attitude could use a little work, Mia," he said dryly.

"Let's not even go there, Mr. Sunshine," she said, eyebrow raised. "Now, as I was saying, the killer expects Margot to show up at ten P.M. My plan is to arrive at ten, dolled up a la appropriate for a decoy and—"

Matthew swung his legs to the floor and leaned back against the sofa. "And what? And wait till some sleazebag—correction, sleazebags—approaches you and starts pawing you?"

"If that's what's going to happen, yes," she said. "The point is that we wait to see *what* happens."

"And in the meantime, someone gets killed in the parking lot or followed down the street and offed in an alleyway."

"No, Matthew," she said. "We'll safeguard against that. Your part, if you choose to join me, is to wait in the parking lot, at the ready to help whoever is about to get—be hurt."

Matthew shook his head. "So this is your great plan."

"Do you have a better one?" she said. "The tenth is only a couple of days away."

"And what if I don't choose to go along with this crazy scheme?" he asked. "Then who helps the cheater in the parking lot?"

"I'll involve the police," Mia said.

"Oh, yeah, they'll let you set up a sting like that, Mia. Give me a break. They'll take you right out of it, set up their own surveillance; there'll be no 'Margot,' and you'll still lose your opportunity."

Mia turned away. "So I'll follow the man or men who approach me into the parking lot and make sure they get safely to their cars."

He laughed. "You mean before or after the killer attacks you first?"

"Stop it, Matthew," she shouted. "Either help me work through this, or just shut the hell up."

He glared at her, then slumped down on the sofa.

She sipped her coffee. "And while you're at it, I'd appreciate it if you would put on some clothes."

Matthew rarely blushed; perhaps once or twice in his life something or someone had made him color. Well, he could add now to the list. He'd forgotten he wasn't wearing a stitch of clothing. After she'd taken the sheet last night, he'd grabbed a blanket from the hall closet and covered himself. He was naked as a jaybird.

Wrapping the blanket securely about his waist, he got up and went into the bedroom. The scent of her was everywhere in the room. He stared at the bed, perfectly made. No one would ever know a stunningly beautiful, sexy creature had slept here last night. Had slept here for the past two weeks.

Had offered herself to him last night.

Matthew sighed and grabbed a pair of jeans and a white T-shirt and headed into the bathroom for a quick shower. A quick *cold* shower.

As he dried himself off and dressed, Matthew knew he had to get away from Mia for a little while, even for just an hour. He had to think through this ridiculous plan of hers, come up with a way to stop her, and come up with a new plan that didn't put her into jeopardy—that didn't put her anywhere near MacDougal's on the night of the tenth.

The phone rang, and Matthew picked up the extension in the bedroom. It was Laurie.

He could hear her sniffling. "Laurie, what's wrong? Are you crying?"

"Oh, Matthew," she said. "I just miss him so much." She broke down into sobs.

"Laurie, just hold on tight, and I'll be there in a half hour, okay?"

"'Kay," she managed through her tears.

Matthew had gone to see Laurie twice in the past two weeks, ostensibly to make sure she was all right and to see Robbie, who was back home from the visit to his grandparents. She'd been quiet and hard to talk to, and when he saw her and Robert's wedding photo back on the mantel in a new frame, he'd breathed a huge sigh of relief. She'd simply been having the photo reframed.

But it didn't diminish the fact that she clearly knew her husband had been cheating on her. And it made the possibility that she had hired a decoy even stronger.

Until he thought about Mia's theory that she would have shown some reaction to her had she been the one who'd hired Margot. Unless he was right and his sister-in-law was one amazing actress.

And a cold-blooded killer.

He left the bedroom and found Mia busily writing on her pad.

"I'm working out my plan, Matthew. My way. I'll be happy to share it with you when I'm finished."

Fine, he thought. Let that occupy her for the next hour or two while he visited with Laurie. He could rest assured she wouldn't leave if she was busy working out the details. And he'd clearly given her a lot to chew on.

"All right," he said. "In the meantime, I've got to go see Laurie. That was her on the phone. She's in tears. She misses Robert."

Mia's expression softened, and she nodded. "Go. I'll be here when you get back."

"You promise you won't go out, Mia?"

She stared at him for a moment, then returned her gaze to the pad. "I promise."

"Okay. I should be back in about an hour and a half. I'll hear the details of your plan then. We'll figure something out for the night of the tenth."

She nodded and sipped her coffee, and Matthew headed out the door, confident that she wasn't going anywhere.

A half hour later, Matthew pulled into the driveway of Laurie's house. Laurie sat on the porch swing, Robbie sleeping against her chest. As he walked up to the porch, he noticed Laurie darting a hand under her eyes to wipe away tears.

Was she acting the part of the grieving widow for his sake because he had shown up with "the decoy" she had hired to set up her husband? Because she figured he was on to her and what she'd done?

Or was she simply the same wonderful sister-in-law she'd always been, grieving for the husband she had loved and lost? Was it a crime to know that your husband was cheating on you? Was it fair to turn the victim into the accused?

Dammit, Matthew thought. What the hell was the truth? Why was everything so upside down? What had happened to his ability to read people, to trust his instincts?

Mia Anderson had happened, that was what.

"Thanks for coming, Matt," Laurie said, reaching up to kiss Matthew on the cheek. "I was just feeling so sad, and you're the only other person in the world to whom Robert was family."

Matthew squeezed her hand and kissed Robbie on the head before sitting down beside them. "I know," he said.

"I thought I was doing okay"—her green eyes pooled with tears—"but then all of a sudden, wham. I break down."

"You don't have to be strong, Laurie," Matthew said, putting his arm around her. "You lost your husband. You need to take your time, grieve whatever way you need to."

"But I feel like I need to be strong for Robbie," she said. "I don't want to cry in front of him."

Matthew put out his arms, and Laurie handed the baby to him. He cuddled his nephew against his chest and breathed in the scent of him.

He and Laurie were silent for a while, watching the occasional car pass by, watching the leaves stir in the gentle breeze, watching the clouds and the sky and wondering if Robert was up there, okay.

"So your new girlfriend is very pretty," Laurie said.

"She's not my girlfriend."

Laurie raised an eyebrow. "Matthew, I saw the way you two looked at each other, and I noticed that you shared some personal things with her. I've never known you to do that with a woman."

He'd shared *way* too much personal information with Mia.

"She looked a little familiar, but I couldn't place her," Laurie commented.

Matthew's back went up. Was she fishing? Or had she simply seen either Mia or Margot around the vicinity?

"So, are you going to spill, or what?" Laurie asked, caressing Robbie's wispy hair.

"There's nothing to tell," Matthew said. "She's just a friend. That's all. Even if I wanted more, which I don't, it wouldn't work anyway. She wants it all—the whole love thing. I'm not into commitment."

Laurie shook her head. "Matthew, there's nothing in being alone. Nothing."

Is that why you put up with a husband who cheated on you?

Before you got sick of it and killed him?

Matthew closed his eyes to will the thoughts out of his head. He had no idea what to think anymore.

"Matthew, not every marriage is like your parents'," Laurie said. "Marriage can be the most wonderful thing in the world. Even if there are problems. And there usually are."

Matthew leaned back against the swing and lifted Robbie higher on his chest. "Did you and Robert have problems?"

"Of course," she replied. "All couples have problems, married or not. But working through problems is what marriage is all about."

"You don't think that some problems are insurmountable?" Matthew asked. *Like being cheated on every Saturday night?* he added mentally.

Laurie seemed lost in thought for a moment. "Not if at least one of the couple is willing to do something about it. Sometimes one person can fight for a relationship, and eventually, the other person comes around."

That's what you've been doing for the past few years, Matthew thought. *Fighting for your marriage. Waiting for Robert to come around.*

You're not a killer. You're simply a woman who was in love with a man who was cheating on her, a woman who, whether through rationalization or whatever, was willing to put up with quite a lot for that love.

But did you give up? Did you take the photos of Margot and Robert kissing in Chumley's and then kill him in the parking lot?

Did you kill three other men?

Dammit! Why the hell would Laurie have killed *three* men and *then* her husband? It made no sense. Why would *any* of the widows have killed other men?

Laurie sighed. "It's been a long time since Gwen, Matthew."

Matthew's stomach twisted. "She has nothing to do with it, Laurie."

"You're right, sweetie," Laurie said. "She doesn't. Nothing at all. Which is why it's high time you forgot about her, too. Forgot the betrayal. Forgot your father's betrayal of your mother and that terrible night. All the terrible nights. You're not your father. And every woman isn't Gwen."

"I thought I came here to talk about you," Matthew pointed out.

"I liked Mia, Matthew," Laurie said. "And I could tell she liked you quite a lot."

"Whatever," Matthew responded. "We're just friends."

"Right," Laurie said. "Just friends. Who look at each other like you're in love."

Matthew shook his head. "How's my favorite nephew, anyway?"

"Nice change of subject." Laurie chuckled. "I'll tell you how he is—he could use a little cousin."

"Laur—"

She patted his hand. "I don't have any siblings, Matt. So it's all up to you. Isn't it?"

Robbie began wiggling, and his mother took him in her arms.

"Someone's cranky and tired," Laurie cooed to Robbie. "I'd better get him to bed."

Saved by a two-year-old. Matthew stood up and hugged Laurie and kissed Robbie on the forehead. "You call me if you need to talk. Any time, Laurie."

"I know. And you, too, Matthew."

Laurie and Robbie headed inside, and Matthew got into his car. But instead of pulling onto the highway, some force made him turn right on Main Street. Ten miles straight up Main and he'd be in Edgeville, the town he'd grown up in.

He drove almost absently, the familiar landmarks barely registering as he left the township of Oak Ridge. *Welcome to Edgeville, population 22,000* read the sign posted on the town green.

Matthew turned on Hill Road and drove past the old, pale yellow house where he'd grown up. He didn't even glance at the house. But something made him stop and back up. He forced himself to stop the car in front of the house and look at it, really look at it. The yard, the porch, the front door.

The house was the same color it had been when he'd lived there; he was surprised the new owners hadn't painted it. His father had died in this house—a heart attack—and though the house had been left to him and to Robert equally, Matthew hadn't wanted any of the money from its sale. He wanted nothing to do with it. And so his share had gone into a trust fund for future heirs. Now, it looked as though Robbie would be the sole beneficiary.

As he stared out the window at the yellow house, it suddenly looked like just a house, just a place where he once lived. No ghosts, no memories. Just a house.

He drove on and turned onto the path that led to the cemetery where his parents were buried. Maybe he could use a talk with them both. But as the graves came into view, Matthew realized he couldn't bear the idea of walking inside the grounds, standing before his mother's grave and making her feel as though her marriage was the reason he'd vowed to never marry, never have children.

Never give Robbie a cousin.

And he didn't have anything to say to his father. He never would.

Bitterness and sadness fighting for dominance inside him, Matthew turned onto the highway. He was in the perfect frame of mind in which to deal with Mia.

Completely closed to her.

* * *

"I think we should stop by MacDougal's tonight to get the layout of the place and the parking lot," Mia said, tapping her pen against her legal pad.

From the moment Matthew had walked in ten minutes ago from his visit to Laurie's and let Mia know that he had no more to go on as far as Laurie as a suspect was concerned, Mia had been talking nonstop about her brilliant plan. God, he hated her plan.

But he'd been right about his frame of mind. Between his endless list of questions that had no answers, his conversation with Laurie—or he should say, Laurie's *monologue* to him about his love life—and driving past the home he'd grown up in and thinking about his parents, he had no room in his mind for Mia or for what had happened last night.

From her expression and tone of voice, Mia had a one-track mind, and it wasn't him or last night: it was the night of the tenth. Fine. That was what he wanted.

"And what if the killer just happens to be there tonight and sees us," Matthew pointed out, exasperated. "That'll blow your plan out of the water."

"Maybe you should have let me finish my sentence without interrupting me, then," Mia snapped.

"Fine, finish."

But he really hoped she wouldn't. He hoped she'd rip up the five pieces of legal pad paper in her hand, toss the heap in the garbage along with her crazy scheme, and just leave the planning up to him.

Problem was, Mia was way stubborn. And perhaps more importantly, he didn't *have* a plan.

"We'll show up in disguise tonight," Mia said. "Scope out the place."

Matthew raised an eyebrow. "Scope out the place? Since when did you become so proficient in the lingo?"

"Since I've had to become an amateur private detective," she tossed back.

Matthew sighed and flopped back against the sofa, kicking a foot up onto his coffee table.

"Can I continue now?" she asked, impatience tinged in her voice.

"Please do."

She shot him a glance, then returned her attention to her pad. "Okay, so then, on the night of July tenth, this Saturday night, you'll arrive at MacDougal's alone—in a new disguise—just in case the killer recognizes you from the night at Chumley's or from your disguise tonight. And then I'll arrive a few minutes later."

"And do what? Sit down at a table and wait for some cheating bastard to slobber all over you? A cheating bastard who may or may not be the killer's target?"

"Yes, exactly," Mia said, her tone completely neutral.

Matthew groaned. "You're really going to do this?"

She nodded, then tapped her pen in the air. "You know, Matthew, I just realized something. Maybe the killer *doesn't* have a target. Maybe he or she just randomly waits for some guy to pick up the decoy and decides for no reason that that man is going to die."

"But why?" Matthew asked, crossing his hands behind his neck.

She gnawed her lower lip. "Right. *Why*? That's what I can't figure out."

"Well, what do we know about the previous victims?" Matthew said. "The only thing we know for sure that connects them is the fact that they were all married."

"But two didn't even have their wedding rings *on* when they were making their moves on Margot," Mia pointed out. "We know from you that Robert wasn't wearing his wedding ring when he was with Margot in Chumley's. And Lisa Ann Cole said that her husband *never* wore his ring, that she remembered he wasn't wearing it when he left that night because they got into a fight about it. She said he carried it in his wallet instead."

Matthew thought about that. "Well, I do know that Robert always wore his ring except when he went out partying. So, if he wasn't a random victim, it's possible that the killer would have seen him with the ring on at some point, somewhere else, perhaps."

"But what about Lisa Ann Cole's husband?" Mia said. "If he never wore the ring . . . ?"

"Maybe our killer knew the victims from somewhere else? Knew they were married men who were cheating?"

Mia tilted her head and considered that. "But knew all of them? And from where? Two live thirty miles distance from each other."

Questions, questions, questions. That was all they had. "And how would the killer know the victims would be going to a particular nightclub on a particular night weeks in the future so as to hire Margot to be there that night?" Matthew shook his head. "Once again, it makes it seem like the killings were random. How could that be planned in advance?"

Mia held his gaze. "You do see that my playing

the part of Margot is our only way of answering these questions, right?"

Damn. She was right about that. Nothing made sense about this case.

"I see it, Mia. I just don't like it."

"I don't like it either," she said. "But it's worth it to me to do it. For both our sakes, for your brother and for my sister. And for whoever is on the killer's list for the tenth. If our plan fails, we tell the police all we know and suspect, even if it incriminates Margot for a while. Agreed?"

Matthew took a deep breath. "All right. So you show up a few minutes after I do, tape recorder in your purse, and sit alone at a table . . ."

Mia looked at him for a moment, and he saw that she was pleased. He had given in.

"Right," she said. "And you'll be sitting alone at another table, watching everyone in the bar very closely to see who's checking me out, who's paying close attention to me."

"We know for sure that the killer expects a cheating husband to be there and to go for Margot. Why I still can't figure—"

He stopped and leaned back against the sofa, his mind working a mile a minute.

"Matthew? What is it?"

"My contribution to the plan just became clear," he said, going over the final bits of it in his mind.

"What are you talking about?" Mia asked.

"*I'm* going to play the part of cheating husband."

Mia's mouth dropped open. "What?"

Matthew leaned forward, his elbows braced on his thighs. "I'm going to show up before you, alone, wearing a wedding ring. Right before I go to make my move on you, I'm going to take off my ring, quite obviously, but not so obviously that it looks like I want to be seen doing it, and then put the ring in my pocket, most likely as Robert did."

The color drained from Mia's face. "Matthew, that's crazy. You're setting yourself up to get killed!"

"But it was okay for you to do that yourself?"

"My plan doesn't make me the target of the killer!" Mia cried. "Margot isn't dead, Matthew!"

"Mia, we suspect that someone is going to die this Saturday night—unless we do something about it. My playing the part of cheating husband and making myself a target saves some poor schlub from getting jumped in the parking lot or from even knowing he was about to meet his maker."

"No."

"The fact that I'm setting myself up allows me to protect myself," he pointed out. "The second I walk out of the bar and head to my car, I'll be expecting someone to creep up behind me. I'll be ready."

"How are you going to be ready for a sudden gunshot to the back, Matthew?"

"I'll wear a bulletproof vest," he countered. "Mia, I'll protect myself."

She shook her head. "Can we get back to my plan, please?"

"Fine," he said, leaning back again. "Your plan requires mine and vice versa."

"My plan does not require you to set yourself up to be murdered!" Mia cried. "Now listen to me and forget all about you being the target. That is not happening."

"Fine, go ahead. I'm listening."

Mia narrowed her eyes at him. "Are you really listening?"

Matthew nodded. He was listening. While he formulated his own plan, that was.

"Okay," she began. "I'll be watching the other patrons, too—especially to catch a guy in the act of removing his wedding ring. I don't know if we'll be lucky enough to catch that, but maybe we will be."

Matthew almost snorted. "You'd think a cheating jerk would be smart enough to take off his ring *before* he even got inside, but I've actually seen Robert remove his ring right in the middle of a restaurant or a sporting event—if there was an attractive woman around."

Mia shook her head. "Unbelievable."

"And sickening."

"Speaking of sickening," Mia continued, "the target will come over, sit down, and I'll flirt with him for a while. Then, if he asks me to leave with him, I'll say yes."

Matthew's eyebrow shot up. "Excuse me?"

"This is how we're going to catch our killer straightaway," Mia said. "You'll see that I'm getting ready to leave with the target, and you'll hurry outside and hide behind a car. The target and I will come out a minute later. I'll make an excuse for having to run back in to get my scarf or go to the ladies' room. The killer will come out looking for the cheater. And when he or she does, we'll tackle him."

"Tackle someone with a gun or a knife," Matthew said flatly.

"Or we'll throw something," Mia amended. "We'll do something to startle the killer. Anything that lets the cheating guy get away safely and leaves the killer exposed."

"Mia, the only way I'll even consider this scenario is if you carry a cell phone and call 911 the moment the killer shows a sign of making a move. There's a police precinct a half block away from MacDougal's."

"I have no problem with calling the police," she told him. "After the killer makes his move."

Matthew sighed. "Now here's *my* version of your plan. I set myself up as the target. I take off my wedding ring and make a move on you. I'm the guy who leaves with you. And then you immediately head back in to get your scarf and *stay* there while I fiddle with my car keys out in the parking lot, supposedly waiting for you. *I* deal with the killer—who I'll be expecting and ready for—*alone,* meaning without your help."

"Matthew—"

He shook his head. "Look, you're insisting on your plan and how you fit in; I'm insisting on my plan and how I fit in. I'm compromising here, Mia. Take it or leave it."

She stared at him. "The minute I go back into MacDougal's, I'm calling the police and telling them something's going down in the parking lot."

"Fine. They can get there in time to arrest the psycho."

Mia was gnawing on her lower lip. "But what if they don't get there in time to save your life, Matthew?"

"Mia, I'm going to be careful. I'm going to take every precaution."

"You can't! There's no such thing as being prepared against a cold-blooded killer who's struck four times. Four times *without* being caught."

"Are we compromising, or not?" Matthew asked.

"Oh, so suddenly you're the king of compromise?" she snapped. "I wouldn't have known that from last night."

"I thought we weren't going to talk about last night," Matthew said.

"Fine," Mia replied. "Let's not talk about it. Let's not talk about anything." Her expression was stony. "Let's just meet in the living room at around six P.M. to go buy some stuff for disguises. We'll change up here, then head over to MacDougal's around seven-thirty or eight, when it starts getting crowded. How does that sound?"

Bossy little thing, wasn't she? "Just fine."

"Good," Mia said. "Until then, I'd like some time alone."

"You can take your pick of the bedroom or the living room," Matthew ground out through gritted teeth.

"I'll take the bedroom," she said, before stalking off with her notes and slamming the door behind her.

There were a lot of slammed doors in their relationship, Matthew thought.

Just the way it should be.

Chapter Fifteen

"We need two wigs," Matthew told the salesclerk at Wig Out, a shop he'd never even noticed, even though it was two blocks from his apartment and next door to the bagel shop he frequented almost on a daily basis.

"We're going to a masquerade party tonight," Mia added. "We'd like to look totally different, but not too way out. Just not like us."

Mia wondered if she had another "look" in her. So far, there was the plain Jane and the Margot.

"How about a blond wig for you, sir," the salesclerk suggested to Matthew, "and for you, miss"—she tilted her head to the left and then to the right, studying Mia's face and the shape of her head—"maybe red curls?"

Red curls. Just like Mia's mom. When Mia was young, she used to love watching her mother comb out the deep red ringlets, see them bounce up as they dried. Mia and Margot, around five or six years old, would squeal with joy as they gave the ringlets a gentle tug and then set them springing. And their mother would laugh with such delight. The twins had taken after their father lookswise, with their fine, medium brown hair and pale brown eyes. Mia had always yearned for her mother's gorgeous red hair.

And tonight, she would have it.

"Red curls sound great," Mia told the salesclerk.

Matthew was eyeing the wig the woman brought over to him as though it were a dead mouse. "This is a little embarrassing," he said, "trying on a wig. *Wearing* a wig."

Mia smiled. "Matthew, it's just for a few hours."

The woman led them to the back of the store to two leather chairs facing mirrors. She fitted the blond wig on Matthew first. "You could pass as a natural blond with those blue eyes," she commented, a flirtatious lilt in her voice.

"I think my dark eyebrows are a dead giveaway," Matthew countered, grimacing at his new, wavy, dark blond tresses.

Mia grinned. And as the salesclerk fitted her with the red wig, her smile turned wistful.

"Wow," Matthew exclaimed, gazing at her reflection in the mirror. "You look great as a redhead."

Mia stared at herself in the mirror, and for the first time in perhaps her entire life, she liked what she saw. The deep red was almost auburn, and the texture was very similar to her own. Mia's hair had never held a curl, except for the time she'd cut it off as a teenager and the release of its weight added waves she never knew she had.

"Your skin tone, your light brown eyes—red really suits you, hon," the salesclerk said.

"Thanks," Mia told her. "I'll take it."

"Yeah, I'll take this thing," Matthew added, grabbing the wig off his head and running a hand through his hair.

He held out the offending hairpiece, his expression twisted into utter misery. The saleswoman took it from him, and his shoulders sagged with relief. Mia couldn't resist a smile.

She took one last look at herself as a redhead, then removed the wig and handed it to the salesclerk, who headed to the front of the store to ring up their purchases.

"Well, we've got our wigs," Matthew said. "What next for our disguise?"

Mia thought for a moment. "How about nonprescription eyeglasses?"

"Great idea," he said. "And we should also pick up a couple of cheap gold wedding bands so we show up at MacDougal's tonight looking like a married couple."

"Why?" she asked. "I mean, I know why you need the ring for tonight, but why is it important that we appear married tonight?"

"Because if our killer is there," Matthew explained, "he or she will see me with my redheaded *wife.* And he or she will then see me again on Saturday night, trying to pick up the *decoy.*"

She nodded. "Ah, I see. Good point."

Fake wedding rings. A rush of bitterness rose in her throat. Her entire marriage had been fake. And now she'd have a fake wedding ring to go with her fake new look.

Fake, fake, fake.

She looked at herself in the mirror, though, and felt anything but fake. She felt *right.*

"It's funny," Mia said, getting up from the chair.

"I've been so used to *not* looking like myself, and the minute I put on a wig that totally changes my hairstyle, I feel completely natural."

"I'm not following," Matthew said. "Not looking like yourself?"

She blushed. "Oh, I just mean—" She glanced at the floor. "Forget it."

"I'd rather not," he said. He cupped his hand under her chin and gently lifted her face to his. "Tell me."

How she wanted to take his hand in hers and press it against her cheek, throw herself in his arms, and feel his strength around her. Feel safe. But he slipped his hand away and reached for his wallet.

"It's just that my husband—my ex-husband," she amended, "preferred me as a blonde like my sister is. So I colored my hair."

Matthew nodded. "Ah. So you were serious when you said you changed your look to suit your ex. I remember you telling me that when you were taking a bath."

"And we were talking through the door just like Margot and I used to—" The tears came, and Mia was powerless to stop them.

"Mia, it's all right," Matthew soothed. "She's going to come home. After Saturday night, she'll come home. Everything's going to be okay."

"I hope so," she said, sniffling.

But would it? Would anything ever be all right again? She was scared to death of Saturday night, no matter how brave a front she put on for Matthew. She was scared to death that Norman Newman was going to kill them both. She was scared to death that Matthew would discover that Laurie Gray was the killer. She was scared to death to dress up as

Margot on Saturday night and walk around as the woman she'd vowed she'd never look like again after her divorce.

And deep inside, she was afraid that Matthew Gray was going to like how that woman looked. Like it a lot.

"So where should we go for fake wedding rings?" Matthew asked as they walked up Bridge Avenue, Mia carrying their wigs in a shopping bag. They'd stopped in Vision Today for nonprescription eyeglasses and had walked out with a pair of horn-rims for Matthew and trendy black frames for Mia.

"Charm machines outside the supermarket?" Mia suggested. "I have no idea."

"Do charm machines really sell rings?" he asked.

She shrugged. "They did when I was a kid. But maybe they were made out of candy." She smiled. "I loved those rings. You could wear them all day and have a treat whenever you wanted."

He smiled. "There's a supermarket a few blocks up with some charm machines out front. Let's look. Maybe we'll find you a candy ring, too."

They walked in silence, and Matthew wondered what she was thinking. He imagined it would be as weird for her to wear a ring on her left hand as it would be for him.

They stopped in front of the row of charm machines full of different kinds of candy and tiny toys.

"I don't think these mood rings will fool our killer," Mia said, chuckling at the colorful, large rings in one of the machines.

"Ah, here are your edible candy rings," Matthew

said. "Let's get a couple. We'll each have a memento, something for us to remember the other by—"

What an idiot he was. What a complete idiot.

He glanced at Mia. She stared straight ahead, her expression tight.

"I mean—"

"I know what you mean," she said, her voice devoid of emotion. "Why don't we try a large drugstore. Sometimes they have a costume jewelry counter."

The candy rings avoided, they went into Reid's Pharmacy a few stores over from the supermarket, and there, wedged between the sunglasses rack and the disposable cameras was a display of cheap jewelry: bracelets, necklaces, rings, earrings.

"These almost look real," Mia commented as she fingered a pair of diamond stud earrings.

Matthew couldn't imagine anything but the real thing, the most precious gems, adorning Mia's body. Suddenly, the thought of a ring that would turn green in a few hours on her perfect finger seemed wrong.

But the real thing seemed *really* wrong.

Matthew put all thoughts of right and wrong jewelry out of his head. They were buying two cheap gold wedding bands as part of a disguise, that was all.

"These look okay," he said, holding out a large and small version of the same gold band. "And only nine ninety-nine each. Who knew anything related to marriage was that inexpensive?"

"I lost almost everything in my divorce," Mia said softly as she took the smaller ring and turned it over in her palm. "I did get the house, but my ex-husband had hated all my furniture and insisted on trashing it or selling it and moving in all of his things when we married. So when he moved out, I had an empty shell."

"Was it like a fresh start?" he asked.

"I guess," she said, biting her lip. "I like the place, but it's never really felt like home. Maybe because I shared it with my ex for so long."

"I've never lived with anyone," Matthew said. "I can't even imagine what it would be like to share my home with someone."

Her expression turned wistful. "It can be really nice when you're in love."

"I suppose," he replied, slipping the ring on his finger to test the size. "Wouldn't know what that's like either."

She glanced up at him. "You've never been in love?"

He shook his head. "This one's a little tight." He twisted it off, grateful the ring came off at all, and selected a larger one from the display.

"Never?" she asked.

"Never."

She raised an eyebrow and slipped her ring on her finger. "This one's too big."

He handed her another one to try and twisted the one on his own finger. "I thought I was in love once."

"What happened?" she asked.

"She turned out to be a lie."

He felt Mia's gaze on him, and he turned slightly, ostensibly to put the ring back and choose another. "It's a relief that none of these fit me."

"Because you never want one on your finger at all?"

He nodded. "I was so taken. She really played me. I had no idea she was setting me up for a fall until I caught her red-handed in my office, taking pictures of very sensitive documents that would bankrupt me if the competition got ahold of them."

Mia looked stricken. "She was working for the *competition?*"

"She was *sleeping* with the competition."

"Oh, Matthew, I'm so sorry."

"Whatever."

"Did you love her?" Mia asked. "I mean, before you exposed her?"

"I thought I did," he answered honestly, his gaze on the display. He stared at a diamond tennis bracelet, so like the one he had bought for Gwen to celebrate their first month as a couple. Before Gwen, he'd dated only casually, never seeing the same woman more than three times. If he did, the woman invariably brought up the relationship question, the "where is this relationship going?"

He'd always wanted to say, *"What relationship? This is our third date. We're just getting to know each other."* But if he and the woman had slept together, and often, there was sex on the first date, Matthew couldn't very well say, *"What relationship."* And so he'd talked honestly with his dates about his problems with commitment. A few times he'd gotten, *"You might have told me this before we had sex, asshole,"* a glass of wine in his face, and a date storming out of the restaurant, but mostly, the woman appreciated his candor and the choice to decide whether or not a casual relationship was something she could handle. Once or twice, it was something the woman could handle. And once, it turned out that the woman couldn't handle it.

And Matthew had broken a heart.

Which was when he'd decided never to sleep with a woman on the first date and never to see the same woman twice. Until he realized that meant no sex, period. He'd amended that to no sex on the first date without telling the woman beforehand that he wasn't interested in commitment or necessarily a second date. That resulted in a few slaps across the face, but enough "fine with me" to keep him from going crazy.

And then he saw Gwen Harriman for the first time. She'd come in for an interview and had taken his breath away. He'd known it was dangerous to hire a secretary to whom he was so physically drawn; but she was so well qualified, and he felt so happy just to be in her presence, that he'd gone against his better judgment and welcomed her to Matthew Gray Enterprises. On her first day, he'd taken her to lunch, and over fancy gourmet salads he'd been surprised by the ease of their conversation, how much they had in common, and how alike their worldviews were. He'd been unable to take his eyes off her, unable to take his mind off her.

And unable to even imagine that she'd done her homework on him. Studied him. Researched him. She'd come to Matthew Gray Enterprises knowing exactly who he was, what made him tick, what appealed to him, and how to earn his trust.

And earn his trust, she did. For the first time in his life, Matthew had believed that love between a man and a woman truly existed, that marriage and family could be something beautiful, that commitment and vows could be honored. And then he came home unexpectedly early from a business trip, planning to surprise Gwen with a diamond engagement ring that he'd placed in his office safe before he'd left for L.A.

But when he opened his office door, he'd found the woman he wanted to propose marriage to sitting in his desk chair, taking pictures of highly secret documents. Her shocked expression, the fear he saw in her eyes, gave her away; it had been easy to see she was lying when she claimed she was taking the pictures for him, for his office safe, so that there would be backups.

And then he'd done his own research and learned who Gwen Harriman really was.

"Matthew?"

He blinked and realized he'd been staring at a very large fake diamond ring on the display for the past few minutes. "Sorry, Mia. Did you say something?"

She smiled softly. "You were a million miles away."

"Nowhere good."

"Well, then how about we get out of here," she said. "I found a ring that fits me. Try this one. It looks bigger than the ones you've tried so far."

Matthew took the gold band and slipped it on the third finger of his left hand. It fit perfectly. "Success."

Mia smiled, her beautiful face lighting up. Gwen used to smile like that all the time, he thought darkly.

"This thing is cutting off my circulation," Matthew all but growled, pulling off the ring.

"But you just said—"

"It fits fine," he said grimly.

Her brows furrowed in confusion. "Ah, you didn't mean *literally*."

He led the way to the cashier. "Sure feels that way."

She glanced at him, her expression once again unreadable. And that was a good thing because he really didn't want to know what she was thinking.

MacDougal's Bar was so ordinary, just another popular hangout along the strip on Bridge Avenue.

But it was a place possibly marked for a murder in three days if their speculations were accurate.

As Mia took a seat at the bar and ordered two club sodas and buffalo wings for the two of them, Matthew headed to the jukebox, ostensibly to play a few tunes, but really to take in the place. He committed to memory the jukebox to the far right, the small dance floor next to it, the circle of tables around the dance floor, and the long, L-shaped bar. The door was to the left. As far as Matthew could see, there was not a back entrance.

The parking lot was on the left side of the bar. At seven-thirty on a Wednesday, the parking lot, along with the nightclub, was very crowded. Women and men were two deep at the bar, a group of young men were playing darts near the jukebox, and two young women were dancing on two platforms on either side of the dance floor, which was empty, save for two couples slow dancing to a Shania Twain song.

The bar was medium-size, small enough for Matthew to keep an eye on everyone Saturday night, yet large enough that he wouldn't arouse suspicion.

How he wasn't arousing suspicion in this getup, he'd never know. He looked ridiculous as a blond, would never have chosen the horn-rimmed glasses, and the fake mustache he'd glued on couldn't possibly look real. Mia had *ooh*ed and *ahh*ed over how real he did look before they'd left his apartment, but he felt like an idiot. He couldn't wait to get rid of the disguise and take a shower. Even the thought of putting on this getup again on Saturday night was making his neck break out in hives.

Mia, however, looked amazing. Her chin-length red ringlets were both sexy and innocent at the same time, and though her black-framed glasses hid her beautiful doe eyes, they somehow added an allure. She looked like an art professor or a film producer.

And she looked absolutely nothing like the woman he'd come to know over the past few weeks. If she passed him on the street in her disguise, he'd never recognize her.

He had no idea how Mia had changed her look for her husband and lived with it for so long. He'd been in disguise for only a half hour, and already he was squirming. Mia had changed her hair, her style, her clothes, everything about her physical self for years.

He shook his head, sickened by what people did to please others, to make relationships work, marriages continue. If you weren't happy with the way someone was, if you weren't happy, period, why not just leave?

Why hadn't his mother left? She'd explained that over and over. *You just don't understand, Matthew. I love him, Matthew. I love you and your brother, Matthew.*

When you're older, you'll understand, Matthew.

Love is complicated, Matthew.

But it wasn't supposed to be. And Matthew had never understood.

A woman put a dollar in the jukebox, and in seconds, music filled MacDougal's. It was his brother and Laurie's wedding song: "Wind Beneath My Wings." What a joke. What a lie.

Marriage was such a damned lie. The whole charade of a wedding ceremony, all that expense, all that posturing. Just to make some vows one of the duo, sometimes both, had no intention of keeping.

One woman for the rest of my life, Robert Gray had often said when Matthew had confronted him about his philandering. *Can you imagine sleeping with only one woman till you drop dead from old age? No thanks, man.*

So why get married? Matthew had wanted to know. Why pick one woman when you wanted several? Why get married when you weren't ready to commit?

Because you love the person, Robert had explained. *You love the woman you marry, you want to share your life with her, you want to go through the daily crap, wake up, fall asleep, weekends, grocery shopping, the mundane daily toil of life. You want to share life with your best friend. That's what a wife is. After a while, it's not necessarily about sex.*

Matthew understood the concept of a best friend. He also understood the concept of desiring that best friend physically. He wanted both. And since it had been made crystal clear to him that you couldn't *have* both, he would never marry. It was that simple.

And what about when the sex goes? Matthew had asked his brother. *How can you be best friends with a woman you're cheating on?*

You just don't understand, Matt, Robert had said, shaking his head.

Matthew didn't want to understand. Ever.

The blare of a rock and roll intro jarred Matthew back to the present. He took a final glance around MacDougal's, and comfortable that he had the lay of the land, he headed back to the bar and took a seat next to Mia.

"I don't see any of our suspects," Mia whispered, handing him his club soda.

He glanced around. "Well, I for one am relieved that at least one person on our list isn't here."

Mia squeezed his hand, her expression soft. It was clear she knew he was talking about his sister-in-law.

He looked down at her hand, the left finger encircled by the cheap band of gold. He glanced at his own left hand, sporting a larger version of the same ring. It itched on his finger.

He swallowed, realizing that to everyone around them, they were a married couple out for a night of wings and beer at a popular hangout.

A married couple.

The back of his neck broke out into a sweat. *Yup, I'm a married man, taking my wife out after work, and then this Saturday, I'll be just like I feared, going out alone and picking up a strange woman. Cheating.*

Matthew felt sick to his stomach, a bit surprised that even the arranged setup of adultery made him nauseous.

"Oh, Matthew, I love this song!" Mia exclaimed as an old Elton John tune began playing. "C'mon, let's dance."

"You've got to be kidding," he said, looking at her as if she were crazy. "You want to dance?"

"Why not?" she asked, her eyes clouding over.

He instantly regretted that he stung her. "I mean, it's just that I wouldn't think you'd be in the frame of mind to dance. Given why we're here," he added.

"Oh, okay, then," she said flatly, grabbing a peanut from the bowl on the bar. "We don't have to dance."

"If you want to dance, we'll dance," Matthew said.

"Don't do me any favors," Mia snapped.

"Our first marital fight," Matthew cooed, taking a sip of his club soda.

"Look, just forget it," she snapped.

She was serious. She actually wanted to dance. Mia was full of surprises, Matthew thought, shaking his head in wonder.

He stood up and put out his hand. "May I have this dance?"

She looked into his face, and her own relaxed when she saw that he was serious. She smiled softly and placed her hand in his. "You may."

They headed to the dance floor, hand in hand, and joined a bunch of others swaying to Elton John. He put his arms around her waist; she put hers around his neck, and their bodies at a comfortable distance, they slow danced.

"I haven't danced in about a hundred years," Matthew said. "I think the last time I stepped onto a dance floor was five years ago."

Four years ago, he corrected mentally. With Gwen. Right before she revealed herself to be a corporate spy for her boyfriend. Right before *he* revealed her, he amended. He'd caught her copying documents with his own eyes. Heard her lies with his own ears.

Matthew closed his eyes to shake off the memory, and without meaning to, he pulled Mia closer. Their cheeks resting against each other, Matthew breathed in the scent of her. The faintest hint of roses, of soap, of green apples. And, unfortunately, *wig*.

"I haven't danced since my marriage ended," Mia said. "It feels nice."

Yes, it did. Too nice.

Suddenly, Matthew could taste Mia, each inch of her creamy, soft body. He could smell her, smell them. He felt his zipper strain against his erection, and he resisted the urge to press her against the wall and dirty dance the way he really wanted to at the moment.

She glanced up at him, and her eyes widened at the desire she clearly saw in his; then they smoldered with her own desire. And before he could stop himself, he leaned down and kissed her, softly at first, and then more passionately.

She looked up at him. "Let's not start something we can't finish," Mia whispered, her voice catching.

"My mistake," he said. "Sorry."

And as he stepped back a reasonable distance, he wondered how something that felt so right could be a mistake. He wished the song would end so that his hands would stop itching to pull her close again, to feel her against him, even just the soft skin of her cheek against his.

Finally, the song did end.

"Your buffalo wings are probably ready, anyway," Mia commented as they headed back to their stools at the bar.

And they were, which gave the two of them a reason not to talk for the next fifteen minutes as they popped wings into their mouths and had another round of club soda.

"Sorry about that on the dance floor," he said.

"Forget it," she replied flatly. "I have."

Cold, he thought. Too cold. Which meant she hadn't forgotten it and wouldn't.

Change the subject, buddy. Just don't go there. Focus.

"So, you hardly seem nervous about being in MacDougal's, Mia," Matthew commented. "I expected you to be a little freaked."

"I don't have anything to be scared about *tonight,*" she said, biting into a wing. "Saturday night might be a very different story. I'm sure it will be. But I've scoped out the place, I know where the bar is and where the tables are and where the door is and where the bathroom is. I know where the parking lot is in relation to the main avenue."

"You've been as busy as I have tonight," he commented.

"I want to be prepared," she responded. "The one thing that bothers me about this place is the parking lot. I wish that fence wasn't there along Bridge Avenue. There's no direct access to the avenue, and we can't see over the fence."

"I know," he said. "I noticed that. Makes the parking lot a little too private."

She shuddered, and he placed his hand on her arm. "You okay?"

Mia nodded. "I'm fine. And I'm ready for Saturday night."

He held her gaze. "You're sure, then. You absolutely want to go through with this?"

"I'm sure," she replied. "Surer than I've ever been of anything. I want to bring my sister home. And I want to see your brother's killer brought to justice."

He downed the last of his club soda. *And then*

what? he wondered. What happened after her sister came home and Robert's murderer was rotting in a jail cell? Would he ever see Mia again?

What would the circumstances be? If they didn't have the case, the investigation to bring them together, why would they ever see each other? That would make them friends or lovers or something in between.

They had become friends, he supposed. And they had become lovers. It was the in between and everything else he had trouble with.

Mia stared at today's date in her appointment book, circled once in red ink.

July tenth.

When she and Matthew had first discussed the plan two weeks ago and then again even three days ago, July tenth had seemed so far away.

But here it was. Saturday, July tenth. Dawning bright and sunny and warm, like any other day. But it wasn't just any other day. Tonight, Mia would either clear her sister's name, or the deaths of four men, to whom her sister was terribly connected, could go unsolved forever. If Margot didn't show up tonight as instructed, the killer might direct his or her rage on Margot herself—if she ever did come home, that was.

Mia shivered, despite the fact that she'd turned off the air-conditioning in Matthew's bedroom and opened the windows to let in some fresh morning air. Goose bumps broke out along her arms.

She wondered what Matthew was thinking. For the past three days, they'd gone over and over the plan for tonight, and when neither of them could keep their eyes open a moment longer, Mia would retreat to the bedroom. If he thought about her, if he wanted her, Mia didn't know. She knew only that he'd been keeping her at arm's length. She'd ask him something even remotely personal, and he'd evade the subject, then change it. She'd try to talk to him about Laurie Gray, and he'd answer woodenly.

She thought of their dance at MacDougal's, the way he'd kissed her so unexpectedly, yet so expectedly. Their kiss was so right, felt so right, but there was no way she was putting herself through that kind of torture again. No way she'd allow herself to sink into a kiss, into his arms, into hope, when he'd pull the rug out from under her.

And so she herself had stopped it this time. Stopped them.

She wondered what would have happened if she hadn't stopped him. Would they have gone back to his place and continued what they'd started on the dance floor? Would they have taken a bubble bath together to cleanse off their disguises and made love in the tub?

Perhaps they would have gotten somewhere along the line, but Mia knew in her heart that he would have called a halt to their passion. To what was between them. That was what he couldn't handle—what was between them. And it was a lot.

When their mission tonight was over, she would be going back to Margot's alone. She would wake up tomorrow morning and return to Baywater and color her hair back to brown, take her yoga class, repot her plants, and stare out the window wondering where Matthew was and what he was doing for the rest of her life.

And Matthew would be right here, in Center City, going back to the business of work, visiting his nephew, walking around alone for the rest of *his* life.

During her divorce, Mia couldn't imagine herself ever falling in love again, ever wanting to marry again, ever wanting to share her home or life or body with a man. She never thought she'd have the strength to demand all that she deserved, so she'd planned never to get involved with anyone. And then she met Matthew.

She felt his arms around her as they'd danced. Felt his lips against hers. Felt his breath stir at her neck.

Oh, Matthew, why does it have to be this way? What we have is the start of something truly amazing.

The start of something that would never be.

Her knees wobbled, and she had to sit down on the edge of the bed, lest her legs give out from under her.

I love him. I love Matthew Gray.

She loved him and couldn't have him.

But, for a few hours a few days ago, he had been her husband. Well, to those at MacDougal's, anyway. They'd been wearing wedding rings, dancing, sharing some wings and club soda. A married couple out for a few hours to have a nice time.

She'd liked the way the ring felt on her finger. She'd been surprised by that. She'd thought the ten-dollar band would remind her of the cheapness, the phoniness, of her marriage to David Anderson. But it hadn't. Matthew had bought her the fake ring, and she'd worn it to pretend to be married to him.

Pretending, if only for a little while, had felt good.

It had taken her out of herself, out of her memories, and allowed her to dream of being married to Matthew, allowed her to imagine what it would be like to be married to him for real.

She glanced down at her empty finger and caressed the spot where the ring had been.

You're an idiot! she yelled at herself. *The fake gold band symbolizes how fake your relationship is. How nothing it is and how nothing it's going to be. Face up to the truth, Mia!*

The candy rings can be a memento, something for each of us to remember the other by. . . .

This ring is cutting off my circulation. . . .

How much clearer could he make it that there was no future for them? That he had no intention of changing his mind or his heart or his life. When they returned home Saturday night—

Correction: when *he* returned to his apartment and *she* returned to Margot's, he would flop on the sofa, watch a late movie on television, and then fall asleep, waking up on Sunday morning to a jog as though she'd never come into his life.

"Good morning, Center City!" exclaimed the disc jockey of the morning radio station to which she set her alarm. "It's Saturday, July tenth, and you're listening to the Z man on a hot summer morning at eight o'clock . . ."

July tenth.

The man she loved was risking his life tonight. The thought of that, of losing him forever, coupled with the knowledge that she'd never have him anyway, was unbearable.

Mia turned off the radio and lay down on the bed, her arms hugged around her.

The tears came, and Mia let them. She put her

hand over her mouth to muffle the sounds. The last thing she needed was for Matthew to hear her crying.

Get yourself together, girl, she ordered herself. *You've got to be strong for tonight. And you have to mentally prepare.*

She glanced at the red wig on the dresser. Her mother's face and her sister's floated into her mind. She'd lost her mother; and Margot had been lost to her for years. But she was going to put an end to that. After Saturday night, when it was safe for Margot to come home, things were going to change between the Daniels sisters.

They were going to be close whether Margot liked it or not. Instead of passively accepting their relationship the way it was, the way it didn't have to be, Mia was going to take charge.

If only she could do the same with Matthew.

Chapter Sixteen

At eight-thirty that night, Mia stood trembling in her sister's walk-in closet. She slowly slid outfit after outfit on the rack, unable to choose anything, unable to even think. Margot's miniscule minidresses and skirts, skin-tight leather pants, and cleavage-baring tight tops were all appropriate for the part Mia was to play tonight. But the thought of putting on any of these outfits and actually leaving the apartment, of turning herself back into the woman she vowed she'd never be for anyone. . . .

But now it's for Margot, she reminded herself. *You're doing this to save your sister. To save a man's life tonight. To bring Robert Gray's killer to justice.*

Mia took a deep breath, closed her eyes, and pulled out whatever outfit her hand landed on. It was a matte jersey red halter top, tight and cropped with a matching miniskirt. Mia selected a pair of Margot's red sandals, low enough to run in yet still high enough to look decoy appropriate, then raided her lingerie drawer for a strapless bra. Margot had at least fifteen strapless bras.

Mia had been a nervous wreck all day—and dressing up as Margot, something she'd vowed she'd never do when her marriage ended, was the least of her concerns. She was putting herself in grave danger, putting Matthew in sure danger, and there was no guarantee that they would catch the killer or save anyone.

Mia dropped the clothing on the bed and sank down, her head between her knees. *Deep breaths, girl,* she told herself. *You're not going out there alone. Matthew will be with you.*

For a few hours, anyway.

"Mia? Getting ready?"

She blushed, despite the fact that he couldn't see her through the closed bedroom door.

"Yes, I'll be out in forty-five minutes or so," she called back.

"I think I put my wig on wrong," Matthew said. "It doesn't look like it did three days ago when you put it on for me."

Mia couldn't help laughing. "I'll fix it."

She heard his footsteps retreat and softly shook her head. *You see, Matthew, you need me. You can't even put on a wig without me.*

Fresh tears welled in her eyes, and she blinked them back hard. It was time to get dressed, put on her makeup, and bring her sister home. There was no time for tears.

She stood and walked over to Margot's vanity table, laden with perfumes and cosmetics. Sitting down on the little upholstered bench, Mia pinned up her hair and examined her face in the oval mirror. *Well, I can't very well play the part of decoy with a fresh-scrubbed face,* she thought.

How would a decoy do her makeup? Porn star-esque? Vamp?

Mia knew only two looks: work and social events. And even her "evening" look met with criticism from her husband: *That lipstick is a little pale, don't you think? Try a sexy red. Are you wearing mascara? I can barely see your eyelashes.*

Mia highly doubted that Matthew Gray even knew what mascara was.

She was going out tonight as a decoy, paid to entice men into cheating. That meant a sexy look, but probably nothing too obvious so as to attract too much attention to herself.

Mia's usual routine was to start with a layer of moisturizer with sunscreen, then dab a little pressed powder at her shiny spots, sweep on a little taupe eyeshadow, whisk a quick brush of mascara on her lashes, dab her pink lip gloss on her lips, and run a brush through her hair. For evening, she added a little brown eyeliner, maybe lipstick instead of the lip gloss.

Tonight, she'd need to look sexy and innocent at the same time. Sexy to attract, innocent to seal the deal. "Hope you don't mind my using your cosmetics, Margot," she whispered.

She started with a layer of moisturizer, then covered her face with foundation, a product she never used. She pressed a puff of loose powder all over her face, then whisked on some rosy-colored blush. Her skin looked absolutely flawless, radiant. She was surprised, actually, that her face didn't look all caked-on and orange. Still, she couldn't imagine doing this every day. After the rosy shade of blush, she then swept a pale, shimmery shadow across her lids and a deeper color in the crease, the way she'd been shown at a cosmetics counter at the mall. She added more liner to her eyes than she was used to, and much more mascara. Finally, Mia selected a perfect red lipstick and applied it, blotted with a tissue, and then leaned back to examine the new her.

Tears welled in her eyes and threatened to destroy the work she'd just done. She looked exactly like her ex-husband had always wanted her to look. She looked like Margot, out for an evening on the town. She looked like she'd promised herself she'd never, ever look.

Mia blinked away the tears and dabbed some powder under her eyes to cover the tear stains. Then she pulled the pin out of her hair and plugged in Margot's hot-roller set.

Twenty minutes later, Mia's blond hair gently waved down to her shoulders. She bent over and threw her hair over her head, gave it a good shake, then threw her head back and let the bouncy strands settle as though naturally windblown.

Time to dress. Mia stood in front of the full-length mirror attached to the walk-in closet and stripped out of her T-shirt and jeans. She put on the uncomfortable strapless bra, then fought a little with the halter top until she figured out how to get it on without ripping it. She pulled on the miniscule skirt, slipped into the sandals, closed her eyes, and then opened them.

Well, I look like a decoy, that's for sure, Mia thought. *I look like a lot of women I've seen over the past few weeks, out on a Saturday night in the city.*

Deep breath, deep breath, deep breath.

"Mia?" Matthew called. "It's nine-fifteen. Almost ready?"

"Be right out," she called back.

She grabbed a little red shoulder bag, transferred the necessities into it, and then pulled open the bedroom door. Ready or not, here she came.

Matthew was standing in front of the sofa, reading the *Center City News*. He glanced up, did a double take, and then dropped down onto the sofa as though his legs had given out.

It was exactly the reaction she expected. She wanted to cry.

"*Whoa*," he whispered. "Whoa." His mouth dropped open. "You look amazing."

The man she loved was staring at her as though she were a porn star ready for a night of hot sex with him.

"I look like a cheap decoy is what I look like," Mia snapped.

"No, you don't," Matthew said. "You look like a beautiful woman going out on a Saturday night. You look absolutely stunning."

He stood and walked over to her. "Turn around. I'd love to get a look at the entire package."

Her heart breaking, Mia blinked back the tears. He took her hand and held it high, and she turned slowly around, just like she used to do for David Anderson.

Her hand flew to her mouth, and she ran to the bathroom. And once again, Mia sank down onto the cool tile floor and threw up.

"Mia? Are you all right?"

Silence.

He knocked softly on the bathroom door, so worried about her. "Mia?"

"I'm fine," she called back hoarsely.

She came out a few minutes later, showing no signs of having just been sick. She looked as stunning, as radiant, as unbelievably sexy as when she'd gone in. Her expression grim, she sat down on the sofa and stared out the window.

"Mia, we can forget this whole stupid plot," he said. "I can see you're scared out of your mind."

"I'm not scared," she said. "I'm just fine."

"You just threw up, Mia."

Silence.

He sat down next to her. "Let's just forget the plan," he said. "We'll go to the police, tell them what we know, and let them take it from here."

"And who is going to play the part of Margot Daniels?" she asked. "Who else looks exactly like her?"

"No one's going to play her part," he replied. "We're calling off the plan. It's that simple."

"We call off the plan, and the killer goes free," Mia insisted. "The police won't ever have an opportunity to set him or her up the way we can tonight."

"But, Mia, it's too much," he said. "You were sick, and we haven't even left yet."

"Maybe something else made me ill," Mia said in such a low voice that he wasn't sure he heard her correctly.

"What do you mean?" he asked.

"Maybe it's looking like this, Matthew. Maybe it was your reaction to me."

Okay, now he was completely confused. "But you look gorgeous."

"I look like my sister," she whispered. "I look like the woman my ex-husband wanted."

"You mean, the one who still wasn't enough for him?" Matthew said. "The one who could never please him, no matter what she did?"

"That was mean," she whispered.

"No, it wasn't, Mia," he told her. "It's the truth. What your ex-husband wanted had nothing to do with the way you looked. It had to do with him and his own insecurities. This look is you as much as the natural look. It's all shades of *you,* Mia."

She glanced down. "But your eyes practically popped out of your head for this look, Matthew."

He took her hand in his. "My eyes popped out of my head when I first saw you, Mia—in paint-splattered sweatpants and a baggy T-shirt. You had your hair in a ponytail and not a stitch of makeup on your face. This is still you, Mia. If you're not comfortable with it, there is no reason for you to gussy up like this, that's all. That's the point."

She glanced up at him, then gnawed at her lower lip. "Let's go," she said. "I'm ready now."

"Mia, we really don't have to do this," he said.

"Yes, we do."

He stared at her, but she wouldn't meet his gaze. They sat in silence for a few minutes.

"Okay, let's go," she said, her voice a bit stronger. "I'm as ready as I'm ever going to be, Matthew."

"You're sure?"

She nodded. "I'm just nervous, that's all. But I'm ready. And I want to do this. So let's get going."

"But what about my hair?" He pointed to the lopsided mop of blond waves on his head.

She smiled. "C'mere. Let me fix it."

Relief flooded him. He was afraid he'd never

see her smile again. He was also afraid he'd never get the opportunity to slam her bastard of an ex-husband against a brick wall. What a number that asshole had done on her.

Did she not realize how absolutely perfect she was exactly as she was? No matter how she looked, whether all dolled up like a movie star, or completely natural like sunshine, she was Mia. His Mia.

That was a startling thought. He had no idea where it came from. She wasn't *his Mia.* She wasn't his anything. And after tonight, she wouldn't even be in his life anymore.

The reason would be no more. And without cause to work together, their relationship would have to be based on something else.

There could be nothing else.

She'd turned slightly and scooted over, her hands in his hair to adjust the wig. He could smell the green apples, the musky perfume she'd sprayed on her neck. Her arms raised, her breasts strained against the tight, slinky red fabric of the halter top she wore.

God, how he wanted her. He wanted to take her right here, rip off the clothes, lick all that makeup off her face, and make love to her until they were both slick with sweat and sated.

"You're all set," she said with a smile. "And I think you make a fine blond."

He grimaced, and she laughed and he was thankfully pulled back into the here and now instead of fantasyland. He had to keep his mind on tonight, not on her body.

"Are you ready?" he asked. "You're sure you're ready?"

"As ready as I'll ever be," she said.

"I won't let anything happen to you, Mia."

"It's you I'm worried about," she said softly.

"I'm going to be fine."

She took a deep breath. "So you'll leave first, and then a few minutes later, I'll follow."

He nodded. "Right. Everything's going to be okay, Mia."

Please let me be telling the truth, he thought. *Please let this go down the way we planned.*

"Don't forget these," Mia whispered, picking up the horn-rimmed glasses from the end table and handing them to him.

He slipped them on, and their gazes locked. His heart moved in his chest, and he took a step back, startled.

"Matthew? What is it?"

He couldn't speak. Suddenly, all he wanted was to tell her how he felt, how his heart felt. But what was the point? He couldn't give her what she wanted.

"I—" he began, but he didn't even know what he was going to say. And so he pulled her to him and kissed her.

She pushed against his chest. "What the hell do you think you're doing?" she asked.

"A kiss goodbye," he said.

"Yes, a kiss *goodbye,* Matthew. Exactly."

"Mia, if I could—"

"Save your breath, Matthew. I know. If you could, but you can't and won't. I don't need you to want me. Especially when it's clear this dolled-up version of me has made quite an impact on you."

"It's made no more impact than you without a stitch of makeup on, Mia."

Mia raised an eyebrow. "Oh, really? Suddenly,

you're dropping down on the sofa and all tongue-tied. Suddenly, you can't find words to express yourself when you were spouting this and that just fine yesterday."

What could he say to make her understand? They were about to embark on a very dangerous mission, and if he was tongue-tied, it wasn't because she was wearing red lipstick and showing some leg. It was because his heart had physically moved in his chest at the thought of leaving her for the next few minutes, at the thought of her in danger, at the thought of never seeing her again after tonight.

But he didn't have words for all that.

"Look, Matthew, after tonight, we're going our separate ways. Let's just get tonight over with, okay?"

"Mia—"

"Just go. It's nine-forty," she said and turned away.

No matter what was in his heart, it didn't matter. They'd both said too much over the past few weeks; too much had happened.

He'd lost her before he'd even had a chance to have her.

At nine-fifty, Matthew pulled open the door to MacDougal's and was greeted by the blare of a Bon Jovi song and the roar of talking and laughter. The place was packed. Every seat at the bar was taken, and a few people were squeezed in between the stools, waving bills to get the busy bartender's attention. The dance floor was full of bumpers and grinders, and most of the tables surrounding it were taken.

My brother's murderer is in this room, Matthew thought, glancing around. He twisted the fake gold ring on his left hand, wondering if the killer was watching him, noticing that a man with a wedding ring had come into a nightclub alone on a Saturday night. He had no idea if the killer had been in MacDougal's Wednesday night. If the killer had been there, he or she had been in as good a disguise as Matthew's and Mia's.

I can't wait to get my hands around your neck, he thought bitterly.

He headed to the bar and ordered a club soda.

"Hi!" chirped the woman standing next to him. A petite brunette with freckles and a low-cut tank top, she held up her wrist under his nose. "Do you like this perfume?"

Oh, Lord. Matthew bent down and sniffed her wrist. "Very nice," he told her and was rewarded with a beaming smile. "Oh, I see someone I know. Nice to meet you."

She shrugged and resumed swaying and stirring her drink, her gaze on the dance floor.

Matthew headed over to the jukebox and glanced at the door. It was ten o'clock, and Mia was due. The door opened, and a group of men and women came in, followed by Mia.

She took his breath away. Her blond hair shone in the dimly lit bar and waved softly to her shoulders. Her red lipstick, so sexy, matched her hot red halter top and miniskirt. And those sandals. Goose bumps broke out on Matthew's neck. Between the miniskirt and the sandals, Mia's amazing legs were a mile long. She was the most beautiful woman he'd ever seen. But not more beautiful than the woman she looked like the first time he saw her.

He watched heads turn as she glanced around and made her way to a table about fifty feet from where he stood. She sat down and perused the cardboard menu of drinks on the table.

"Wanna dance?" asked a woman standing next to him. "I love this song."

Matthew glanced at the attractive tall blonde. "I would, but I have two left feet. Anyway, I'm meeting someone. But thanks."

"Well, she's not here yet," the blonde countered.

Jesus. Pushy. "But she will be here soon, and if she comes in and sees me dancing with another woman, I'm in big trouble."

The blonde rolled her eyes and turned to another guy and in five seconds was shaking her butt on the dance floor.

Matthew mentally shook his head and took stock of the place. From where he stood, he could see the entire bar. With Norman Newman's, Lisa Ann Cole's, Theresa Healy's, Ashley Davidson's, and yes, Laurie Gray's faces clear in his mind, he searched every inch of the place for the five suspects. Unless they were in disguise themselves, none of them was in MacDougal's.

Maybe our killer is simply late, Matthew thought.

He glanced at Mia. She'd adopted a neutral expression. *Good job,* he sent telepathically. *If you're nervous or uncomfortable, and I know you're both, you'd never know it by looking at you.*

He noticed two young men staring at her and whispering between themselves. Probably betting each other on who'd have luck with the hot blonde.

Matthew was right. One of the men approached her, and was back in position next to his friend in four seconds. The other man laughed, straightened his shirt, ran a hand through his hair, and made his way over to Mia. Matthew shook his head. Mia said something to the man, her expression remaining neutral, and the guy was back with his friend in moments. Both men were scowling. Neither man was wearing a wedding ring, and she'd clearly gotten rid of them quickly.

Where are you, you bastard? Come out, come out wherever you are. I am so ready for you. So ready to take you down.

His gaze roaming the bar, Matthew noticed a man staring at Mia. A gold ring shone on the third finger of the man's left hand. Matthew watched him take a deep breath and run a hand through his hair before making his way in Mia's direction. *I'd better nip this in the bud,* Matthew realized, *or this guy just might end up the target.*

But someone was blocking his path.

"Would you like to dance?"

Damn. It was the petite brunette again. She was looking up at him so earnestly that her freckles almost seemed to be dancing.

"Uh, sorry, but I was just about to—"

Her smiled faded. "Yeah, I know. You see someone you know, right?"

Get the hell out of my way, he wanted to scream at her. Wedding Band was advancing, and Matthew had to beat him to Mia's table.

"Actually, yeah," Matthew told the brunette. "I'm sorry. I really would like to dance. How about later?"

Her face lit up. "I'll hold you to that."

He smiled, then weaved his way to Mia's table as fast as he could. But the tall man had beat him to it.

Dammit!

"It was a gift, but you can probably find it at Macy's or Bloomingdales," Mia was saying to the man.

Huh?

"Thanks," the man replied. "My wife would love that outfit. And I'm useless when it comes to picking out clothes for her, so thanks. I don't want to mess up our first anniversary by buying her something she'll hate."

Mia smiled, and the man left. Matthew let out the breath he'd been holding.

"Would you like to dance?"

Not the brunette again, please, Matthew prayed. He turned around to find an attractive redhead standing in front of him.

"I love this song," she said, swaying her hips suggestively.

"I would," Matthew said, "but I was just about to—"

The redhead glanced behind him at Mia, then returned her gaze to Matthew. "Ah, I see. Your loss." She thrust out her chest and turned to another guy.

I don't think so, Matthew thought. Man, was he grateful he'd never have to enter a place like this after tonight. Between the music and the constant come-ons, which felt faker to him than his wig, mustache, and wedding ring, he was about at the end of his rope.

Why doesn't the ring deter these women? he wondered. He wished he had the audacity to ask the next woman who asked him to dance. It wasn't as though he was hiding his hand in his pocket; he held his club soda in his left hand specifically to showcase it every time he took a sip.

Yet, they still came on to him. What the hell?

He glanced around again, this time specifically looking for one of the four widows. He knew in his heart that he wouldn't find Laurie Gray here. So who would he find? Lisa Ann Cole, decked out in her leopard print? Theresa Healy, a murderous glint in her cold eyes? Or Ashley Davidson, distraught and sobbing?

The thought of Ashley Davidson brought the image of his mother to mind. Letitia Gray had also been distraught. She had also been sobbing. And she had picked up a gun, pointed it at her philandering husband, and cocked the trigger. In his mind's eye, Matthew saw the gun wavering in her hand, saw the tears falling down her lined cheeks, saw the desperation, the inability to take any more. He wondered if the killer was like his mother, a woman who'd lost it, who'd snapped, who'd gone off a cliff in her own head.

No. His mother hadn't killed anyone. She hadn't pulled the trigger. And Matthew would never, ever believe that she would have if the police hadn't come.

He wondered sometimes if his father had known that, known that his wife didn't have it in her to hurt anyone. Robert Gray Senior certainly hadn't tried to keep her away from Robert and Matthew after "the incident." Once, Matthew had asked Robert why he thought their dad didn't press charges or legally demand that their mother not be allowed in their home or to see the boys. Robert had thought that their father knew their mother was too weak to ever hurt anyone, especially her children, who had never caused her any pain.

Too weak.

Matthew had countered that their mother was anything but weak, but Robert had reminded him that she hadn't left their father during years of philandering and ill treatment. She hadn't left him even after the final incident. *What's your definition of weak, little brother?* Robert had wanted to know.

Norman Newman is my definition of weak, Matthew thought. A man who harassed women when they said no. A man who grabbed women into hotel rooms. A man who didn't understand that *no* meant *no.* That was the definition of weak.

The definition of *strong* was sitting just a few feet from Matthew, looking so beautiful, so brave. His heart swelled, and he wanted nothing more than to go to her, take her out of here, away from this, away from danger, away from ugliness.

Focus, man, he ordered himself. *Focus! There's a killer in this room, and you're thinking about romance?*

Matthew called himself every name and curse there was, then looked around MacDougal's for anyone who was looking at Mia. A lot of people were checking her out, men and women. The women with a hint of annoyance, the men with lust.

Holy—

Someone was staring at Mia with burning hatred.

It was Norman Newman.

Chapter Seventeen

Mia squeezed her lime into the club soda the waitress had just brought her. Her stomach had started churning the moment she'd walked into MacDougal's and had been turning over nonstop since she sat down. She felt so conspicuous in this getup, so exposed. She'd been aware of the eyes on her when she'd entered the bar and walked to her table. Men looking at her with unbridled lust in their eyes. She was sickened. She would bet anything that not one of those men would be interested in a conversation, what she thought of the crisis in the Middle East, or what she did for a living. They were interested in a score, to show their friends they'd "picked up" a pretty woman. They were interested in sex. A one-night stand. Maybe a few-nights stand. The way they looked at her, what they wanted from her revolted her.

Focus, Mia. Remember why you're here. You're supposed to look like an object. They're supposed to look at you as though you're nothing more than that. This is what will lead you and Matthew to the killer.

The killer.

The killer was somewhere in the room. Watching her. Waiting. Preparing to pick victim number five.

Fear gripped her by the throat, and suddenly she couldn't breathe. *Calm down, Mia. Calm down. Everything is going to be okay. Matthew is here. The killer will be caught. Neither of you will get hurt. Trust in that.*

Mia closed her eyes and willed Matthew to come over and get this over with; then she changed her mind and willed him away so that he wouldn't put himself in danger. She'd glanced in his direction a few times since she'd sat down, and she'd been shocked, as she had been three days ago, to see him in his disguise. Yet despite the blond wig and the mustache and the horn-rimmed glasses, he was Matthew. Her Matthew. The man she loved. She would know him, know those dark blue eyes, anywhere.

The disguise did nothing to lessen how attractive he was. Each time she'd spotted him, he'd been talking to a different woman. Given the circumstances of why they were here, Mia had no doubt that the women had initiated the conversation, but Mia was still bothered by seeing him with other women.

Get used to it, she told herself. *He's not yours.*

Correction: she *wouldn't* have to get used to it because after tonight, she'd never see Matthew Gray again.

A gray blob of sorrow formed in her heart, and tears stung the backs of her eyes. What the hell was wrong with her? She was in the middle of a very dangerous sting operation, and she was crying over a man she couldn't have? A man who didn't want her?

Actually, he did want her. Only sexually.

Sex. That was certainly the name of the game in MacDougal's tonight. Men and women were bumping and grinding on the dance floor as though they were having sex with clothes on; women with very little clothes on were shimmying their stuff as though they were on display for the men standing around watching. All around her, people laughed and talked and drank. She supposed they must be having a good time, but as she watched people individually, she got a very different impression. She watched a young man stick his fingers in a woman's drink, pick up an ice cube, and slip it down the front of the woman's shirt, much to her glee. She hooted and pretend punched him; then they started making out. But how much fun could it have been to feel an ice cube down your blouse? How much fun could it be to be with a man immature enough to do that? These weren't teenagers in MacDougal's; the drinking age was twenty-one, and a good many of the people in MacDougal's looked to be in their thirties and forties.

Maybe you're being too judgmental, she thought. *Miss Self-Righteous strikes again.* Her ex-husband had constantly thrown that line in her face whenever she told him she wanted to go home from whatever social event he'd taken her to.

She watched another woman at the next table run her hands up and down her date's thigh until the man grabbed her hand, placed it on his crotch and vigorously rubbed up and down. The woman looked mortified and tried to wriggle her hand away, but the man wouldn't let go. He was staring into her eyes like an animal and rubbing. Mia saw panic in the woman's eyes, then acquiescence. The woman began kissing the man's neck and rubbing on her own. Now that she was doing what he wanted on her own, he slipped his hand up under her shirt and groped her breast. Mia glanced around, wondering if anyone else had noticed. But everyone else seemed wrapped up in their own dates.

Mind your own business, Miss Priss, David used to say. *Stop worrying what other people are doing and start* doing *something yourself.* Then he'd yank her close and press himself against her, shoving his tongue in her mouth. Humiliated, Mia would run out of wherever they were, a party, the bar of a restaurant as they waited for a table, the park. After enough of that kind of humiliation, Mia had refused to attend events with David. At first he was angry, but then he was only too glad to go out alone. She learned why when he began coming home with lipstick stains on his neck, phone numbers in his pocket, and once, a condom wrapper inside his underwear.

It was then that she'd told David she wanted a divorce.

Stop thinking about David Anderson, she ordered herself. *Stop thinking about anything but the matter at hand. Getting through this sting operation and catching the killer.*

All right, Matthew. It's ten-twenty. Time for you to come over so that no one else does. Time for this terrible night to end.

Where was he? she wondered, glancing around for him. He'd been over by the jukebox, and then she saw him heading in her direction, only to be waylaid by an attractive redhead. He'd been standing relatively close by the last time she looked, but now he was nowhere to be found.

Perhaps he went to the bar to get another drink and take a look around at the front of the place, Mia thought. She was sure that was it.

She craned her neck to see around a tall man, but it wasn't Matthew she saw.

Someone else she knew was coming toward her.

It was Norman Newman!

"Mia!" Norman exclaimed. "So clumsy. Allow me to clean that up for you. I always carry some tissues in my pocket."

She stared at the club soda she'd spilled all over the table. Her heart had started booming in her chest the moment she laid eyes on Norman, and she'd jumped in her chair with such force that she'd knocked over her drink.

Norman reached into his pocket, and Mia felt the blood drain from her face and saw a flash of black and then little white dots behind her eyes.

Don't black out, dammit, she told herself. *Don't faint with Norman Newman as your rescuer!*

He pulled out a pack of pocket tissues, and she let out a whoosh of air. She felt warmth return to her cheeks.

Breathe, Mia. Just breathe. It's a pack of Kleenex, not a gun.

While Norman mopped up the mess, Mia frantically searched MacDougal's with her eyes for Matthew, but she didn't see him anywhere.

Where the hell are you?

Oh, God. Had Norman somehow recognized Matthew's disguise and gotten to him?

No, she told herself. *That isn't possible. Stop letting your mind go places it doesn't have to go. Shouldn't go. Matthew is unrecognizable.*

But why wasn't he anywhere in MacDougal's? Why wasn't he standing nearby, listening and watching? Where *was* he?

Norman threw the wad of wet napkins under the table and sat down. She wasn't about to comment on his manners or behavior.

"I've been hoping to run into you again," he said, straightening his tie.

Suddenly, the wide navy-and-cream tie looked less like a tie and more like an instrument of strangulation.

She wondered if that would be his weapon of choice tonight, if that was what he had in mind for his victim.

Oh, God. Norman Newman was a cold-blooded killer. The creepy little man who'd been teaching at Baywater Middle School, running the physics and chemistry lab, monitoring the chemistry club and directing the school science fair, was a cold-blooded killer.

How had he appeared so normal all these months? Norman was a model faculty member of Baywater Middle School, and the principal often spoke highly of him. *The students like him,* the principal had said. *He's patient with them. And he's a wonderful teacher.*

She'd seen evidence of that, actually, during one of the vice principal's more annoying ideas for staff development. Each teacher had had to sit in on another teacher's class in an entirely different subject, and Mia had pulled Norman Newman's name out of the hat. She'd watched two class periods, a seventh and eighth grade chemistry class, and with her own eyes she'd seen Norman relay complicated information in an engaging and patient manner. The students even laughed a few times at corny jokes he made; it had been clear to her that they did indeed like him, even if they considered him, to use Amy Farley's term, a nerd.

But he wasn't a "nerd." He was a crafty murderer.

Norman scooted his chair closer to her. "Mia? So quiet! I must say that you look lovely tonight. Ravishing, really."

She swallowed. Should she humor him? Assure him that she'd gotten all dolled up for the assignment he'd hired her for?

No—all the manila envelopes that had come for Margot had no return address, no name, no nothing. Norman had clearly wanted to remain anonymous, and if she let him know that she knew he was the one who'd hired "her," it could ruin tonight's entire operation.

She should simply be herself, the Mia she always was with him—and the Mia she should be based on their last interaction. "I want you to know that I filed a complaint against you with the police," she lied. "I have a restraining order. You're not to come anywhere near me."

"But, Mia," he said, dropping his gaze to her breasts. "I only want to apologize for my terrible behavior a couple of weeks ago. I'm really sorry for how I acted."

Mia's hands shook, and she clasped them in her

lap. "A restraining order means you can't come within fifty feet of me, Norman."

He raised his gaze to her face, a hurt expression in his beady eyes. "But, Mia, isn't my apology worth anything to you?"

He was psychotic, she realized. Truly sick.

Mia shuddered. What an actor he must be. To hide his psychosis so well, to carry on his teaching duties, parent-teacher conferences, mundane conversations in the faculty lounge. She'd never guessed that he was unhinged. She'd simply thought that he was annoying, a pest, socially inept. She'd never been so wrong.

She didn't understand why he'd been asking her out every Monday morning for the past six months when he believed that she was an undercover decoy. When he'd hired "her" four times to test the fidelity of other men.

When he'd killed those men.

Oh, God. Was it her fault that four men were dead? Had Norman killed them because they'd tried to pick her up when Norman wanted her for himself?

No! No! That made no sense. Norman was the one who'd hired them to try to go out with her in the first place! But why? What drove him? Norman was a single man, and if she wasn't mistaken, his parents had been happily married for thirty-five years before his father passed away from cancer two years ago. Mia and many other teachers at Baywater Middle School had gone to the funeral, and so many people had gotten up to eulogize his father, each mentioning what a loyal and devoted husband and father he was. His mother had been sobbing during the entire funeral, and afterward, at her home, she'd been inconsolable. Mia remembered Norman guiding her upstairs to rest.

So if he wasn't a victim of a philandering wife because he wasn't married, and his parents weren't philanderers, what would drive him to seek out married men, set them up to be tested by a decoy, and then kill them when they failed that test?

And what was *her* connection to it all?

Fact: he thought she was earning extra money as a decoy to supplement her teacher's salary. Fact: he had a "crush" on her. But why hire her, though? Just to see her test the vows of married men? For what purpose? *Why?*

She was back to square one. If he thought she was a decoy, *why* would he get so upset about seeing her in Center City bars with other men? He would know that she was only working, doing her job.

Why are you trying to figure him out? she asked herself. *He's psychotic! What more do you need to know about how his mind works?*

Norman tilted his head and stared at her. "Mia, aren't you going to accept my apology?"

Panic slammed into her stomach. What was she supposed to say? How was she supposed to handle this?

Why hadn't she prepared for Norman Newman?

Because you didn't want to believe that he was the one, she realized, ashamed of herself. *Just like Matthew didn't want to believe that Laurie Gray was the killer. The difference is that Laurie is family to Matthew, the mother of his beloved nephew, and someone very special to him. You didn't want Norman to be the killer because of how guilty it would make you feel.*

But she did feel guilty. Intellectually she understood what Matthew had meant when he said that no one was responsible for the actions of another person. But if it wasn't for her, Norman wouldn't have hired Margot. Wouldn't have killed Robert Gray. Wouldn't be preparing, unbeknownst to him at this point, to kill Matthew Gray.

A sob rose in her throat, and Mia tamped it down.

Where are you Matthew? Where are *you?*

Norman was impatiently looking around MacDougal's. Making sure that Matthew hadn't come back from the dead to challenge him? she wondered frantically.

Stop it, she told herself. *Stop it. Matthew is fine. He's in disguise, and there's no way that Norman could possibly have recognized him.*

"Where is the waitress," Norman snapped, twisting his fleshy neck to look behind him. "The service in here is terrible! A waitress should have been over here to replace your drink, free of charge, the moment it spilled."

Mia breathed a sigh of relief. He was only looking for the cocktail waitress—not for Matthew.

"That's okay, Norman," she told him. "I'm fine."

"No, no. I want that drink replaced now," he responded.

As Norman continued to look around, Mia dared a glance to her left and to her right, hoping to catch a glimpse of Matthew in her peripheral vision. But there was no sign of him.

Norman turned to face her. "Ah, there she is, at that large table. I'm sure she'll be over in a minute."

Mia nodded around the lump in her throat.

"I don't understand why you were so afraid of me when all I wanted was to share a cup of coffee with you," Norman said. "I would never hurt you, Mia. Ever. I *love* you."

Oh, God. Oh, God. Oh, God. Her heart was racing so fast she was sure Norman could hear it. It was her fault. Norman had killed four men because he was in love with her.

"But then that *per-son* had to come ruin our day," Norman continued. He glanced around him again. "Where the *hell* is that waitress? I've been sitting here for at least five minutes and I haven't been served and your drink has not been replaced!"

Deep breath, Mia. Just relax. You're in a public place. If he pulls out a weapon, two hundred people will help you. No one will get hurt.

Oh God, please. Let no one get hurt.

"Are you dating that man?" Norman asked, staring at her, his cold, beady eyes narrowing. "That he-man who barges into private motel rooms and destroys public property?"

"We're . . . just friends, Norman," she said.

He began running his hands up and down his tie as he stared at her. "I don't believe you."

She had no idea what the right answer was anymore. Was she supposed to try to soothe him, make him think she did like him the way she did in the Center City Motel?

Wait a minute. Goad him. Make him angry. And then he'll go after Matthew, you'll call the police, and they'll come and take Norman Newman away. He'll never hurt anyone again.

He'll go after Matthew . . .

Fear gripped her again, and she fought against it. *You've prepared for this,* she reminded herself. *It's all planned down to the last detail. Trust in Matthew.*

She glanced up at Norman, forcing an aggressively sexual glint to her expression. She smiled coldly. "Actually, Norman, you're right. I'm lying. I *am* dating him."

He looked as though he wanted to spit. "I thought so. I could tell by the way he was acting all possessive of you that day. And busting into my hotel room like that. I hope they made him pay."

"Oh, I'm sure they did," she told him. "He's *very* possessive. He hates it that I date other men."

Norman's face brightened. "You date other men?"

She wasn't sure if that had been the right thing to say, but he seemed pleased all of a sudden. Perhaps he thought he had a chance.

"Ah, yes, of course you do," he said. "I've seen you with other men around the city." His gaze dropped to her breasts and stayed there.

Mia took that opportunity to glance around again, hoping, praying to spot Matthew.

There he was! He was standing not two feet away from her table, behind Norman, and partially hidden by a rather large man. Matthew caught her gaze for a moment and nodded, as if to tell her that he was watching and that everything was okay. That she was doing exactly what she should be doing.

Relief flooded through her, and her shoulders sagged.

Of course you're dating other people. I've seen you with other men around the city. . . . She didn't get that. He knew that the men he'd seen her with in Center City bars were the men he'd targeted for death. The men he'd hired her to entice. Was he just playing a game with her? Or was he truly delusional—or whatever psychological term fit him?

"Mia, you're looking a bit tired," Norman said. "Are you sure you're all right?"

"I'm just fine," she snapped. "I just had a late night last night."

His face fell. "That jerk you were with the other day?"

Mia smiled. "No, someone else. A new guy I met a few days ago. I really like him."

"Oh," Norman muttered, a pout forming on his fleshy lips.

"I think he might even be the one," Mia exclaimed. "I mean, things between us are *amazing.*"

She glanced up at Matthew; he flashed her a thumbs up so quickly she wasn't sure he'd done it at all.

"Amazing?" Norman repeated.

"A-ma-*zing*!" she confirmed with a sexual smile. "If you know what I mean."

Norman coughed. "Why will you date these other guys and not me?" he asked, running a hand through his wiry brown hair. "What's wrong with me?"

"Why, nothing, Norman," she told him. "You're very . . . nice. Just not my *type.*"

His beady eyes narrowed. "Not your *type?*" he repeated coldly. "What *is* your type?"

"Hmm . . . *that* guy!" She pointed at Matthew, who walked up to the table as though he'd just arrived. He was sipping a tall drink that looked like vodka or gin, but was club soda.

"Excuse me," Matthew said, gesturing at the empty chair across from Mia. "Is that seat taken?"

Norman glanced up at Matthew, annoyance in his beady eyes. "You can take it."

"Thanks, guy," Matthew said and sat down, his gaze on Mia.

"What do you think you're doing?" Norman asked, staring at Matthew as though he had four heads.

"What?" Matthew asked, all innocence. "You just said I could take the seat."

Norman sputtered. "I thought you wanted the *chair*—to bring to another table or something."

"Why would I want to sit at a different table when the most beautiful woman in MacDougal's is right here?" Matthew responded, looking Mia up and down.

Mia blushed on cue and giggled.

Norman glared at Mia, then stared at Matthew. "Well, you can't sit there. We're in the middle of a private conversation."

"Oh," Matthew said. "Sorry. But there's no other seats. Go ahead, talk. I won't listen."

Steam was coming out of Norman's ears. He was glaring at Matthew with an expression that Mia had never seen before. Beyond hatred.

Don't be scared, she told herself. *You're safe. Matthew is safe. Norman is going to be locked up very soon. Just do what you have to do. Follow Matthew's lead.*

"We're having a conversation here," Norman snapped at Matthew. "Do you mind?" It wasn't a question.

Matthew smirked. "Yes, I do. Sorry, buddy. Why don't *you* take a hike?"

Norman's face turned beet red. He glared at Matthew, then turned his attention to Mia. "Do you believe this jerk?" Norman asked Mia.

"Oh, Norman, don't be like that," Matthew taunted. "Why don't we ask the lady who she'd prefer to sit with and talk to."

Norman looked to Mia. "Well, Mia?"

"Norman, look, I accept your apology, okay? I think our conversation is over."

"So I guess I'm dismissed," Norman hissed, a vein popping out of his neck.

"Guess so, guy," Matthew said in a singsong voice. "The lady hath chosen."

Matthew crossed his arms over his chest and laughed.

Norman's eyes settled on the gold wedding ring on Matthew's finger, and his mouth fell open. "He's *married*, for God's sake!" Norman sputtered. "Is nothing sacred to you, Mia? If not the sanctity of marriage, what about setting an example for your students?"

"Oh, Norman, please," Mia said, rolling her eyes good-naturedly.

Norman looked as though she'd slapped him. "I'm appalled. Absolutely appalled."

Mia giggled. "C'mon, Norman—don't be such a fuddy-duddy!"

"Yeah, *Norman*," Matthew said. "Don't be such a fuddy-duddy."

Norman stared at Matthew, hatred and rage darkening his beady blue eyes. Then he looked at Mia with contempt and stood up.

"Leaving after all, buddy boy?" Matthew asked. "I was hoping you'd stay."

Norman shoved his chair under the table so hard that people around them turned to look. "I don't like you," he said to Matthew. "I don't like you at all."

"Should I cry here or when I get home?" Matthew replied. He chugged his drink and signaled the waitress for another.

Norman ignored Matthew and turned his attention to Mia. "And you. You are just a continual disappointment, Mia."

"Norman!" Mia chided. "Why so serious?"

Norman shook his head. "I really feel sorry for you, Mia. But I feel the sorriest for your students. I'll be sure and discuss your behavior with Principal Ashton."

"Run along, scout," Matthew taunted, slinging an arm around Mia. "I'd like to get to know this lovely lady a lot better."

Norman stared at Matthew for a long moment, then turned and stalked away.

"Where's he going?" Mia whispered to Matthew. "What if he leaves? We won't be able to prove anything!"

"I doubt he's going anywhere," Matthew assured her. "He's probably just going to the bar to cool off."

Sure enough, Mia watched Norman retreat to the bar and squeeze in between two women. He said something to the blonde and gestured at the stool between her and her friend. The blonde glanced at him, rolled her eyes, then removed her purse from the stool. Giving the woman a dirty look, he picked up the stool, carried it over to the L-shaped portion of the bar and sat down, then glanced over at Mia. She realized he wanted to put himself in position to watch her and Matthew.

She let out the breath she'd been holding.

"You all right?" Matthew whispered.

She nodded. "Where were you before?" she

asked. "I was so scared he'd gotten to you. I didn't see you anywhere, then saw him, and I panicked."

Matthew adjusted his glasses. "I'd spotted him earlier, and he was moving around a lot, so I was just keeping an eye on him. He was standing by the bar earlier, staring at you, and I wanted to be able to watch him without being seen; so I moved behind him."

"I was so scared," she repeated, her voice trembling.

"I'm sorry, Mia," he whispered. "But I'm all right. And I *will* be all right. We *both* will be. We're going to get him, okay? In a little while, the police are going to take him away, and it's all going to be over."

She nodded. "You're right. I know you're right."

He covered her hand with his own, the hand with the wedding ring. It was so shiny that it gleamed in the low-lit nightclub. "We've got to put on a show for him, Mia. Piss him off royally. Put him in a very bad mood."

"Oh, I think you took care of that, Matthew."

"You didn't do too badly yourself," he told her with a smile. "Look, Newman's moving again. Probably wants to position himself so he can hear our conversation."

Mia glanced at Norman. He was struggling to move the bar stool to the corner of the L-shape so that he could both see Mia and Matthew *and* hear their conversation.

Matthew reached up with his left hand and caressed her cheek, then scooted his chair even closer and kissed her full on the mouth. Mia closed her eyes and gave in to the kiss, allowing herself to forget for a moment that Matthew was playing a role. His lips were warm and soft, and he smelled so good, like man and soap. As he broke the kiss, she slowly opened her eyes and gazed into his.

His dark blue eyes smoldered with desire. Mia inched closer to him and softly pressed her lips to his. She touched his cheek, cupping his jaws with both hands and putting everything she had into the kiss.

She wasn't acting. She wondered if he could tell. *Jesus, Mia, you're not supposed to seem like a woman in love!* she chided herself. Norman might actually "approve" of the depth of her emotion and soften. She had to act as though she was only interested in a good time, all too happy to "put out" and satisfy her married lover.

Mia pulled back from the kiss and giggled. "Yum-yum," she cooed. "Did I ever tell you you're the *best* kisser?"

Matthew took her hands and caressed them on the tabletop, whispering into her ear with a lascivious expression. He was actually saying, "We're gonna get him, Mia. We're gonna get him." But Norman didn't know that.

A waitress came by to take Matthew's order, and the moment she left, he resumed his role. Gazing at her. Whispering in her ear. Caressing her hand. He was almost too good, though. Too affected by her slinky red outfit and her sexy makeup. He hardly seemed like he was acting at all. But it wasn't love that Mia saw reflected in his eyes; it was lust.

Because he wants you and doesn't love you, she reminded herself. *He doesn't have to act at all. Just play your part, Mia. Do what you need to do.*

And so she did. She giggled, flipped her hair,

winked, and blew into Matthew's ear. She was making herself sick.

How did Margot do this? she wondered. *How could she stand it?*

"I think I had a little too much to drink," Matthew said, slurring his words for, she was sure, Norman's benefit. A drunk target was an easy target. "You're show boot-a-ful." He caressed her shoulder. "And your hair smells like wildshowers." He laughed. "Upps, I mean wild*flowers.* Guess I did have a little too much gin tonight, baby doll."

"That's okay, honey," she cooed. "I can be the designated driver."

"Hmmm, I would definitely like a ride from you, babe," Matthew said.

Mia was a little taken aback at how blatantly sexual that was. *Okay, he's acting a little,* she reminded herself. *You can't take anything he says here tonight personally. It's all show for Norman's benefit. Just remember that.*

Mia glanced at Norman, and they locked gazes for a moment. A vein was pulsating on his forehead. He looked as though he was literally going to explode at any second.

"I think he's good and worked up," Mia whispered to Matthew.

Matthew leaned back in his chair and took her hand, bringing it to his lips for a kiss. "Good," he whispered. "Because I am so ready for a showdown."

Mia's stomach rolled.

"So, babe," Matthew said more loudly. "I know a boot-ee-ful hotel just a wee drive from shere—here, I mean," he said. "Wery, wery romantic. We could check out their nightslub—I mean nightclub." Matthew downed the rest of his club soda, which Mia was sure Norman thought was vodka or gin straight up.

Mia smiled at Matthew and caressed him under his chin with a fingertip. "Maybe, sweetie. Just maybe."

"C'mon," he pressed, slipping his elbow off the edge of the table as though he were too drunk to sit up by himself. "It's Saturday night. We'll dance, ship . . . I mean *sip* some champlagne, and see what else the night holds for us . . ."

"Okay," she said on a giggle. "Let's go."

"Wait a minute," Matthew whispered so only she could hear. "I just realized that we shouldn't leave together. It might deter him from following us. It's me he wants to hurt, not you. If he thinks we're both out there, he might not come after me."

"You're right," she whispered back. "Sweetheart," she said loud enough for Norman, "why don't you go rev up the car and get the air-conditioning all cranked up for me. I'll just go powder my nose in the ladies' room."

"You got it, darlin'," Matthew replied. "But I'm not letting you out of my sight without a kissie-wissie."

She looked into his eyes, hoping to see that he really meant it, that he wanted one last kiss before they had to separate—for the showdown and forever. But all she saw in his gaze was lust.

Why do you keep expecting more? she asked herself. *Just let him go.*

If only it were that easy.

Mia stood and forced a smile. "See you soon, sweetie," she said, and turned toward the women's bathroom. With her peripheral vision, she could see Norman watching her. And she felt his gaze boring a hole into her back.

At the bathroom door, she dared a glance at Norman. He was watching Matthew. Matthew threw a few bills onto the table, then got up, and Norman practically jumped out of his seat. Matthew walked out the door of MacDougal's, and Norman stood by his stool at the bar, frantically waving a ten-dollar bill.

"Service!" he shouted to the bartender. "I need to settle my bill."

But the bartender was ignoring him while he filled two mugs of beer at once. Norman was turning beet red.

Now, she told herself. *Slip out the door while he's waiting to pay!* Mia ducked behind a large party that was leaving and got herself in the middle of them. Norman was still at the bar, waving his ten, shouting at the bartender to give him his bill.

Mia slipped out the door and let out the breath she was holding. She saw Matthew up ahead, walking to his car very slowly. She ducked down behind a minivan midway between the door to MacDougal's and where Matthew had parked his car way in the back. She slung her purse across the front of her body and grabbed the cell phone, gripping it in her fist. Okay. Everything was going to be okay. *The minute Norman comes out and heads toward Matthew, I'm calling the police. They're just a block from here. They'll come in two seconds.*

Please let this go down okay, she prayed again.

Please.

* * *

Matthew leaned against his car, breathing in the warm summer air. In, out. In, out. In, out. He was calmer than he expected. Perfectly calm actually.

Because he was ready. So damned ready to beat the hell out of Norman.

His brother's murderer.

The murderer of three other men—and who knew who else.

And the psycho who'd tried to hurt Mia.

He couldn't wait to get his hands on that psychotic, creepy twerp. What a sicko. Matthew had no doubt that Norman would come after him. If the wedding ring wasn't enough bait, the taunting he'd received from both Matthew and Mia surely had put Norman over the edge.

Not that Norman was appropriately dressed for murder. He wore an ill-fitting tan suit with a wide navy-and-cream-striped tie. Perhaps Norman liked to dress up for such occasions, Matthew thought darkly.

It had taken all Matthew could do at the table earlier not to shove his fist in Newman's doughy stomach and pummel him.

And it seemed that it had taken all Mia could do not to throw up all over Newman's suit. Truth be told, Matthew knew Mia well enough to recognize the subtleties of her facial expressions, and it had been clear to him that he'd gone a little too far at the table. She was sensitive about his coming on to her when she was all decked out in her Margot look. He needed to respect that, yes, but he also needed her to realize that no matter what she looked like, she was Mia. Not Margot. Not a fantasy woman her ex-husband wanted. Just Mia.

He'd put on quite a show of desire back there in MacDougal's, but it had been for Newman's benefit. Matthew hoped Mia knew that. The more jealous Newman became, the angrier he'd get.

Matthew wanted to make damned sure Newman was in the mood for murder. Because tonight was Matthew's only opportunity to nail the bastard.

Mia, he's married, for God's sake . . . Is nothing sacred? Newman's words echoed in his mind, and he wondered what motivated the sicko to murder married men who tried to pick up the decoy he himself hired. From the moment he'd first spotted Norman inside, he'd been wondering about motive. He couldn't figure out the connection between hiring Mia in secret as a decoy and then killing the men who were enticed by her. Why target married men? If it was the idea of Mia as a decoy or as a woman he wanted and couldn't have that motivated him to kill, why not kill any man who tried to pick her up? Why *married* men? Why, why, why, why?

Perhaps the fact that the victims were married gave the sicko some sort of weird justification in his mind. *They're committing adultery, so they're no good, anyway.* Was that Newman's way of thinking?

It's yours, Matthew realized, a knot forming in his stomach. *It's you who think adulterers are among the worst forms of humanity.* But weren't they?

People make mistakes, Matthew, he'd heard his brother say over and over. *People sometimes choose wrong when they marry. People fall out of love. Sometimes innocent people get hurt because of it. Yes, it's "wrong," but so is denying yourself what you really want.*

Denying yourself what you really want. Perhaps that was the only thing his brother had ever said that made sense. But there *was* right and wrong. And denying yourself *wrong* was *right.* Which was what Matthew was doing. He had a cheater's blood in his veins; his father had proven it, and his brother had corroborated that by his own actions. Denying himself a wife, a family, so as not to hurt them, was right.

The only kink in that line of thinking was that Matthew couldn't imagine himself cheating. Cheat on Mia? Not in a million years.

So if you wouldn't cheat on her, why would you have to deny yourself the pleasure of her company in your life?

You could go slowly, see how it feels.

It didn't feel comfortable already, and he was just *thinking* about it.

God, he was frustrated. Frustrated by his feelings for Mia, frustrated by the case. He ran a hand through his hair and glanced up at the night sky. The moon was a crescent—

The moon!

Suddenly Matthew realized why Norman had hired Margot once a month: for the *new moon,* which rendered it invisible. The lack of moonlight would have provided a cloak of darkness in a parking lot that might be lit by streetlamps. But tonight, only three weeks after the last murder, the moon shone brightly overhead.

Why didn't Norman wait until next week for the phases of the moon to complete themselves? Why risk being seen?

He shook his head. Again, question after question after question, and no answers.

Except for the killer's identity. Matthew's hands itched. He wanted them around Norman Newman's neck so bad—

He heard the door to MacDougal's open, and he

forced himself not to look. He wanted to appear as though he wasn't the least bit interested in who was coming and going, and he wanted Norman to think creeping up on him was possible. But he was positioned so that he could see out of his peripheral vision once someone got just a bit farther in the parking lot.

Dammit. The person who'd left MacDougal's wasn't Newman. It was that perky brunette with the freckles, the one who'd asked him to dance twice. Damn. Was she the one he'd promised a dance to, or had it been the redhead?

He turned slightly away so that she couldn't see his face. The last thing he needed was for Newman to see him talking to another woman. He might go berserk on Mia's behalf and try to kill both him and the brunette.

He dared a glance out of the corner of his eye. No one was in the parking lot. He breathed a deep sigh of relief. The brunette had either gone back inside or she'd headed to the other side of MacDougal's for the pass-through to Bridge Avenue.

Tick-tock. Tick-tock. Where the hell was that cretin?

The door opened again, and a couple came out and quickly turned the corner for the avenue.

Where the hell was Newman? Had he decided to forgo a chance to kill Matthew to have some time alone with Mia? Holy hell. Did he have her cornered in the back of the bar? Matthew's heart suddenly palpitated—did he have her trapped in the men's room? The bathroom seemed to be Newman's favorite place for his idea of romancing a woman.

Stop letting your imagination run away with you, he

told himself. *Newman wouldn't miss the opportunity to come after you. It's you he wants dead, not Mia.* If he wanted Mia dead, he would have made his move at least four times already. Newman wanted him six feet under. Matthew had seen it in his eyes. Still, he wanted to check on Mia, make sure she was safely inside.

There weren't any windows on the front of the building. Not that Matthew could risk running up toward the nightclub to sneak a peek for Mia anyway. If he and Norman met along the way, Matthew's plan could be ruined.

He'd just have to wait for the cretin.

Come out, you spineless weasel. I'm right here.

Chapter Eighteen

Her heart thumping in her chest, Mia glanced at her watch. Five minutes had passed since Matthew had left MacDougal's and Mia had ducked between the minivan and the sports car, but Norman still hadn't come out.

What was he waiting for? Wasn't he worried he'd miss his opportunity to murder the married man who'd failed his test with the decoy?

Cell phone in her fist and tape recorder on in her purse, Mia took a gulp of the hot, sticky night air, barely able to breathe as it was, and darted on her haunches to the front of the minivan. She peeked around the huge tire at the door to MacDougal's. Not a soul was around. She glanced in the opposite direction at the far end of the dark parking lot for Matthew. She caught a glimpse of his wavy blond wig and breathed a sigh of relief.

Mia darted back out of view and sagged against the tire. Her thighs were killing her from crouching, but it was either that or skin her knees against the hot, rough pavement. She looked at her watch. Only another minute had passed since the last time she looked, but she didn't understand why Norman hadn't come running out after Matthew. Was he still trying to pay his bar tab?

Damn. Where *was* that psycho?

She wouldn't be able to keep poking her head around the tire to see if Norman was coming; that was too risky. If Norman spotted her. . . . But she could *hear* the door to MacDougal's open and close, and she could quickly take a peek to see if it was Norman coming out. Then she could call the police.

Deep breath. Everything was going to be all right.

So far, only a couple holding hands had left MacDougal's, preceded by a petite brunette wearing espadrille sandals that tied halfway up her leg. Since Mia didn't hear them coming her way, she assumed the couple and the woman had gone the other way, toward the Bridge Avenue pass-through on the other side of the nightclub.

The door whooshed open. That must be him! Mia thought, her heart racing a mile a minute. She darted over by the edge of the tire, then craned her neck to see if it was Norman.

But it wasn't. Only another couple, hand in hand, turning to the right for the Bridge Avenue pass-through.

"La, la, la—ye-ah, ye-ah," came the drunken voices of young women singing at the top of their lungs. The cacophony was coming from over the fence, on Bridge Avenue. *"Ye-ah . . . ye-ah, ba-by."*

Please stop singing, she sent telepathically. *Please! I need to be able to hear the door open and footsteps!*

Panic gripped her by the throat, and she dared

to peer around the tire one more time. And suddenly everything went black.

Strong hands had clamped around her neck and were squeezing, squeezing. Squeezing harder. The cell phone fell from her fist and barely made a sound as it hit the ground.

Mia saw white dots in the black, then all white, then black.

Fight! she told herself. *Fight anyway you can.*

She jabbed her elbow back as hard as she could, and the hands loosened for just a second, enough for Mia to gulp in some sticky air.

It's me he wants to kill, she thought. *Me.*

Matthew! she screamed in her head. *Help me!* But she had no voice. No air.

Get an arm out of his grip and elbow him in the face, anywhere! Mia told herself. *Save yourself so that you can save Matthew when he goes after him. He sneaked up on you—he'll sneak up on Matthew.*

Mia wrested her arm out of his grasp long enough to jab it back in his stomach, and the hands around her neck released. She quickly turned over and prepared to kick Norman in the face.

"Ye-ah, ye-ah, baby. La, la, la . . ." sang the women on the other side of the fence.

But it wasn't Norman Newman who was staring at her with a murderous glint.

It was a woman.

A woman she'd never seen before in her life.

No, wait a minute. The espadrilles! It was the woman who'd come out of MacDougal's five minutes ago.

The woman pulled out a gun and pointed it at her.

Mia went completely still.

"What are you doing, hiding out here, you slut!" the woman hissed.

"What. . . What?" Mia managed to croak as the woman lowered to inches above Mia's face.

The woman narrowed her eyes and sneered, the gun inching closer and closer to Mia's forehead. "What is that damned racket?" The woman lifted her head and seemed to be training her ears for the direction of the singing.

"Ye-ah, baby . . ."

The woman spit on Mia's cheek. "Planning on going home with that blond man when I'm not looking, Margot? You're such a dirty whore!"

Sickened, her heart pounding in her chest, Mia stared at the angelic-faced woman before her. The woman was all of five feet four with a smattering of freckles across her nose and cheeks, pretty green eyes, like a cat's, and bouncy, shiny brown hair. She was petite, yet strong, compactly built, like a gymnast or a bodybuilder, even. Mia was at least three inches taller, yet the woman was much stronger.

"He wasn't even the one I wanted to go after you! You've ruined everything, you stupid bitch!" The woman cocked the trigger and put it to Mia's temple.

For a moment, she saw black, then stars, then black; then everything came into focus again. Her head was spinning.

"But today's your lucky day, Margot," the woman continued, "because he'll do. What a pig, trying to pick you up when he's clearly married. I saw his wedding ring! He's a pig!"

"Yes," Mia said, hoping agreement would calm the woman down enough for Mia to try to reason with her. "He is a pig."

The woman backhanded Mia hard across the face. "But you were going to have sex with him anyway, you filthy whore! I don't pay you to sleep with anyone. I pay you to *test* them."

The force of the woman's slap slammed Mia's head against the pavement. "No," she croaked. "No. I wasn't going to sleep with him. I swear. I was leading him out here for you! Why do you think I was hiding here?"

"What are you talking about?" the woman asked, narrowing her eyes.

"I know what you do," Mia said. "I know that you stop those bad men from ever cheating on their wives again. I know that's why you send me the pictures."

The woman stared at Mia, her expression softening just slightly. "They deserved to die. Each and every one of them. No one else was stopping them from their cheating ways. It was up to me. It's filthy whores like you with your tight, skimpy clothing and makeup who steal them from their wives. You should be ashamed of yourself, you disgusting bitch."

"I only dress like this when I'm working," Mia said. "When you hire me for a job. When you want me to test the fidelity of a married man. A woman doesn't steal away a married man; he chooses to cheat. That's why you kill the men, isn't it? Because they *choose* to cheat."

"That's right. They choose to cheat. And I choose to kill them."

Relief flooded Mia at the confession.

"That blond man came on to me so hard, in

such a disgusting way," Mia said, adding an expression of revulsion. "So I led him out here, then told him I left something inside. But I really just ducked here, waiting for you to come and do what you have to do."

"That is what I do," the woman whispered. "I do what I have to do. I had to kill all four of them."

"I know you did," Mia said. "The last man, Robert Gray, the one at Chumley's, he also came on to me very strongly." *Confess*, Mia prayed. *Confess for the tape recorder.*

"I watched that pig pick up different women every Saturday night at eight o'clock for six months, sometimes several women a night. What a pig! Disgusting pig. He was married, but what did he care? He just cheated and cheated!"

"I know," Mia said softly. "I understand."

The woman's eyes darkened with rage. "Cheaters never prosper!" she woman hissed.

"No," Mia agreed. "They don't. Thanks to you."

The gun still rested against her temple. Mia's breath was so shallow, she could barely hear herself.

The woman was staring at her. "They all cheated, weekend after weekend. I watched them all, time and again. I saw the way they'd take off their wedding rings—if they bothered to wear them at all—and go pick up some slut like you." She reached into an open pouch at her waist and pulled out a large square of electric tape.

Mia's heart began booming in her chest. She tried to find her voice to scream, but no sound came forth. The singing from the other side of the fence was so loud that any sound Mia managed to croak would be drowned out anyway.

I love you, Matthew, she mentally told him. *I love you so much. . . .*

The woman plastered the tape hard against Mia's mouth and smoothed it out. "They didn't even care who saw them with their tongues down your throat," she continued. "Like clockwork, they'd show up at their favorite bars, same time every weekend, get drunk, and go after women. Bastards." She spit on Mia's forehead.

Again, everything went black; then a flash of white sparked behind Mia's eyes, followed by stars. She felt the woman blowing in her face and gently slapping her cheek.

"Don't you faint on me, you filthy whore," the woman said. "You're a slut! You're disgusting. It's all your fault that they cheat. I thought I could trust you. I thought you were a good girl who never went with a married man. But you're just like *her.* You were going to leave with that blond man and have sex with him. But instead, you're going to die."

Shut up! Matthew mentally yelled. *I can't hear if the door opens!*

A group of young women on Bridge Avenue were singing a pop song at the top of their lungs. Dammit! He wished he could jump the fence and tell them to shut their traps.

Calm down, man. They would either quit singing or keep walking eventually. But they'd been stationary for so long that Matthew sensed they were waiting in line to get into one of the more crowded nightclubs. The singing continued. *Shut up!* he yelled in his head again. *Shut the hell up!*

"You big jerk!"

Matthew spun around to find Norman Newman stalking toward him, his hands hidden behind his back.

Here we go, he thought. *Here we go.*

"Where's Mia?" Norman demanded. "I want to talk to her!"

Relief coursed through him that Mia was clearly safe. "She's using the ladies' room," Matthew said, gesturing to MacDougal's.

"You don't deserve her," Norman growled.

"Oh, I think I do," Matthew said, wiggling his eyebrows to really piss off Newman. "The wife won't do what I have a feeling Mia will do—and do *well.*"

A vein popped out in Norman's temple, and his face turned beet red. "Don't talk that way about Mia! She's an angel."

"Whatever," Matthew responded. "I don't know her. I only know she looks damned good."

"You're vile!" Norman said. "You make me sick. You're married. What does your wife think of you cheating on her?"

"What do I care?" Matthew shrugged. "As long as I get some hot sex on the side."

Norman took a swing; Matthew moved his shoulders a fraction and avoided the clumsy punch.

So he doesn't have a weapon in his hands, Matthew thought. *But that doesn't mean he doesn't have one hidden in his waistband or sock. Don't get careless.*

"Why did you do it?" Matthew asked, locking eyes with Newman. With the man who killed his brother.

"Do what?" Norman snapped.

"Kill those men," Matthew said. "Why?"

"What are you talking about? What men?"

"There he is!" shouted a male voice up along the side of MacDougal's. He must have come from the Bridge Avenue pass-through. "John, I found him!"

"Oh, no!" Norman whimpered. He began stamping his feet. "They're gonna take me back, and I haven't squared things away with Mia!"

Matthew stared at Norman, wondering what the hell was going on. "Who are those guys?"

Norman continued to stamp his feet, but then he waved at the men. "They're my friends," he told Matthew. "They're the only ones who care about me."

"Ye-ah, yeah! Baby, baby. La, la, la! Ye-ah!" Dammit, would those drunken women ever shut up?

The men, wearing white shirts and white pants and white shoes, jogged over. "Roger, we've been combing Center City all night for you. You know the rules. You keep running away like this and we'll have to take appropriate measures to protect you."

"What the—" Matthew looked from the men to Norman and back again. Who the hell was Roger?

"Roger, do you know this man?" one of the men asked Norman.

"No," said Norman. "He was trying to pick up the woman I like."

Matthew leaned over to read the patch sewn onto the men's shirts. *Center City Gardens Hospital.*

Gardens Hospital? That was—

"Why do you keep calling him Roger?" Matthew asked one of the men. "His name is Norman Newman."

"I'm only Norman Newman outside!" Norman

screeched. "Inside, I'm Roger Shea. Like Shea Stadium. Oooh, I know this song! *Yeah, baby! La, la, la!*" Norman began to sing along with the women, still crooning on the other side of the fence.

Matthew's head was spinning. Inside? *Huh?*

"Norman Newman?" the other man repeated. "Is that your real name, Roger?"

Norman swished his lips from left to right, then hung his head and nodded.

"He admitted himself with identification that said Roger Shea," one of the men explained to Matthew.

"Center City Gardens Hospital is for the mentally ill, isn't it?" Matthew asked as one of the men soothed Norman and held him firmly by the arm. "Norman is a patient?"

The man nodded. "He's run away five times now, but yes, he's a patient. He checked himself in three weeks ago."

Five times? Three weeks ago? Robert had been murdered three weeks ago. "Is it possible to find out if he was accounted for on a certain night?" Matthew asked.

"Sure, if you have proof you're a close relative." the man said. "You can stop by the records office and see Bobbie or Mary, depending on whether it's a weeknight or weekend you're talking about."

"It was a weekend," Matthew said absently. "A Saturday night. June nineteenth."

The man soothing Norman glanced at Matthew and seemed to decide it would be harmless enough to give him some information. "Oh, I can tell you right now that he was accounted for from six P.M. until two A.M. June nineteenth, a Saturday night. That was the night he checked in. I know because it was my first night on the job, and I was assigned to his ward. I sat with him for eight hours straight. He was crying like a baby."

"Was not!" Norman whined. "I wasn't crying!"

"It's okay to cry, Norman," the other man said, punching his coworker on the arm.

"He's despicable," Norman hissed, pointing at Matthew. "He's married, but he's cheating with the woman I'm in love with."

Matthew shook his head softly.

"He'll get his, Roger," one of the men said to Norman. "They always do. C'mon, big guy. Let's get you back to your room. We're going to have to talk to Dr. Field about the best way to keep you from running away again. You have to be protected from yourself, Roger. That's the rule. We explained that when you checked in. You're on serious medication, Rog. You can't just run off."

"Sorry," Norman said. "But how am I going to convince Mia to marry me?"

"Hey, Norman, I thought you were living with your mom," Matthew said. "Did you tell the principal that because you were embarrassed to tell him the truth? That you'd checked into the Gardens Hospital?"

"I didn't want Mia to find out," Norman said, stamping his feet again. "If I told Principal Ashton, Mia would have found out. So I told him I had to take care of my mother after her stroke. I had two weeks' vacation coming to me."

"Your mother didn't have a stroke?" Matthew asked.

Norman started to cry. "She did, too! But she has an aide. Part of my salary pays for it!"

"Let's go, Rog," the man said to Norman. He

slipped Matthew one of his cards. Matthew glanced down at it. *Center City Gardens Hospital. John Dumont, Senior Orderly.* Then the men led Norman, who was singing along with the women again, away.

Jesus. Matthew shook his head.

And then he froze.

If Norman wasn't the killer, who was?

And where the hell was Mia?

Chapter Nineteen

"You're going to die, you filthy whore!" the woman hissed over and over. She straddled Mia, one knee pressed hard into her stomach. "You slept with my husband. You slept with *so* many women's husbands. And you're going to suffer terribly for your behavior, you slut!"

The woman shoved the gun harder against Mia's temple, and again, Mia saw black, then stars.

"You know what, you dirty slut?" the woman said. "I'm going to kill you with my bare hands. I want to squeeze the life out of your disgusting, whoring body." One hand clamped tight against Mia's neck, while the woman dropped the gun in the pouch at her waist. "I'm going to choke the life out of you, you scummy bitch."

Mia grabbed the woman's hand and tried to push her away, but the woman was too strong. Both hands were now around Mia's neck, squeezing, squeezing, squeezing.

I love you so much, Matthew . . .

I love you, Margot.

I tried. I really tried. . . .

"Die, you filthy slut!" the woman snarled. "Die!"

The hands squeezed and squeezed, and everything went black. And then suddenly, the hands released. Mia sucked in air, her own hands flying up to her neck to gently rub it. She gasped for air, coughing and choking.

"What the hell!" the woman yelled as she was dragged off Mia.

Matthew!

Mia got to her feet. Matthew and the woman were wrestling on the ground.

"She has a gun, Matthew!" Mia choked out.

The gun was in the woman's hand, and Matthew was struggling with her, the gun pointed up in the air. Mia saw the cell phone just under the minivan; she lunged for it and scooped it up, then dialed 911 and hastily gasped out the information.

"She's a filthy whore!" the woman screamed. "And you're a dirty cheater!"

"Oh, my God, it's you!" Matthew exclaimed. "You asked me to dance!"

"But you only had eyes for the whore," the woman shouted. She kicked up in the air, but Matthew sidestepped her.

"You killed my brother," Matthew said flatly. He tried to twist her arm, but the woman was strong and held her own.

"I killed a lot of cheaters," the woman said.

Sirens wailed. As the police cars raced up Bridge Avenue and turned into the parking lot, the singing finally stopped. "My brother was Robert Gray. You murdered him outside of Chumley's."

The woman's eyes gleamed. "Ah, yes, three weeks

ago. He was so easy. Stab, stab, and down he went like the spineless jellyfish he was."

A surge of adrenaline shot through Matthew, and he smacked the gun out of her hand. It clattered under the sports car, and Matthew pinned her to the ground.

"Cheaters never prosper!" the woman screamed.

"And killers don't get away with their crimes," Matthew responded.

"You ruined my chance to get Benjamin Slovel!" the woman shouted as two police cars raced toward them. "He was the one I wanted, not you! I watched him at MacDougal's every Saturday night at ten o'clock. Right after your filthy brother. I watched him show up here, take off his wedding ring, and have sex with women in the backseat of his car for a month!"

"So why did you have to hire a decoy?" Matthew asked. "Why not just go after the men themselves? Why hire Margot?"

The woman tried to spit at Mia again, but now Mia was too far away. "Because that dirty whore looks exactly like the woman who stole my husband. He'd come to these bars, too, picking up women, taking them to motels. Screwing them. I watched him do it. And then I killed him. Shot him right in the nuts."

"So you were killing your husband over and over by killing these men?" Mia asked. "And using Margot—me—to make you angry enough?"

"So, the eye-candy has a brain," the woman snapped.

"What's going on here?" a police officer called, gun drawn. His partner and two other cops had surrounded the threesome.

"I have the whole confession on tape," Mia shouted. "This woman killed Robert Gray in Chumley's parking lot three weeks ago. She's killed three other men, too. She was going to kill tonight, but we set her up and stopped her."

"Cheaters never prosper," the woman screamed. "Those men deserved to die! You deserve to die," she shouted at Matthew. "He's a married man! Look at his wedding ring. And he tried to pick up that whore!"

The police handcuffed the woman and read her her rights. "Let's all head to the station," an officer said, leading the woman to the police car. "You two go in the other car."

Mia's legs buckled, and Matthew caught her. "It's over," he said. "It's all over."

Yes, she thought, tears stinging her eyes. *It's all over.*

"We should arrest you for withholding crucial evidence for solving these murders and for conducting an investigation on your own," Detective Osgood snapped at Matthew and Mia.

They'd been in the Center City precinct for two hours, telling their story, sharing the tape. The woman confessed every detail of her crimes to anyone who'd listen. Her name was Ginny Loomis, and she lived on the other side of Baywater.

"You're both damned lucky everything turned out okay," the detective continued. "Both of you could have been killed."

"We had to try," Matthew told him. "We knew we had one night, one opportunity, to catch a cold-blooded killer."

"You should have come to us," the detective countered.

"We're here now," Matthew said. "And all we want is to make sure that psychopath is put away for the rest of her life."

"She'll probably end up in Center City Gardens after her trial," the detective said. "If she's considered *sane* enough to stand trial. She's totally gone."

"Well, she and Norman Newman can be roommates," Mia said numbly.

Matthew glanced at Mia, who'd been very quiet till this point. She'd corroborated what Matthew had told the police, adding in details when necessary, but for the most part, she remained silent. Matthew had filled in Mia about Norman Newman during their ride to the precinct. She'd been shocked to learn the truth about him.

"He checked into the Gardens on his own under an assumed name with fake identification," the detective said. "He has now been formally charged with the kidnapping of Mia Anderson and will be arrested at the Gardens in about a half hour."

Mia nodded, her gaze on the scarred wooden table.

"The two of you can go," the detective said. "We'll take it from here."

Matthew reached over to help Mia up, but she darted away from him.

"I'm fine," she said. "I just want to get out of these clothes and take a long, hot bath."

As they walked out of the precinct, there was finally a breeze stirring the warm, muggy night air. "Well," he said. "We did it."

She nodded.

"You must be exhausted," he said. "I know I am."

"We should get some sleep," she said flatly. "You don't have to walk me back to Margot's. Now that both Norman and the killer are behind bars, I feel safe again."

"I'll walk you," he offered. He didn't want to let her go, but he didn't want to push. She had been through quite a lot tonight.

"I'd really like to walk alone," she said. "Digest everything that just happened. Or maybe just forget about it."

Forget about it. Of course she wanted to forget about it, Matthew realized.

"Goodbye, Matthew," she said, holding his gaze.

He had so much to say. But he was exhausted and wiped out, and when he opened his mouth to speak, nothing came out. He clamped his mouth shut. If only he could just grab her in his arms and hold her, then take her home with him and snuggle with her in bed and wake up fresh.

But wake up to what? He couldn't give her what she wanted.

"Goodbye," he said softly.

He thought he saw tears well up in her eyes, but she turned away before he could be sure.

And then she walked away.

Straight out of his life.

"This just in from News Channel Six—earlier this evening police arrested a woman who's been dubbed the Nightclub Killer by media at the scene. Ginny Loomis is charged with allegedly killing at least four men in and around Center City . . ."

Mia stared numbly at the television, at the blond newscaster relating the few details about the arrest. She sat on the sofa in Margot's huge, empty apartment, her knees drawn up to her chest.

"The brother of one of her victims," the newscaster continued, "together with a female partner whose connection to the case is as yet unknown, set up a sting operation in which the alleged killer was caught. Center City police are grateful to the Good Samaritans for their help in this investigation . . ."

It was truly over. And as good as that made Mia feel, she couldn't stop the tears from falling down her cheeks.

Goodbye . . .

He'd let her go, just like that.

And she knew she would never see him again.

"Mia! Mia, wake up!"

Someone was gently shaking her shoulder. Mia's eyes popped open; she bolted upright. "What the—

"Margot!"

Mia jumped up and flew into her sister's arms. She stepped back and looked at her sister, into her eyes, then grabbed her into a fierce hug. "Oh, Margot! I was worried sick about you!"

"I'm so sorry, Mia," Margot said. "I hope you know how sorry I am."

"I'm going to make us a pot of tea. You sit down and don't budge." Mia saw tears well in her sister's eyes.

"Okay."

Margot did as she was told, and Mia took a long look at her. Her sister was pale and looked way too thin, dark circles under her eyes. She wore tight, faded jeans and a black tank top and sneakers.

Her hair was in a low ponytail, and she didn't have on a stitch of makeup. For once, Margot Daniels looked a lot like Mia Anderson.

Mia headed into the kitchen and put a kettle on to boil. Her sister was home. Safe. Mia lifted her gaze to the ceiling and sent a silent prayer of thanks.

"Let me help," Margot called from the living room. "I think you've done quite enough for me. I saw the news reports."

Mia had hoped that Margot would be watching the news regularly for any reports about Robert Gray's murder. As she'd drifted off to sleep on Margot's couch, she'd prayed that her sister had been watching television tonight and had heard that the killer had been caught. That it was safe for her to come home.

Mia walked back into the living room with a tray containing the teapot she'd given Margot as a housewarming gift, plus the two lumps of sugar each of the twins liked in their tea.

As Mia set down the tray on the coffee table, Margot put her hand over Mia's. "I never meant for you to get involved." Again tears welled. "I don't even know what you did or how you did it, but thank you."

"I had help," Mia said. "A lot of help."

"That man—the brother of . . ."

"Robert Gray," Mia said flatly.

Margot's gaze was on the floor. She nodded. "So I guess you know everything, then."

"Not everything, Margot." Mia poured two cups of the chamomile tea. "I don't know *why*. Why would you want to be a decoy? And why in the world would you choose being a decoy over a man like Justin Graves?"

Surprise passed over Margot's face and then sadness. She stood and walked over to the wall of windows. "I've been a decoy for a long, long time, Mia. For about five years."

Mia was shocked "*Five* years?"

"I had trouble making ends meet as an interior decorator when I first moved to Center City," Margot explained. "My first client was a very sweet woman with very little funds—which was why she hired me. Her husband was demanding a divorce, and when he moved out of their home, he took all their furniture with him. Even though she put him through dental school, he was refusing to pay alimony."

"That hardly sounds fair," Mia commented, adding the sugar cubes to their tea.

"Oh, Mia, you should have seen this woman. Tears streaming down her face, she told me about his affairs, and how she'd finally gotten up the courage to confront him. But she didn't have proof for the divorce proceedings that he was cheating."

"So she hired a decoy," Mia said.

Margot nodded. "She'd contacted a private investigator, who put her in touch with an independent undercover decoy."

"And that's when you decided to become a decoy, too?"

"I was drawn to the idea of providing women with the proof they needed of their husbands' infidelity."

Put that way, the job almost sounded like a worthy cause. "But what you had to do to get that proof . . ."

Margot dropped her gaze to the floor, then looked up at Mia. "I know. But at first, I felt empowered. I felt like Superwoman, Mia. I was twenty-four and didn't have a care in the world, or so I thought."

Mia put her hand on her sister's shoulder. "You didn't want to have a care in the world, you mean."

Margot nodded. "I'd been living on my own in Center City since I was eighteen, since Mama and Daddy were killed. I was broke, lonely, had boyfriend after boyfriend who didn't really care about me, and the nature of decoy work requires that you desensitize to a lot of things, a lot of issues."

"And that's exactly what you needed then, to desensitize yourself?"

Margot nodded. "To life."

"Oh, Margot. I wish you'd turned to me."

"You had your own problems, Mia."

That was true.

"Your way was to marry a man who was completely wrong for you, and I was helpless to stop you. I used to comfort myself by assuring myself that one day, you'd see the light, and that you'd be okay. I always knew you'd be okay. But I wasn't so sure about myself."

Mia thought about the combination lock to Margot's metal box, the anniversary date of Mia's divorce from David Anderson.

"I hated that man so much," Margot said. "What a shit he was."

"I know—now," Mia said, a gentle smile on her lips. "I had a lot of growing up to do."

"Me, too."

Mia sipped her tea and leaned back against the sofa. "So when did your work as a decoy lose its appeal as empowering?"

"After about two years," Margot replied, leaning

back with her tea herself. "I'm surprised it took that long."

"What happened?" Mia asked.

"Well, it started with little things," Margot said. "For example, I gave a client the proof of the pictures, and she tore them up in front of me. Said it wasn't her husband, that she'd made a mistake in hiring me. She wanted the negatives, and she threatened me. Said if I didn't give her the negatives and forget I'd ever laid eyes on her or her husband, she'd kill me."

Mia's teacup trembled in her hand, and she set it down on the coffee table. "Weren't you scared out of your mind?"

Margot nodded. "I suppose the job was always dangerous, but I started to become aware of how dangerous at that point. Suddenly I realized that married men were groping me in public places, coming on to me. That I'd hired myself out as an object. My job was to be an object."

"Your job was to provide women with proof of their husbands' infidelity," Mia said, surprised that she was defending her sister's line of work. "Your intentions were very honorable."

Margot glanced at Mia and bit her lip. "But I stopped feeling that part of the equation. The job was so sleazy, and after a couple of years, I began to feel sleazy. I began to feel that all I was was sexy, a sexual object, a fantasy. Nothing more."

"But, Margot, what about Justin? He seems like a terrific guy, and he loved you."

Tears welled in Margot's eyes, and she put down her teacup. "When you think you're nothing, it's hard to believe that anyone can love you."

Now tears welled up in Mia's eyes. "Oh, Margot. Is that really how you think of yourself? As nothing?"

Margot was silent for a moment, then nodded and burst into tears. She covered her face with her hands, her body wracked with her sobs.

Mia pulled her sister into her arms and rocked her. "Honey, you're more than something. You're everything."

"To who?" Margot managed through her sobs.

"To me, for starters.

"But more importantly, you need to be everything to you. You've got so much going for you, Margot. You're so intelligent and kind and funny. You're such an individual. And you're one of the most talented interior decorators I've ever seen."

"You've never even seen my work," Margot said through her sniffles, and Mia knew her sister was feeling a little bit stronger.

"I have, too, seen your work," Mia said. "At Justin's."

Surprise flashed in Margot's eyes. "How did you come across Justin anyway?"

Mia took a deep breath. "I'm sorry about this, but in order to help you and get to the bottom of Robert Gray's murder, Matthew and I had to root through your stuff. We found the letter from Justin."

Margot burst into tears.

Mia grabbed her sister's hand and rubbed it. "Margot, he loves you. He still loves you."

"I'm not worthy of him," Margot said in such a low voice that Mia wasn't sure she heard correctly.

"Margot, you are worthy. You're worthy of anything and anyone you want. He sure thinks you're worthy."

Margot sniffled and picked up her teacup. She took a sip and then wrapped the cup with her hands. "You think he'd talk to me if I went to see him?"

Mia smiled. "I'm sure he would."

"I'm ready to change my life, Mia. I just don't know where to begin."

"I'll help you," Mia assured her. "And I do know where to begin."

"Where?" Margot asked, her pale brown doe eyes shimmering with tears.

Mia smiled softly. "With us, honey. We're both going to change our lives, and we're going to do it together. And we're going to start with being sisters. Real sisters. We'll help each other through."

"But you don't need help," Margot said. "You're so together, you love your work, you have that cute house."

"I hate my life," Mia confessed. "I'm not together. Look at me—I don't even look like myself. I changed my appearance to suit a man, for heaven's sake. And I'm not comfortable in that house! I like teaching—in fact, I love teaching. But I hate Baywater. I really do."

"I do like Center City," Margot said. "I always have. I love the glitter of the city, all the cultural activities, and there's so much interior decorating work to be had, if I get my act together to drum up business."

"Then Center City is where you should stay. And I think your first client should be yourself and this austere apartment."

Margot glanced around. "Yeah, I always hated this apartment. So cold. I guess I kept it this way so that it would never feel like home. So that my *life* wouldn't feel like I was home. Do you know what I mean?"

"Oh, Margot. I know *exactly* what you mean."

Over scrambled eggs, bacon, and a lot of strong coffee, Mia filled in Margot on the investigation and her relationship with Matthew.

"And he just said goodbye and walked away?" Margot asked.

Now tears pooled in Mia's eyes. "Just walked away."

"So go after him!" Margot exclaimed. "Go after the man you love like I'm going to go after the man I love."

"But the man you love loves you back, Margot," Mia pointed out.

"It sure sounds to me like Matthew loves you," Margot said, sipping her coffee.

"Even if he does love me, it doesn't matter," Mia said. "He *won't* love me." Mia pushed her scrambled eggs around on her plate, her appetite gone.

"There's somewhere I want to take you today," Margot said, a twinkle in her eye. "Two places actually."

"Where?" Mia asked.

"You just leave that to me."

Matthew sat on the porch swing at Laurie's house, Robbie sleeping peacefully against his chest. He'd told Laurie that Robert's killer had been caught, some crazy woman who attacked men in parking lots of nightclubs. Robert had probably been playing darts, gone out to his car to drive home, and been attacked at random. Because the news reports were so vague with details, Matthew hadn't had to worry about Laurie finding out about the decoy business or exactly how he and Mia had set up the sting operation. Laurie had cried for the senselessness of it all, and Matthew had held her, letting her sob on his shoulder for as long as she needed. Finally, she'd said she was relieved that his murderer had been caught, that Robbie wouldn't have to grow up knowing that his father's killer hadn't been brought to justice.

Laurie had asked Matthew if he'd watch Robbie for a little while so that she could go lie down and rest. For the past hour, he'd cuddled his precious nephew against his heart. He would be happy to sleep out here all night with Robbie asleep in his arms.

You could give Robbie a cousin, that's what you could do. . . .

Laurie's words came back to him as Mia's face flashed into his mind. He wondered where she was right now, what she was doing.

Robbie stirred in Matthew's arms. "We got her," he whispered to Robbie. "She's behind bars where she'll stay for a long, long time. She'll never hurt anyone again. Your daddy's death has been avenged by justice."

Robbie's beautiful blue eyes opened, and he grabbed at Matthew's nose. Matthew let his nephew squeeze and grab at his face and ears, inhaling that delicious scent of baby powder.

Of life.

Robbie pulled Matthew's ear and laughed.

I'll tell you what you could do—you could give Robbie a cousin. . . .

Matthew closed his eyes and stared up at the

bright blue sky and thought about baby cousins and a woman named Mia.

"Okay, open your eyes!" Margot said, swiveling Mia's chair around. Mia opened her eyes and stared at herself in the mirror of Margot's hairstylist's station at Hot Cuts. Her mouth dropped open. "It looks exactly like the wig!"

"I told you Maria was a wizard," Margot said.

She certainly was. Margot had brought Mia's red wig to her hairstylist in Center City and instructed her to cut and color Mia's hair exactly like it. And exactly like it was what Mia had. Cut chin-length and released of its weight, Mia's usually straight hair now gently waved, just like the wig. And the color—the color was that of their mama's. The color that Mia had always wanted.

She now looked in the mirror and saw herself. The woman *she'd* always wanted to be. The woman she *was.*

"You look so much like her, Mia," Margot said, tears welling.

Mia smiled at Margot's reflection in the mirror, then hopped out of the chair and pulled her sister into a tight hug. "We don't look much like twins anymore," Mia pointed out.

"But we are," Margot said. "Inside."

Mia smiled.

"C'mon," Margot said, "I have one more surprise for you."

"What is it?" Mia asked.

Margot grabbed her hand and led her to her car. "It's about a forty-minute drive. So buckle up and enjoy the ride, sister dear."

They settled in Margot's sports car, and Margot turned on the radio and began singing along. Mia smiled. Her sibling seemed happy, and Mia knew Margot was going to be okay. They were both going to be okay.

But the moment Mia turned to glance out the window, all she saw was Matthew. Her heart lurching, Mia blinked back the tears stinging the backs of her eyes. She wondered what he was doing, what he was thinking.

If he was thinking of her.

Probably not.

Mia closed her eyes and tried to block his face from her mind, but those dark blue eyes, that shock of thick chestnut hair, that face, those shoulders, that chest. . . .

She loved him. She loved him so much her heart hurt. And instead of trying to rid his image from her mind, she gave into it and *felt* him. Felt his touch against her skin, felt his soft, strong lips against hers, felt his arms around her, his hands on her. . . . Suddenly, she felt better, lighter. . . .

"Okay, sleepyhead, you can open your eyes," Margot said.

Mia started. Had she actually fallen asleep? She glanced at her watch—almost an hour had passed since they'd left the hair salon. She glanced out the window. Margot had parked her car in front of a town green.

A large sign with white letters on a background of peaches read, *Welcome to Peach Haven.*

Mia smiled. "You wanted to see the old house?"

"Yes. But more importantly, I think you're going to want to see the old house."

Mia glanced at her sister in confusion, but Margot

only smiled cryptically and drove on to Bell Lane. She pulled up in front of the pale blue house, its white shutters and white porch gleaming in the early afternoon sunlight. "Oh, Margot, look. There's a *Sold* sign in the grass. The house was for sale, and someone bought it."

"Yeah, *you*," Margot said.

"What?" Mia asked, staring at Margot.

"I bought it in your name," Margot explained. "And yes, you can pay me back!"

"But how did you know, how did you—"

"I saw that it was for sale about a month ago, and I set the wheels in motion then," Margot said. "I wanted to surprise you."

"Surprise me, you did," Mia said. "Oh, Margot. It's my dream to live here, and to live in this house!"

"I know it is," Margot replied. "Let's go check out your new home."

"I love you so much, Margot," Mia said, grabbing her hand and squeezing it.

"I love you, too."

Chapter Twenty

Two weeks later

Mia taped the last of the moving boxes and wrote *Dishes and Delicate* across the top. She wiped her forehead, then arched her back. Packing up the contents of her house sure was hard work.

But it was worth every minute for where she was going. Home. To Peach Haven.

For the past two weeks, Margot had helped her pack. The twins had talked about everything and anything, and the work had gone by fast. In two weeks, Mia felt as though she'd gotten to know her sister for the first time.

Margot was in the midst of redecorating her apartment, and the changes were amazing. Where there was once cold beige leather, there was now plush red velvet and colorful throw pillows. There were fresh flowers, brightly colored rugs, and the watercolors that Margot had always loved. Her bedroom was now hot pink, and one extravagant boa was draped around her vanity. Margot had made new business cards for herself and was handing them out at every opportunity. So far, she'd gotten herself two clients.

And most importantly, she'd gotten herself back on track. She was on her way, and she was happy.

Mia smiled for her sister. They were *both* on their way. Mia had managed to score a job as a seventh and eighth grade English teacher at Peach Haven Middle School, and she'd given notice at Baywater. The principal had been sorry to hear that she was leaving, but under the circumstances, he understood at least one of the reasons for Mia's wanting to move out of Baywater. The police had alerted him to Norman Newman's arrest. There would be no more escaping for Norman, no more teaching. No more harassing of anyone.

Mew. Mew-mew. Mewwwww.

Mia spun around. The stray kitten she'd been feeding for the past two weeks had somehow sneaked into the house and was sitting on the kitchen table, lapping up the remains of the milk in Mia's bowl of cold cereal. "Cutie, milk is bad for your tummy! Here," she said, picking up the kitten in her hand and petting it. "Have some nice cool water. And how about I open you a can of tuna? Would you like that, Cutie?"

"Sounds like you've adopted yourself a pet."

Mia turned around. Matthew Gray stood in the doorway, separated from her by the screen door.

"Cutie's a good name for her."

Mia could only stare at him.

"Can I come in?" he asked.

She nodded, cuddling the kitten against her chest for support.

"Why do I have the feeling that that's not the wig," Matthew said, looking at her hair. "It's the real thing, isn't it?"

"Yes," she said.

"It looks great." He reached over and touched the gently waving ends, then ran his hand down the length of her head. "Oh, Mia."

She held his gaze, scared to death that he'd come to tell her he was thinking of her, that he missed her, but of course, he still couldn't be with her. Couldn't make a commitment.

She wasn't ready to hear that. She knew it already, but she couldn't hear it all over again.

"Margot came back," she told him. "In the middle of the night. She's okay now."

He nodded. "Good."

"She and Justin are together again," she told him. "They're taking it slow, but they're both so in love with each other. The three of us went to dinner last weekend."

And she'd never felt Matthew's absence so acutely as she had that evening. Seated at a table for four, Mia had been so aware of the empty chair, the chair that her man should have been sitting in. Her Matthew.

"Mia—"

"Don't, Matthew," she said. "Please. I know already, okay?"

"You know that I love you and want to spend the rest of my life with you? The rest of my life showing you how much?"

Her mouth dropped open, and she stared at him.

"If you and Cutie there will have me, that is."

She couldn't speak. She tried to utter words out of her open mouth, but nothing came out.

"Mia, will you marry me?"

"Oh, Matthew," she breathed and ran to him. He enveloped her in a hug.

Mew. Mew-mew.

Matthew chuckled. "Better put Cutie down before we crush him with too much love."

"There's no such thing as too much love," Mia replied. "Not from you."

"Or from you."

Matthew held her in his arms and gazed into her eyes. "I thought maybe after we got ourselves hitched, we could start on giving Robbie a cousin."

Mia nodded, unable to speak. "I love you so much, Matthew."

"I love you, too, Mia. I'm only sorry it took me so long to realize what an idiot I was being. My own worst enemy."

She squeezed him tightly. "All that matters is that we're going to be together."

"Not here, apparently," he said. "Moving somewhere I should know about?"

"Margot bought my parents' house in Peach Haven for me," she explained. "The town and house of my dreams. Do you think you could be happy there?"

"I think I'd be very happy there—I think *we're* going to be very happy there for the next sixty or so years."

Mia beamed. She was going home, and taking a new husband—her true love—with her.

AUTHOR'S NOTE

If you would like to receive a current Janelle Taylor newsletter and list of all of her books, please send a self-addressed, stamped envelope (SASE) to the address listed below. A legal size/long envelope is needed for these materials. Or you can print them from the website listed below, along with newsworthy updates.

Readers Heart
P. O. Box 285
Buford, GA 30515

To learn more about Janelle Taylor, her past works, future releases, and topics special to her, visit the Janelle Taylor website at: www. *readersheart.com.* It also contains a photo gallery. You can send her e-mail to readersheart@aol.com or to JnATaylor@aol.com.

Fun reading and Happy Holidays from Janelle Taylor.